The
Knowledge

The Knowledge

Steven Pressfield

• a too close to true novel •

BLACK IRISH ENTERTAINMENT, LLC
New York/Los Angeles

BLACK IRISH ENTERTAINMENT LLC
223 EGREMONT PLAIN ROAD
PMB 191
NORTH EGREMONT, MA 01230

COVER DESIGN BY DERICK TSAI, MAGNUS REX
EDITING BY SHAWN COYNE

FIRST BLACK IRISH ENTERTAINMENT EDITION
DECEMBER 2016

FOR INFORMATION ABOUT SPECIAL DISCOUNTS
FOR BULK PURCHASES, VISIT WWW.BLACKIRISHBOOKS.COM

ISBN 978-1-936891-51-1
eBook ISBN 978-1-936891-48-1

1 2 3 4 5 6 7 8 9 10

FOR DENISE GOLINGER
AND FOR MO

"... your application to become a licensed London taxi driver [has been] accepted and [you] have received a booklet entitled *Guide to Learning the Knowledge of London*, known as the Blue Book. Remember, the Examiner will rarely ask you the precise routes in the book, but [others that] nearly correspond to those routes. For example, you will not be asked [the route] from Manor House Station to Gibson Square No. 1 because you could have memorised [that] route, but instead you could be asked John Scott Health Centre to Barnsbury Gastropub ..."

from *Blue Book Runs and Pointing Maps*,
Taxi Trade Promotions, Ltd., London 2015

Book One

1.

Gotham Cab

I had a boss named Marvin Bablik when I drove a cab in New York City. This was in the seventies when the city was dirty and dangerous. One afternoon when I came in to start my shift (I drove from six in the evening till two in the morning), the hack manager waves me over and tells me, "The Turk wants to see you."

Bablik is a Turkish-American Jew who has owned the company since the 50s. He drives in once a week from Westchester in his white '72 Eldorado, which he parks in his own private spot on a concrete pad directly above the river. The company is called Gotham Cab. The garage is in the Bronx, in the industrial section smack on the water east of Southern Boulevard.

Bablik and his brother own four other taxi companies with garages scattered around the boroughs, but the Bronx shop is the one I work out of. I take the subway up from Manhattan and ride back each night around two thirty. I've never met Bablik or even seen him. Like every other driver, I got hired by the hack manager.

Me: "Why does the Turk wanna see me?"

Manager: "Who knows? But he axed for you personally."

The manager sends me up the back stairs to Bablik's office, which overlooks the interior of the garage. There's a solid steel door with a camera peep; you have to buzz to get in. The big window that looks down on the shop is an inch thick and bulletproof.

The Turk is on the phone behind an enormous, fortress-like desk when I enter. I note an army cot in the corner, made up with blankets and a pillow, a little fridge and a hotplate. The Turk waves me in, friendly, and motions me to sit.

Turk (holding hand over phone): "You're Charlie's nephew, right? Charlie Moses."

I confirm this and take a seat. Bablik finishes his call. He apologizes for pulling me in at the start of my shift. He promises he won't keep me long.

Bablik tells me he's an old friend of my uncle Charlie; they were in the army together in World War II. "I was on the horn to your uncle yesterday. Charlie mentioned that his nephew was driving a cab. For me! Who the fuck knew?"

I notice that the Turk keeps a gun on his desk, a nickel-plated .45.

The Turk is amused that his friend's nephew is driving a hack.

"You went to college, right? Whaddaya doing working in a shithole like this?"

I tell him I got laid off from a job in advertising.

"Are you stealing from me?"

"I beg your pardon."

"Are you running fares off the meter?"

In those days every cab company in New York that employed drivers (as opposed to individuals who had bought a medallion and owned their own vehicles) had installed a device called a "hot seat." This was an electrified wire mesh that was embedded under the back seat. When a passenger got into the cab and sat down, his weight completed a circuit and started the meter running automatically.

Before hot seats, the way cabbies stole from taxi companies was they'd ask a fare when he got in, "Wanna run this trip off the meter?" If the guy said yes, you didn't crank down the flag on the meter. You left it up. It was a win-win. The passenger paid less, and you got to keep every penny he gave you.

That's why the companies started putting in hot seats. It took the cabbies about fifteen seconds to figure out how to defeat the system, of course, with a second wire and a couple of alligator clips. I knew how too. A mechanic named Kingie showed me my second night on the job. I didn't do it though. I was probably the only honest cabbie in the city.

In those days, white guys drove cabs. In media businesses like advertising or publishing, you'd get laid off all the time when the company lost clients or hit a slow patch. While you looked for work or waited for your old job to call you back, you could pay the rent by driving a cab. It was easy then. You didn't need a special license. There was no test. You could show up at six and be behind the wheel by six thirty. Tips went straight into your pocket, so you had money from Night One.

And you met women. Girls would proposition you every night. Nice girls. "What's a clean-cut guy like you doing driving a cab?" In that era, taxis didn't have that plastic partition between the driver and the passenger. Girls would start talking to you from the back seat and pretty soon they'd be hanging their elbows over into the front. When you dropped them off, they'd hand you their business card or scribble their number.

You had to phone them fast though cause when you introduced yourself as "the guy driving the cab," you didn't want them to confuse you with the next laid-off book editor they'd also given their numbers to.

The seventies in New York was a dangerous time. Crime. Lots of crime. Hookers in doorways, creeps on every corner. People would rob you on the street. Burglars would break into your apartment. You walked around with your eyes in the back of your head.

There were real murderers out there. Innocent people got beaten to death every night, or shot or stabbed or thrown in the river. No one went into Central Park after dark. Even in a cab you kept your doors locked and made sure you always had a getaway lane. You never took a fare up to Harlem. I did a couple of times when I first started driving; the passengers themselves would warn you when you dropped them off. "Turn around and get the hell outa here." They were trying to protect you.

You got big tips taking passengers above 110th Street but, as I said, after the first few times I gave it up. Stopping for red lights was the worst. Hitters would pull alongside you and flash a piece. They'd chase you. I ran a toll booth one night at the north end of the West Side Highway, crashed through the wooden barrier at fifty just like in the movies, with a Chevy full of black kids with guns hot on my tail.

Sounds crazy now, but you didn't think anything of it then. You'd get back to your place and you wouldn't even tell anybody. The first time I got held up, at one in the morning under the 59th Street Bridge on the Queens side, the guy stole everything in my pockets including the folding corkscrew I used for my other job tending bar. As he got out, I shouted hey at him.

Me: "How 'bout leaving me a dime?"

Robber: "What for?"

Me: "So I can phone the cab company."

He tossed me the coin. I called in and said I'd just been jacked up at gunpoint.

Window Man: "So?"

Me: "I can't keep working. I got no money. I can't make change."

Window Man: "That's your problem."

Me: "I'm coming in."

Window Man: "You do and you'll never drive again."

So I'm not surprised, now, to see that my boss Marvin Bablik, the Turk, has a steel door, a bulletproof window and a .45 sitting in the open on his desk.

The Turk apologizes again for calling me into the office as my shift is starting. He says he just wanted to see what his friend Charlie's nephew looked like.

Turk: "How much you make a night?"

I tell him between twenty and thirty bucks.

Turk: "I might have something better for you."

The Turk asks if I'm free in the daytime. I say I could be.

He says, "Lemme work out a few details. I'll get back to you."

He stands. I say it's nice to meet you. We shake hands. He walks me to the door.

Turk: "You sure you're not stealing from me?"

Me: "I swear."

The Turk considers this.

"Well, if you ain't, you're the only one."

2.

The Girl with the Hair

That next Thursday was Thanksgiving. I took my friend Nicolette up to my uncle Charlie's house in White Plains. Charlie and his wife Peg have a big family and they always put on a good spread.

After dinner I told Charlie about my encounter with his friend Marvin Bablik. "He left me a note that same night, taped to my locker when I got back from my shift. He wants me to come in early next Monday. Says he might have a job for me."

Charlie: "Be careful with that fucker."

Me: "I thought he was your friend."

"He is, but he's into more crooked shit than anybody I know. Even as a sergeant in North Africa, he was turning over thousands of bucks a week. And he's a pathological liar. Don't believe a word he tells you."

After dinner Nicolette and I take the train back to the city. She's an artist and has a gallery showing first thing Friday morning.

I met Nicolette as a hand-off from my friend Jake Granger. Jake is only two weeks older than me but he's my boss at Young & Rubicam, the ad agency, making about ten times as much as I am, or was. It was actually Jake who fired me. He had to. We lost an account. I was low man on the pole. Jake swore that he had never slept with Nicolette or even kissed her.

"She's a little too artsy-fartsy for me, Stretch. But you might like her."

I do.

Nicolette is five-foot-two with a massive mane of shiny brown curls. Her hair weighs half as much as she does. She lives in a tiny apartment off Abingdon Square (Jake lives just across the square) that doubles as her studio. You walk in and your knees immediately begin banging into canvases. The place is just her bed and two hundred canvases. When I first met Nicolette she was painting miniatures. They were dark and depressing and they all looked the same.

Nicolette is the first artist I've ever known whose work has actually gotten better. This is tremendously encouraging to me because every other writer and painter I know, including myself, is stuck and going nowhere. Nicolette is on a whole other level. She has gone from aspiring artist to real artist. The transformation has been miraculous.

Nicolette wouldn't go on a date with me at first. She wouldn't even meet me for coffee. Instead she insisted that I take a French class with her. Later she explained that she knew Jake was handing her off to me, and she didn't want us to get off on the wrong foot. "So I broke your balls a little, sorry."

Nicolette and I meet every Tuesday and Thursday night, take the No. 1 train up to Times Square and the R over and up to the French Institute-Alliance Francaise on East 60th Street. After, we go for dinner at Maurice's or walk down and across to Joe Allen's. That was when I still had a job, of course.

My apartment is a few blocks north of Nicolette's, on Fifteenth between Eighth and Ninth. I have two rooms compared to her one. The front room is my bed, a kitchenette, and, amazingly, a working fireplace. The back room is a table and chair with my typewriter. The reason I picked this apartment is because it's on the third floor with an external staircase that runs two flights down into the rear courtyard. The open area between the buildings on Fifteenth and Fourteenth is as long and wide as a football field. It runs the whole length of the block. The dining terrace of a Portuguese restaurant sits right across the way beneath my window with a Chinese takeout next door and all kinds of interesting stuff going on after dark.

I took the apartment for my cat, Teaspoon, whom I call Tee. Tee is an outdoor cat. I didn't want to imprison him indoors just because we had moved to New York. I cut a cat-sized hole in a piece of plywood and stuck it in the window frame in the back room right above the external staircase. In summer I leave the hole open for Teaspoon to come and go. In the winter I stuff an old sweater into the hole for insulation. Tee tugs the sweater out with one paw when he wants to go outside. It's not too efficient heat-wise, but it's low-tech and it works.

Jake is always telling me to get rid of Teaspoon.

"Stretch, you gotta lose that cat."

He repeats this every time I see him.

"A single guy with a cat. It doesn't look right."

There's no way I'm gonna get rid of Teaspoon, single guy or not. He's the only person who gives a damn about me and who I, myself, care about. I found him when he was a tiny kitten on a street in London four years ago and paid five hundred and seventy-five bucks to get him home to the States. Teaspoon has been with me through many, many changes, as they say on the West Coast, and has always been true blue. He's the kind of cat who would lend you money, no questions asked, if he had it.

I respect Teaspoon because he is his own man. I have no idea where he goes at night. I see him sometimes from the apartment window, padding across the faux vine arbor above the patio of the Portuguese restaurant. I hear him other nights fighting with various cats in the courtyard behind the Szechuan takeout. He roams as far afield as Nicolette's basement apartment, which is six city blocks away. I have no idea how he gets there. He navigates by cat radar and has since the first time Nicolette cat-sat for him. He shows up at her window and scratches till she lets him in. Nicolette is constantly insisting that I make Teaspoon an indoor cat ("He's crossing Eighth Avenue, for God's sake!") but I will never do that. My cat accepts the risks of city life and so do I.

The only person besides Teaspoon who cares about me and vice versa is Nicolette. Nicolette is not technically my girlfriend but she decided a year ago that we should move in together. Her plan was to keep both our apartments and use hers as a studio for the two of us. She thought it would help her work not to have to stare at her canvases twenty-four hours a day.

We tried it. The problem was I couldn't stop chasing other women. There were two on the third floor in my building, right next door to me, roommates, one incredibly luscious blonde who worked on Wall Street and the other a spooky but very sexy neon artist who worked out of a studio on Spring Street in Soho. This second one, whom I call in my mind the Scary Girl, wears her hair in a super-severe Jazz Age page boy with black lipstick and black nail polish.

Nicolette and I would run into these two in the elevator or the hall and it was clear that I was desperate to get Nicolette out of there so I could bring one or both of them in for a drink. Not to mention nights when I didn't come home at all. Theoretically Nicolette had no right to get upset about any of this. She was free to go her own way. But the situation was not comfortable for either of us and we both knew it.

We had an excruciating breakup in a coffee shop on Mercer Street called The Wise Owl. I didn't see her for months. Then one day I ran into her at Balducci's on West Ninth. She had a new and very stylish cropped cut. She looked like Audrey Hepburn. "I got tired," she said, "of being The Girl With The Hair."

That night Nicolette showed me her new work. I was dumbstruck. She had started painting full-scale. Her stuff wasn't dark anymore or miniature. It was packed with color and force. The pieces had energy; they leapt off the canvas. The style and palette were still recognizably "hers," but it was a "her" that radiated confidence and mastery of technique. They were beautiful.

"See?" Nicolette said. "All I had to do was get away from you."

I was proud of her. "Whatever you did, it worked. These are fucking great, Nicolette."

Now, riding the Penn Central in from my uncle Charlie's, Nicolette starts rummaging through her bag for her insulin kit. She hasn't said a word in the past half hour and neither have I. "So," she says, "when's she coming in?"

Another reason why things haven't worked out between me and Nicolette, or me and anyone else for that manner, is I'm still married. My wife's name is Tracy. She lives in Los Angeles. I haven't seen her in two years but she's a force in my head, if you know what I mean.

I tell Nicolette three weeks next Tuesday.

She asks me where I'm gonna get the money.

"What money?"

Nicolette stands, tucking her kit.

"To show her how well you're doing."

3.

Missizombie

Yeah, okay. I do need money. And yeah, I'm already terrified that Tracy will get into town without warning me and I'll pick her up by accident in my cab. It'll be like the scene at the end of *Taxi Driver* when Cybill Shepherd flops down in the back seat behind Travis Bickle, played by Robert De Niro. If that happens, I'll drive straight to the Turk's office, snatch his .45 and see if I can hit my brains from the inside of my mouth.

I'm desperately in love with Tracy. Plus, I did some terrible, disgraceful shit when we were married that drove her to hate me and have zero respect for me. So I'm tortured by guilt on top of everything else.

Nicolette is right though. I do want to see Tracy. Why she's coming to town, I have no idea. Maybe something to do with Columbia, where she was going to law school before she dropped out to support me as I tried to write my first novel.

Tracy was born in Larchmont, about twenty miles north of the city, though she went to secondary school at the Marlborough School in Los Angeles. Her father lives out there; Tracy chose to stay with him when her parents divorced. She has family in the metropolitan area—two cousins in Manhattan and a married sister in Pound Ridge. Her mother has a place in Annapolis, Maryland, near the Naval Academy.

I met Tracy at Duke. She was a year ahead of me. People think of Duke as a Southern school, but more of its students come from New

York than any other state except North Carolina, and most of those Yankees come from the city.

Why Tracy married me, I still have no idea. When I met her she was engaged to a guy whose family owned a national-brand soft drink. Not Coke, not Pepsi, but right behind. You probably have a couple of cans in your fridge right now. The family was so rich they had their own island in the Bahamas. I knew the guy too. He was a good guy. But somehow Tracy fell in love with me.

I married her as fast as I could, before she changed her mind. I felt like I'd won the lottery. But within three years, we were setting world records for making each other miserable. I wound up on the road with ten bucks in my pocket. Tracy headed for Pacific Palisades to move in with her father.

Tracy's dad is an entertainment lawyer. Somehow Tracy started working in the movies. I never heard the full story. She was reading scripts for William Morris and somebody spotted her. She got cast in a low-budget horror flick. Tracy has old-fashioned features, with high cheek bones and a classic jaw, like screen beauties from the forties. It's the perfect look for those noir/slasher/sci-fi splatterfests that they shoot in Yucca Valley in twelve days for $250K. The roles Tracy got were usually the villainous lawyer who the hero outwits in the final reel or the intense, humorless scientist in the lab coat who takes off her horn rims in Act Two to reveal she's a knockout and the hero falls in love with her just before she's devoured by the monster from Mars.

Tracy's greatest on-screen moment came playing the lead in a surprisingly cerebral brain-eater called *Missizombie*. The plot was *Zulu*, with zombies instead of African warriors. The movie takes place in New Orleans; the climax comes on a levee at night with the lights of the Mississippi River Bridge framing the action. Tracy is alone, the last woman standing. She's in heels and padded shoulders with a long-barrel automatic and a Barbara Stanwyck up-do, gunning down the undead as they hurl themselves at her with the Big Easy in the b.g.

I saw the movie with Jake in the middle of the day at the Thalia on Broadway and 95th Street. The moment when Tracy thumbs the magazine release on her .45, dumps the empty clip into the mud and heels a fresh mag into place is one of the coolest action/chick beats in "B" cinema history. She looked like Helen Mirren holding off the Hottentots.

I take a demented pride in Tracy's film career. She, of course, is appalled by it. "My one goal is to live long enough to accomplish something else in life, so that I won't be memorialized as the Zombie Queen."

So, I'm guessing: Columbia Law.

Tracy is coming back to finish her degree.

Nicolette returns from the ladies' loo. She has gotten coffees for both of us from the guy with the cart. She sits. The train passes 125th Street and slides underground to the rumbling subterranean passage to Grand Central Terminal. "Your wife will be proud of you and how hard you're working," Nicolette says. "I know I am."

How hard I'm working.

I make a mental note to call the Turk. Whatever job he's got for me, I want it.

4.
Death Warmed Over

I told the Turk when we met in his office that I had gotten laid off from a job in advertising. This is true. But my two main obsessions have nothing to do with the ad biz. The first is writing. The second is managing a band.

The name of the band is Death Warmed Over. They're four of them and that's exactly what they look like. This is by no means a negative. Girls wet their panties for these guys, particularly the lead singer whose stage name is Roach but whose real name is Garrett Auslander. I know him from high school. At thirteen Garrett was a geek with sub-zero social skills—a stoop-shouldered, pock-faced loser who couldn't talk to anyone and who nobody wanted to talk to. One day he went into his room and locked the door behind him. When he emerged ten months later, he could play like Jimmy Page. I'm not kidding. He weighed 126 pounds with a prodigious Pete Townshend honker and greasy hair that fell to the middle of his back. He was dynamite.

Death Warmed Over had one legitimate hit, "Skank Magnet." The tune was Billboard's number eight with a bullet for one week.

Skank Magnet is my calling card when I make pitches for the band. I drop the name and people's eyes get wide.

Bar owner: "Skank Magnet. Your guys sang that?"

Me: "They wrote it too. They're creative."

The band is actually much better than I'm making it sound. Two of the members are classically trained, with degrees from Julliard, and the other pair, Roach and our drummer Johnny Schwantz (née Daniel Bisceglia), have worked so hard on their craft that they deserve everything they get.

Music is oxygen to these guys. To get twelve tracks for a new album, they write 100, 200 songs. They would slash their wrists before covering another band's material. And they're good guys. They don't drink and they don't do hard drugs. They have a red '71 Dodge van; they'll drive to Pluto to work a gig and never ask about the take. I've sent 'em to Detroit and even to Kansas. They spent a month playing barefoot bars and crab shacks in Florida, Louisiana, and Mississippi.

What I love most about the band is their level of aspiration. They don't think in songs, they think in albums; and they don't think in albums, they think in careers. In their mind they're Led Zeppelin, they're Black Sabbath, they're The Who. I believe in them. I believe they can be as big as they want.

The main problem with the band is me. I'm the least likely person to promote gigs and negotiate deals. But the guys trust me. They believe in me. They refuse to work with anyone else.

Here's the one thing I know about the music business. You never make any money off your songs. The single greatest thing that Death Warmed Over has going for it is a skull logo that Schwantz, who graduated from Parsons, designed and drew himself. We make five times more money off T-shirts than we do from music.

The back room in my apartment has four things in it—my writing table, my chair, my typewriter, and forty-seven boxes of Death Warmed Over tees. Forget tending bar or driving a hack; those shirts are the only thing standing between the band and me and starvation.

There's one evil fact I have to tell you about the band. Not the band actually, just one guy.

Roach slept with Tracy. Or maybe I should say Tracy slept with him.

It happened twenty-eight months ago after a show at a bar called Monroe's in Ocean City, Maryland. Tracy had driven over from her mother's place in Annapolis. To this day it tears my guts up to think about her and Roach, even though I was the first one to break our vows of marital fidelity, years earlier, and I deserve to be horse-whipped for it. Still I couldn't believe Tracy would be so low as to fuck Roach, and I couldn't accept that he'd be such a scumbag as to nail her. But they did it. If I let myself conjure even .001 of a second of that visual, I feel like the top of my head will explode.

How can I stand it? What keeps me from murdering both of them? Even I hate the answer:

Because I believe in the band's music.

I know, I know. The art world sucks. New York sucks. And the music business sucks more than both of them combined.

Here's one crazy sidebar on the Tracy/Roach thing. My cat, Tea-spoon, used to like Roach. He would hop up into his lap and purr like an outboard motor. Then one day, the very day I found out about Roach and Tracy, like a light switch Tee wouldn't go near him. If it's possible for a cat's face to radiate homicidal hatred, that's what happened with Teaspoon the next time he saw Roach.

How to explain it? There's obviously no way a cat can "find out" that So-and-So fucked So-and-So or even give a shit if they did. Did Tee pick up something from me? He hated Tracy after that too. If she walked into a room, he'd get up and leave. If she chased after him, making those little goochie-goo sounds that non-cat people make when they're talking to cats, he'd jump out the window.

5.

My Cat

I found my cat when he was a tiny kitten, at midnight on a street called Cheyne Walk in London, the Chelsea Embankment. Mick Jagger had a house there (No. 48), and Keith Richards did too (No. 3). I was riding home on the back of my friend Peter's Triumph Bonneville when somehow, I have no idea how, I heard a tiny, plaintive meow coming from the side of the street. I made Peter pull over and stop.

The kitten was so small I could cup him in one palm and fit him into the breast pocket of my jacket. In England they call this the "teaspoon pocket." So he became Teaspoon. I slipped him in next to my heart and he curled up and went to sleep.

The next day I wrote out a hundred 3X5 cards.

FOUND KITTEN. CALL ME.

The cards had my number and a description of Teaspoon. I went door to door around Cheyne Walk, sticking a card in every mail slot. Nobody called. That same day, someone told me they had seen other similar-looking kittens seeming forlorn and abandoned, and even a dog, in that same lane. Someone must have been moving and dropped their animals off in an affluent neighborhood, hoping they'd wind up in a good home.

When my friend Peter died, Teaspoon and I came back to the States.

Tee was with me in Texas and Louisiana, in Kentucky, in North Carolina, and in California when I finally finished my first novel (that I couldn't sell). Wherever I was living, I would bolt together my writing table and set my ancient Smith-Corona manual typewriter on top. Teaspoon would jump onto the tabletop and curl up on the left side of the machine so that the carriage trundled back and forth over his head as I worked. He would stay in that spot for hours. He became my lucky charm. As long as Teaspoon was there in his spot, I could work like a bandit. One time in California he got sick and had to stay at the vet for four days. I was paralyzed. I couldn't write a word till he got back.

I had a '65 Chevy van in those days. Still do; it's in storage at my uncle Charlie's factory in Stamford, Connecticut. When Teaspoon and I were on the road I would set up the back like this:

I'd put four heavy plastic milk crates (stuffed with the dozens of paperbacks I was reading), one in each of the corners of the truck bed. On top of these went my box springs and mattress, which I made up into a bed with sheets and blankets and pillows. The head of the bed was at the back of the van. It was just the right height that you could look out the rear windows so you didn't feel claustrophobic. Enough space remained under the box springs to hold my clothes, which weren't many and which I kept in one suitcase and a couple of cardboard boxes, plus my tools and oil cans, my typewriter, Teaspoon's litter box, and whatever other junk I happened to have at the time. I had an old steel-sided cooler that fit under there too.

"You should have a gun," people told me in the South. But my moods were nothing to joke about. I felt a lot safer knowing the most lethal device in my van was a Phillips-head screwdriver.

On the road, Teaspoon's post was at the very back (the head) of the bed. This was his favorite spot. He liked the pillows and he liked to look out the rear window. After he and I had been living a settled life in one place for a while, I could tell when he wanted to get back on the road because he'd hop up into that spot and look at me expectantly as if to say, "Let's blow this pop stand."

6.
My Agent

I have a literary agent. His name is Martin Fabrikant. Marty is ninety-six years old. That's not a typo. Marty is Dutch and speaks with an accent. He's about four-foot-ten and likes to joke that he used to be six-four.

Marty was prominent about forty years ago. He represented Jack Kerouac and William Burroughs. Now I'm his only client. "Your career is the only thing that keeps me from lying down each night and not getting up." Marty has a way of joking that can be a little too close to the truth.

Marty phones me that Sunday, the Sunday after Thanksgiving. He wants to meet for dinner. He has big news, he says. He wants to know when I'm going to be finished with the book I'm working on now. "When will we have a draft I can take out to the town?"

"Three weeks or a month. I just have to crack the ending."

Marty has already told me the big news, about a week ago, but he has forgotten that conversation. The word is that a hot young editor, Christopher Brand (the son of Everett Brand, who edited Faulkner) wants to read my new manuscript. Christopher had wanted to publish an earlier book, my second one, titled *The Knowledge*, but he couldn't sell it to his bosses at Random House. Well, says Marty, now Chris is at Houghton Mifflin in Boston with his own imprint; he's looking for a young writer whose first work he can bring out. "But you gotta get it to me fast," Marty says. "Half a dozen other agents are trying to get their clients in to Chris too. We have to beat 'em! There can only be one Hot New Writer. How soon can you meet me for dinner?"

Marty loves to meet for dinner. He and I get together every two or three weeks. I always pay. We've done this probably thirty times. Marty lives in the Murray Hill Towers at Madison and 40th. We go either to the Yale Club on Vanderbilt between 44th and 45th (Marty was on the faculty in the 50s) or the Oyster Bar on the lower level of Grand Central Terminal. Marty orders the same meal every time: a martini up, extra dry, then sole or trout meuniere with haricots verts and pommes vapeur (new potatoes boiled), of which he eats no more than half and takes the rest home in a doggie bag. I always walk him to his door. I slip a buck or two to his doorman, Oscar, who is also the elevator operator. Oscar makes sure Marty gets to his apartment without mishap. I have Oscar's number and he has mine, just in case.

"I like to eat out," Marty says, "because I get to speak French." Marty also speaks Russian, German and Polish along with Dutch and English.

I enjoy meeting Marty for dinner. He tells me stories from the old days that are packed with wisdom and encouragement. Marty believes in me. "I'm going to get you going, my boy. You'll see. All you need is one break."

I could never get an agent under ninety-five years old, so I'm very grateful to have Marty.

"How's your gorgeous wife?" he asks now as we're hanging up. "We'll get an offer on this new one and she can go back to law school."

Marty thinks Tracy and I are still together. It's not a senility thing with him. He would think so even if he were twenty-five. Marty is optimistic. He looks on the bright side.

Marty is a death camp survivor. He's got the tattoo. He never speaks about the experience directly (I only know through my friend Pablo, who originally introduced me to Marty) but he'll make remarks from time to time whose gist is, "Appreciate life. Never complain. Work hard and do your best."

Marty has one other mantra: "Talent is bullshit."

"I seen a million writers with talent. It means nothing. You need guts, you need stick-to-it-iveness. It's work, you gotta work, do the fucking work. That's why you're gonna make it, son. You work. No one can take that away from you.

"And I'll tell you something else," Marty says to me now over the phone. "Appreciate these days. These days when you're broke and struggling, they're the best days of your life. You're gonna break through, my boy. And when you do, you'll look back on this time and think this is when I was really an artist, when everything was pure and I had nothing but the dream and the work. Enjoy it now. Pay attention. These are the good days. Be grateful for them."

Knowing Marty has taught me one important truth—never look at an older person and dismiss them because they're infirm or slow. That individual may have gone through hells you can't imagine and be a vessel of wisdom beyond anything you can comprehend.

"Tracy's great, Marty. She sends you her love."

"You hang onto that girl."

"I will, Marty. I will."

The truth is I just got divorce papers from Tracy's lawyer. The return address is Raleigh, NC. Because Tracy and I were married at Duke, the dissolution of union has to happen in North Carolina. Opening the envelope, I was half-dreading seeing Tracy's signature and then a blank line awaiting mine. But she hadn't signed the papers yet.

Why I take hope from this, I don't know. In any event I don't sign on my line. I put the papers aside for the moment.

I hang up from Marty and cross to the back room, my office. I keep the phone in the front room so it won't disturb me when I'm working. Teaspoon is just coming in from the fire escape as I enter. He pads across the floor and hops up into my lap. His coat is cold from being outside. He's purring.

The book is finished really, except for one critical section in the climax. I've got the overall ending. The beginning is done. So is the middle. I'm on Draft #7; I'll probably do eleven or twelve in all. The last few will be minor.

This is my third novel. None of them has sold, or even come close. I blew up the first one after working on it for two years. That was the one that destroyed my marriage to Tracy. The second one took three years. I finished it in Carmel Valley, California. I had a neighbor there, a Mexican novelist named Pablo X. Sifuentes. Marty was Pablo's agent. That's how he came to represent me. "We got this close," Marty always says about that manuscript. "We'll break through on the next one."

This is the next one. The one I'm finishing now.

One thing I know for certain. If Marty can't find a publisher for this one, I will never be able to summon the will to write another. I will have to kill myself. The only issue is who will take care of Teaspoon. Nicolette maybe. I make a mental note to speak to her.

Back at my desk, I get to work. There's a secret that writers know and the secret is this—writing is fun. It can be dangerous, yeah. You can go in too deep. Ask Hemingway or any other novelist who boozed or drugged himself to death. But what does that prove? Not that the work itself is hell. Once you've gone through the changes and acquired self-discipline, once you've identified the interior demons of Resistance and self-sabotage and learned that it's possible to face them down one day at a time, writing becomes fun.

One thing you learn though, if you're a writer, is that nobody gives a damn. My friend Jake will ask me, "How's the book going?" and it's all over his face that he couldn't give less of a shit. If anything, he's hoping I'll fail. When I report any setback, I can see him fighting to keep from grinning.

My uncle Charlie's the same, even though he loves me like a son. "Still writing those books?" he'll ask, in the same tone he'd use to say, "Still squeegee-ing windshields at the entrance to the Midtown Tunnel?"

Except Nicolette and Marty, only one person has ever believed in me and that was Tracy. In the divorce letter from North Carolina, the lawyer specifies the date—December 21—when Tracy is scheduled to arrive in New York. I jot this on my Sierra Club calendar with two notes to myself:

1. Finish book and deliver to Marty 12/7 or sooner.
2. Meet Turk tomorrow re job.

Book Two

The Russian

7.

Terminal Bar

I'm following a fox fur and a pair of black leather Cossack boots.

Abigail.

Abigail Bablik crosses Eighth Avenue at 40th Street and turns up the block on the west side. I fall in, fifty yards behind her.

I'm following Marvin Bablik's wife.

This is the job the Turk wanted to talk to me about.

He bails on our Monday meeting but leaves me a note to meet him Wednesday at noon at the Horn and Hardart's at Sixth Avenue and 57th Street. He specifies this place because he doesn't want any of his cabbies to see him talking to me.

Horn and Hardart's is an automat. There's no counter or table service. The meal selections, the actual items themselves, are displayed behind little glass doors built into the walls. There's a coin slot beside each; you shove in nickels and dimes and the lock on the door opens. You reach in and take your tuna and cottage cheese or your ham on rye. It's on a plate, a real china plate, freshly made and delicious.

The Turk and I sit. He explains the job. My first thought is I can't believe he's serious. Tail your wife? Me?

"You're perfect," says the Turk. "I knew it the minute I saw you."

From his jacket pocket Bablik unfurls a sheaf of clippings—pix of his old lady from the social pages of *The Times*. "She's a high-class dame. Goes to lunch at the Oak Room, meets her girlfriends for drinks at Windows on the World. If I put some thirty-dollar-a-day gumshoe on her, she'll make him in two minutes. Not to mention he won't get past the first doorman or maitre d'."

The Turk says he'll lend me a cab to use for the job. "Take it home," he says. "Park it on your street." He says he'll let me gas up for free at the garage, from the pumps by the underground tank in back, but I have to do it late or between shifts so no one sees me.

I'm thumbing through the news clippings. Mrs. B. is a knockout. She looks like Jane Greer from *Out of the Past.* I have to bite my tongue to keep from saying to the Turk, "This is *your* wife?"

"But you, kid?" he says. "You're the Ivy League type. You look like you belong." He eyes my construction boots and hooded sweatshirt. "You got something decent in your closet, right?"

He'll buy me a jacket, the Turk says. He'll get me some good shoes. He'll pay for a haircut.

"The job is a piece of cake," says the Turk. He assures me it requires no experience and no specialized skills. "Abigail has lunch? You have lunch. She attends a lecture? You sit three rows behind her. I pay."

"How much?"

"Fifty a night."

"Cash?"

"I ain't writing no checks."

Wow.

Fifty bucks is real money. Even if the job only lasts a couple of weeks it'll give me enough cash to quit my bartending gig and work full days finishing the book. I can get it to Marty before Tracy arrives. I'm calculating time to completion. I don't know how many hours each night the Turk's job would require, but for sure it'd be less than driving a hack. I could get some actual sleep.

Except already I'm starting to feel guilty. What if Mrs. Bablik really *is* cheating? I don't want to be the cause of a divorce.

The Turk waves this off. "I'm probably just paranoid. This thing could all be in my head. If it is, you'll be saving me a fortune in lawyers' fees. Maybe my old lady's not banging this Russian skank like I'm 100 percent certain she is."

Bablik gives me a photo of a burly, bald-headed mug who looks like an Eastern European gangster. This is "the Russian." Bablik wants to know if the Russian is having an affair with his wife, and if he is, he wants the Russian's whereabouts. His address. Apparently the guy keeps moving around, slipping from place to place like a Third World dictator.

I hear real emotion in the Turk's voice. I know what it means to be jealous. It's a terrible feeling.

"Kid, I need you. I got no one else who can do this for me."

So now here I am, skulking north on Eighth Avenue at four o'clock on a freezing December afternoon, watching Mrs. B., in fox fur and Russian cavalry boots take a hard ninety off the sidewalk and duck into the Terminal Bar.

I've been tailing Abby for two days and three nights now and, if I do say so myself, I'm starting to get the hang of it. Yes, I have started thinking of her as "Abby." Or "Mrs. B." You can't shadow someone, I have discovered, without developing an attachment for them.

From the way Mrs. B. slips through the door of the Terminal Bar, I can tell she is no stranger to this joint. Nor does she have the slightest suspicion that she's being followed. I give her forty seconds, then push in after her and cross straight to the bar without looking right or left. I take a stool at the end nearest the exit, facing it. That way no one can get out without me seeing 'em.

The Terminal Bar is such a shithole it's actually cool. It's the kind of dive Charles Bukowski would hang out in. I order a Bud and ask for change for the cigarette machine. I still haven't looked around. I gather my quarters and cross to buy a pack of smokes. It's the best way to scan a room. You move through. It doesn't seem obvious that you're looking around.

Suddenly through the window I spot Mrs. B.

Outside!

Crossing Eighth Avenue!

What the fuck.

She's moving fast. Long strides. She crosses the avenue, turns the corner and dives down into the subway.

I'm sprinting across in traffic.

The entrance at Eighth and 42nd leads to the Port Authority Bus Terminal and the subway complex underneath. It's one of the busiest hubs in the city with passageways linking to the 1, 2, 3 and 7 trains, to Times Square and the shuttle to Grand Central, plus the A, C, and E uptown and downtown, not to mention connections to the N, Q, R and S radiating everywhere. It's a mess.

Mrs. B.

She's gone.

8.
Tito

"She made you," says Tito.

"Impossible."

"She knew exactly what she was doing. She ducked in the front and went straight out the back."

No way. "No way she saw me!"

"You're a ghost. You're invisible."

Tito's full name is Partito Cerrone. He's the thirty-dollar-a-day gumshoe that the Turk had hired (and fired) before he brought me on. Now Tito is back on the payroll. We're partners.

Tito is an ex-cop. Twenty-six years, two citations for valor, and a bum leg from getting pushed off a roof in Bed-Stuy in '67. He's about five-nine with no neck and no wrists. I don't know what Tito weighs but when he deposits his tonnage into the passenger seat, the whole cab lists to starboard.

I'm glad Tito's with me. He's tough. He's got a lot of funny stories. And he knows what he's doing.

I have acquired an appreciation for how difficult surveillance can be. You can't do it alone, not in a city, and certainly not in New York. You need a team. You need vehicles, you need communications.

In addition to their digs in Northern Westchester, the Turk and Mrs. B. share a three-bedroom in University Village at West Houston and LaGuardia Place, in the 505 Tower, designed by I. M. Pei. My first night I'm on foot, with the cab Bablik lent me parked on Bleecker, just a few steps away. This is before Tito returned to the job. Abby emerges from the lobby at quarter past seven, strides out the south walkway to Houston Street and hails a cab. In ten seconds I've lost her. By the time I can get my own vehicle into traffic and around the corner, Abby's cab has turned toward Canal and vanished. I feel like an idiot.

Where do you hang when you're shadowing somebody? Night Two, I pick the lightless doorway of an NYU dorm across from Abby's building. Within ten minutes the same two Japanese grad students have walked past me three times, eyeballing me like I'm a mugger or a rapist. Five minutes later the campus cops arrive. They chase me out. I'm back in the same roost five minutes later. Except now some freak in chains and leather is making googly eyes at me. The real cops show up this time. They bust the guy for possession of a weapon (he's got a Boy Scout hatchet under his Marlon Brando jacket) and almost take me in with him when he claims I'm his boyfriend. Why am I hanging out in this doorway? "Officers, it's all right, I'm just surveilling someone."

Plus it's cold. I haven't eaten. Do I dare dash for a Coke and a slice? In the fifteen minutes the cops take hassling me, Abby could've come and gone ten times and I wouldn't have even seen her.

Next morning I phone the Turk and quit.

"Wait. Kid! Don't hang up …"

Somehow he convinces me to stay.

So now it's me and Tito. Tito couldn't make it yesterday. His grandson had a football game. That's how come I was tailing Abby on my own when she ducked into the Terminal Bar.

"It's good that she made you," says Tito.

"Why?"

"Because now we know she's hip. And we know she's hiding something."

9.

Brighton Beach

Abby goes out six of the next nine nights.

Tito has taught me to keep a surveillance log. The documentation will keep us organized, he says, and it gives us something to show Bablik so he keeps paying us (though so far neither of us has seen a dime.)

All six nights Abby attends charity events or fundraisers (MOMA once, the Ballet Company of the Metropolitan Opera once, Save the Children twice, Friends of the Israeli Defense Forces once, Rebuild Stuyvesant Town once) either with girlfriends or a mixed group, of which the Russian is not a member.

Night Seven she goes out alone. She takes a cab to the Ethel Barrymore Theater on West 47th and enters the lobby with the crowd. I'm about to follow her in when Tito's ham-sized mitt stops me. "Be patient," he says.

Sure enough, three minutes later Mrs. B. re-emerges, alone, strides half a block east to the corner of Seventh to beat the various tourists and restaurant-goers competing to hail cabs, snags one herself, and takes off again.

Tito and I are in my own cab, the one Bablik lent me. I'm driving; Tito's in the back seat so our silhouettes don't look suspicious. We tail Abby down Seventh and across town on 42nd where she catches the FDR Drive just below the U.N. and heads south to the Brooklyn Bridge; on the far side, her cab catches the BQE to the Gowanus to the Prospect Expressway, rolling deep, deep into Brooklyn.

"Where the hell is she going?"

At Ocean Parkway and Avenue J, Abby's taxi pulls over. She pays and gets out. A black '62 Chrysler Imperial sits at the curb. Two men are in the front seat. Abby crosses straight to the Imperial and gets in the back. The car pulls out into traffic.

Ten minutes later she's sitting with the two men in a window booth of a Russian restaurant called Cafe Dacha on Neptune Avenue in Brighton Beach. The men squirm awkwardly for a minute or two, trying to make conversation alone with Mrs. B. Then a third man appears from the back of the restaurant. It's the Russian. I recognize him from the photo the Turk gave me, and Tito knows him by sight from previous surveillance. The two guys get up and make way for the Russian. They move to the counter. The Russian sits. He and Mrs. B. are alone in the booth by the front window.

Our cab is parked across Neptune Avenue, about thirty yards up the block. You can actually find parking spaces in Brighton Beach. Are Abby and the Russian lovers? Then what are they doing ordering zakuski and Dr. Brown's Cel-ray Tonic in this Mom 'n Pop dive in Little Russia? Why not someplace romantic, or an apartment or a hotel? Nor does their body language indicate an illicit liaison. They're fighting. I see Abby stub out a cigarette, hard, and immediately light another. I'm watching all this through Tito's 10X binos. I don't dare go into the restaurant myself. Abby has already spotted me once at the Terminal Bar. Tito certainly can't do it. He reeks of low-class flatfoot.

In fact he's half a block up the street now, in a phone booth, calling in the plate numbers on the Chrysler. He's got a friend at the DMV from his police days. We'll know the car's owner, Tito swears, by noon tomorrow.

We sit for an hour. The goons at the counter have time to order a full meal of pirog pie and dumplings, plus dessert and coffee. For the first ten minutes Abby and the Russian remain in animated conversation. She's trying without success to convince him of something. Then he does the same with her. She becomes sullen and silent. He gets up and makes a phone call. She reapplies lipstick and smokes two cigarettes. When the Russian returns, he and Abby get into it again, a shorter dust-up that de-escalates only when the waiter, who seems to be the owner as well, delivers a pair of espressos and a plate of angel wings.

It's not easy doing this stakeout stuff. It's tedious. You have to pay attention and be ready to improvise in the moment, but meanwhile nothing is happening. To fight the boredom, I ask Tito how he came to be connected with Bablik.

"I used to drive for him, after I left the force. Then a little side work."

"What kinda work?"

"The kind that don't go on no W-2."

A final argument between Abby and the Russian flares up and dies down. He pays the bill, stands, and exits alone through the back of the restaurant. Abby lights one more cigarette. The taller of the Russian's two associates, the one with a ponytail, fetches the Chrysler Imperial. The other one holds the door for Abby.

They drive her all the way back across Brooklyn to Atlantic Avenue, turn west and slog through the run of lights to the Brooklyn Academy of Music, where a performance of *The Glass Menagerie* is in progress but hasn't gotten out. A queue of cabs waits on Lafayette Avenue. The Imperial pulls alongside the first in line. Abby gets out and knocks on the windshield. She boards the cab. The taxi drives up the long block and takes a hard left onto Fulton, heading toward Flatbush Avenue and the approach ramps for the Manhattan Bridge.

"Stick with her?"

"What for?" says Tito. "She's just going home."

"Good, cause I'm outa gas."

By eleven fifteen Tito and I have arrived back at Gotham Cab and I'm filling up from the pumps above the underground tank by the river. Tito lights a Lucky Strike standing beneath the NO SMOKING WITHIN 50 FEET sign. The night's taxi shift is out working. The garage is dark and empty, except a few lights on in the repair shop and one in the dispatcher's office.

Tito relieves himself in the weeds, squinting from the smoke rising from his cigarette. "How much you think Bablik makes outa this joint in a year?"

I have no idea. "Couple hundred grand?"

Tito's shoulders rise and fall. He concludes his business and comes back to the cab. It's still early. I ask if he wants to go for a bite before I take him home.

We grab coffee and pie at the Amsterdam Diner on Southern Boulevard. Tito tells me about the gall bladder operation his wife has coming up. Bablik is putting him on Gotham Cab's medical policy. Apparently there's some reason Tito is not covered under the NYPD retirement package.

"The old lady's surgery is why I'm doing this job," he says.

I drop him home on Steinway Street near Ditmars Boulevard in Astoria on the stroke of one. Tito opens the passenger door but doesn't get out.

"Bablik don't make a dime outa the cab company. All his dough comes from that underground tank."

"What tank?"

"The one I was just pissing on."

I don't get it. Gasoline?

"Not that tank," Tito says. "The one next to it. The other one."

10.

Library Lions

On the nights when Abby has no plans to go out, the Turk leaves a message to that effect on my answering service. That way I can take my normal shift driving a cab. I have to for money because the Turk still hasn't paid me. In fact he hasn't come in to the garage at all.

Days I'm working full-tilt on the book. I had thought I could grind hard for a week or two and crack the ending, but it's going slower than I anticipated. Tracy will be in town in another ten days. I've got to get the manuscript to Marty. Good news on that front would go a long way with Tracy.

One of the fun parts of writing is research. I'm a regular at the main branch of the New York Public Library on 42nd and Fifth. So is Nicolette. We go together. She pores through Art History texts while I'm doing my research.

I love everything about the library. I love the lions out front and the steps leading up to the great vaulted neo-Roman facade. I love the Reading Room with its towering ceiling and high cathedral-type windows and its green eyeshade lamps along the rows of tables packed with scholars and students and bums getting in out of the cold. I love scouring through the rows of filing cabinets with their long, oaken drawers that you slide out by pulling on the brass handles, and poring through the file cards, all with their Dewey Decimal System numbers, till you find the book or books you're looking for, or stumble onto some other tome that you didn't even know existed but that sounds even better than the one you were originally seeking; then grabbing one of the stubby little pencils that the library provides beside the cabinets, which are so worn to the nub that you don't even want to steal them, and writing down the books' numbers on those ragged-ass scraps of paper that look like the librarians' assistants tore them up with their own hands to save money.

Now you walk up to the window and turn in your requests, which the clerks slip into a pneumatic tube and send down with a satisfying hiss to the bowels of the library, where, you imagine, other even more pallid and near-sighted clerks wheeling ancient wooden book carts trundle through stacks miles long in all directions and dozens of floors deep below the streets of Manhattan to find your book(s). Meanwhile you have taken a seat back in the waiting room. The seats are oak pews like in a church or a train station. There's an old-fashioned electric board above the Request Window with rows of numbers on it. When your book arrives via dumbwaiter from the library catacombs below, your number lights up. It's a great system.

While I'm doing research for my own book, I decide to do a little on Abby, and on the Turk as well. Tito has completed the license plate trace on the Chrysler Imperial. The owner's name is Ivanov—Dimitri Ivanov—apparently one of the bodyguards, if that is in fact what they are, with an address (out of date, Tito and I discover when we scout it out two nights later) in Brighton Beach, Brooklyn, the neighborhood Tito and I tailed Abby to when she met the Russian.

I look Brighton Beach up in the library. The neighborhood we were in is called Little Russia, sometimes Little Odessa, though the two blocks contiguous to the restaurant are apparently Little Lithuania. Lots of Jews. Searching the archives of *The Times* and the *Daily News,* I come upon two convictions for Ivanov, one for arson, the other for second-degree manslaughter. As for the neighborhood of Little Russia, the area appears to be a quiet, respectable province of the outer boroughs, with no extraordinary citations other than its notoriety as a favored residential enclave for several generations of Russian and Eastern European mobsters.

Then I stumble upon this in *The Times*, from just a few weeks ago:

TAXI MOGUL TO BE HONORED

The article features a photo of Bablik, smiling, flanked by a pair of dignified-looking elder gentlemen identified as officers of an organization called Friends of the IDF.

> Marvin A. Bablik, businessman and philanthropist, has been selected as Man of the Year by Friends of the Israel Defense Forces, a charitable organization to which Mr. Bablik has made significant financial contributions over decades.
>
> The award will be presented to Mr. Bablik by Robert Moses, the Port Authority chief, at the FIDF's annual banquet, January 12, at the Waldorf Astoria. Mr. Bablik, who escaped persecution in Eastern Europe as a small boy, is well known for his fund-raising work on behalf of the Jewish state, particularly during and in the immediate aftermath of the Yom Kippur War of October 1973.

The newspaper archives are delivered to you on reels of microfilm, in little cardboard boxes. The film has sprocket holes on each side; you feed the reel into a manual track in a viewing machine that looks like an oversized TV. Each reel covers three months of newspaper. The machine magnifies the image. You scroll sideways and up and down by using two crank handles on the machine. It takes a little dexterity.

Abby, I discover, is the daughter of an Army three-star general. Abigail Martine Duchevres. She's from Franklin, Tennessee. She went to the University of Virginia, where she was on the Homecoming Court in '43 and '44. She did not finish her degree. In '48 she married a West Point graduate, Lt. Archibald Musgrave Hollings, who was killed three years later in Korea, an infantry company commander, posthumously awarded the Silver Star for valor.

The Times of October 7, 1953 has out-of-town coverage (without photos) of Abby's wedding to the Turk. The ceremonies took place in the chapel at UVA. The officiant was Abby's uncle, Dr. Ernest V. Bissell, an Episcopal bishop.

Bablik and Mrs. B. have been husband and wife for twenty-one years.

The only other article I find that concerns either Abby or the Turk (though I'm sure I'd find more if I had more time) is about an investigation into corruption in the drywall contracting business in Staten Island and the Bronx. Bablik and his brother, who is identified as "Louis" in the article, are named as co-defendants along with officers of two other contracting entities. The companies are accused of doing unlicensed and uninspected business in a covert partnership with Leonard "the Lip" Lipranzio, a notorious gangster reputed to be responsible for dozens of murders over the course of several decades. Among the Lip's alleged eccentricities are 1) he goes to confession once a day, insisting on confiding his sins to the same priest, who has been absolving the Lip's escapades for three decades, and 2) those associated with him regard him with such fear and awe that they dare not even speak his name aloud. When referring to him, they either point to their own lips or form the letter L with their thumb and forefinger.

Bablik and his brother accepted a plea bargain on the corruption charges and were permitted to escape prosecution by paying a fine and by donating labor and drywall contracting services to two public schools then under construction on Staten Island.

I've been avoiding telling Nicolette about my job for the Turk. I know what she'll say. She'll say I'm ducking my real work, which is finishing my book and delivering it to Marty.

Now she comes in while I'm scanning the microfilm files. "What's this?" she says, indicating the story about Leonard the Lip. In five minutes she's gotten everything out of me.

"How dangerous is this job you're doing?"

"What? It's nothing."

Nicolette trails a finger across my scribbled notes.

Arson.

Manslaughter.

Multiple murders over decades.

"Are you an idiot," she says, "or what?"

11.

Buster Weems' Club Inferno

Christmas is two weeks away. I've missed my first self-imposed deadline, December 7, for delivering the manuscript to Marty. Meanwhile I have a second note from Tracy's lawyer. Something unexpected has come up; Tracy won't be in town till January 3.

Good. I can use the extra time to work.

I get in four days straight, at the Library and at home, with no calls from the Turk and no nights tailing Abby. Then, arriving home on the afternoon of the fifteenth, there's a panicked message on my service from Roach, née Garrett, my vocalist and lead guitarist, and two other hysterical screeches from our drummer Johnny Schwantz, aka Danny Bisceglia.

I phone them back. They both come over immediately.

Me: "What's the problem?"

Both: "Tonight's gig."

The date is for a place at 128th and Amsterdam called Buster Weems' Club Inferno. I booked it a month ago and had forgotten all about it. The club owner (Buster Weems has been dead for forty years) phoned me himself, an unheard of occurrence, very, very hot to get the band. The offer was $200, huge money for the guys, and my percentage, thirty bucks, was no-turn-down dinero for me as well. Not to mention the fact that the owner said he'd send the check *before* the date, which he did, also unprecedented, and which I immediately deposited, holding the band's share till after the date. I was so excited I tried to get two nights, offering the band for $350 for both, but the owner, who gave his name as Jackie Q (the check was signed by his secretary), said one night was fine, that was all he wanted.

Suddenly my guys are balking. They refuse to play the date.

Roach: "It's Harlem, man."

Me: "So what? It's a club."

Schwantz: "What do they want with a band like us? Black audiences hate the kind of music we play. They'll hate us. We don't feel comfortable. We don't wanna go."

Me: "The club owner called me!"

Twenty minutes later the truth dribbles out. Jackie Q, who owns Club Inferno, is Javier Quinones, Esq., a hip black lawyer who works for the same downtown firm as Roach's dad. Roach and Jackie Q met at a party in Scarsdale a month and a half ago.

"And ... "

Roach says he and Quinones got to talking. Roach was hyping Q about the band. Quinones' hot fox girlfriend was hanging on Q's arm, fascinated.

Me (to Roach): "You're banging her."

Roach: "This date is a setup, man! They're gonna fuckin' kill me."

Schwantz: "They're gonna kill all of us."

The second thing I know about the music business (beyond the fact that it sucks) is that you NEVER fail to show for a date. It's career suicide.

Roach (to me): "Then you're coming with us."

"Me? What good am I gonna do?"

"You're the grownup," says Schwantz. "You'll protect us."

Five hours later, nine thirty at night, I'm watching Schwantz park the band's '71 Dodge van in the alley behind the club and handing fives to the two six-foot-four, 260-pound bruisers who assure me they've been placed in their posts by Jackie Q himself and that if any passing mofo so much as breathes on the van, they will kneecap his ass and staple him to the utility pole for us to work on after hours at our leisure.

The club is in a basement beneath a dry cleaner and a pizza joint. It's not bad—low ceilings, dark wood decor with a mirror-backed bar and a dance floor, a small stage. The dressing room is adjacent, in the alley under a tent.

Sound check goes fine. The club is empty except for the manager, who's Puerto Rican, a bartender prepping the bar and three women, all black, working the kitchen. Apparently the club serves food as well as liquor.

Around ten the crowd starts filtering in. Backstage three more bone breakers have joined us, all black, and all packing heat as openly as if this were Tombstone, 1881. Two are wearing leather coats and black military-style berets.

Schwantz (tugging me aside): "Jesus Christ, it's Eldridge fucking Cleaver."

The band is terrified. They start getting drunk in self-defense. I do too. Where's Jackie Q? I'm at the bar now. There is no mistaking the air of menace in the room. People have come out tonight for something other than music. The mood is festive, like the Puritan days in Salem before a witch burning.

"You must be Stretch."

I turn to discover a tall, slender black man in an impeccably tailored sharkskin suit. Jackie's hand is cool to the touch when I shake it. I note a gold Rolex and manicured fingernails.

"How do you like the club? Can I get you something? The band need anything?"

"Just alcohol."

"Tell 'em to fuel up. Talent drinks free."

Jackie is the least-black black guy I've ever met. For some reason this scares me more than if he had been an out-and-out militant.

Jackie tells me he admires the band's music. He asks me which one of the band members writes the songs. I tell him Roach. Jackie smiles. "He's gonna get at least one new song out of tonight, I promise you."

Where's Jackie's girlfriend? Could that be her at the table stage-right? If it is, she's a traffic-stopping bombshell. I don't blame Jackie for being furious at Roach.

The emcee is a comic. He's onstage now, ten thirty, warming up the crowd. Four cocktail waitresses work the room. Trays of Manhattans and Screwdrivers pass. No one's drinking beer. I see the bartender pouring Remys and Courvoisiers and Hennessy V.S.O.P.s.

Me (to Jackie): "Any specific numbers you want the band to play?"

"Skank Magnet. But not early. Tell 'em to build to it."

I excuse myself to go back to the guys. As I'm crossing the floor, the curtains part by the entry and in walks the Scary Girl from my apartment building. My next door neighbor, the neon artist. She spots me instantly. She's with a sharp-looking black guy. She herself is dressed head to toe in black with black lipstick and black nail polish. She looks sensational.

The Scary Girl crosses to a table with her date. Other than the first instant of eye contact, she offers no indication that she and I share any acquaintance.

The show starts. I stand where I always do—at the bar as close to the band as possible and directly in their line of sight. You'd be amazed how insecure musicians are and how important it is to them, onstage, to see at least one friendly face.

The abuse starts during the first song.

"I thought they was gonna be music tonight."

"Augggh … I can't stand this shit!"

"What the fuck are you motherfuckers playing?"

The band finishes Song #1, "Alpha Bitch," a crowd-pleasing rocker that has killed in every other venue. The Buster Weems crowd HATES it. The band stays cool. But in the thirty-second transition time between songs, every one of them downs whatever drink they've got and signals for more. I do the same.

Song #2 is "Blindsided," another reliable ass-kicker. The audience hates this even more. The women start up this time.

"He's sweatin'! Look at that boy sweatin'!"

"Hey, boy! Don't you sling no smelly-ass sweat on me!"

Roach is out front on stage, literally two feet from the first tables. The dude has certain moves, stuff he does with his long, greasy hair. He tries them now. The crowd boos and hisses.

People are throwing coasters and ice cubes. They start slinging pennies. If you think this is harmless, try getting hit in the eye with a flung Lincoln-head.

I'm on my feet now. "Hey, hey, hey!" I move in front of the band, facing the crowd. I'm holding both palms up, smiling a thirty-two-toother. "C'mon, you guys! These are hard-working musicians! They came up here to entertain you!"

"Siddown, cracker!"

A woman in back shouts, "Hey! Bob Dylan! Park it!"

Bob Dylan? I don't look anything like Bob Dylan!

A babe up front throws a drink on me. "Get out the way, boy!"

Man in Shades (to me, flashing a .38): "Sit the fuck down 'fore I cap yo ass!"

The band has not stopped playing

Me [to audience]: "C'mon, you guys … cut the boys some slack!"

I have to give Roach credit. Finishing "Blindsided," he thanks the audience, tells them how happy the band is to be here. "We were nervous, I confess. We were anxious coming up here …"

The congregation is howling now.

Roach launches into the next song, "Starship Trooper," a full-tilt headbanger. The audience starts throwing shoes. Guys are flicking lit cigarettes. A side table sails into one of Roach's amps. "Trooper" features a four-minute guitar solo. Roach plows into it. His eyes are rolled back. Sweat is pouring off him. Schwantz on the drums is wailing like John Bonham.

Ridicule and abuse pour from every corner. It's not funny anymore. The guy with the .38 is shouting to Roach, asking him if he is a girl, and demanding that he, Roach, blow him. Somebody slings a bottle. It shatters on the rim of the stage, showering the band with glass.

I'm onstage now, seizing the mike. The band has stopped playing. "That's enough! That's fucking enough!"

The abuse begins centering on me. I can see Jackie Q's g.f. She's squirming. Jackie sits beside her, ogling her with burning eyes. People in the audience are standing now. An assault wave is starting to flow toward the stage.

I've got both hands up, shouting for Q to call this off ...

Suddenly behind me I hear Roach's Stratocaster strike a tender G minor 7th. The band has one ballad in its songbook. It starts with a sweet series of minors. The bass comes in softly. The intro lasts about twenty seconds.

Before it has finished, the mood in the room has altered spectacularly.

Roach glides into his vocal. It's a clean lead with lots of air around it and a simple three-part harmony behind. The song is called "Claire." Claire is Roach's mother. It's a love song, written as if from Roach's dad.

"Claire" is a song of wartime. Roach's father was killed in the German counteroffensive at St. Vith, Belgium, in the winter of 1944. Roach never knew him.

What remains is your face
In the last trace of light
Claire, would you
Remember me too
If I appeared on your doorstep tonight?

I'm not saying it's a great song. But the melody and lyrics, the way Roach and the guys deliver 'em, drains every vibe of malice from the room.

Ninety minutes later the doors have closed but the club is still packed. Half the audience is onstage. I have never seen human beings so intoxicated, or been more so myself. One dude with a shaved skull has taken over Schwantz's drum set and is pounding out a respectable Chick Webb impression; another pair in mohair suits hold Guy the bass player in an embrace like a brother. Schwantz himself has vanished. I'm so wasted I can't remember where I am, and Roach and Guy are not far behind. All I can see, for some crazy reason, is the Scary Girl. She's still here, in the crowd, with her black lipstick and black eyes zeroed in on me.

Minutes pass. Ten? Thirty? Somehow my body has migrated to the top of the bar. I'm on my back. I have no idea how I got here. A pretty black girl in a Diana Ross wig straddles me from above. She has unbuttoned my jeans and is tugging them down toward my ankles. I'm watching, paralyzed. I feel like one of those guys in the movies who wakes up on an operating table with a ring of faces hovering over him.

"Get it up, brother!"

"Show us some bone!"

My jeans have jammed on my cowboy boots. The girl in the wig can't get them off. No matter. She seizes my skivvies and pulls them down below my knees. Simultaneously she hikes her skirt. Either she is wearing no panties or they have somehow dematerialized.

Her eyes lock onto mine. The realization dawns that I'm being called upon to perform sexual intercourse in public. Voices are shouting at me from all sides. It seems to be an issue of honor.

"Up, man!"

"Show a girl some wood!"

The mood in the room is equal parts menace, glee, and derision. I'm just embarrassed. The girl in the wig can't get enough of the attention. She's the star. She weighs about 230 but she's hot and she knows it.

"Whassamatter, darlin'?"

I see Jackie Q. I see the dude with the .38. I see the Scary Girl. I'm trying to rally but there's no way.

Suddenly, for the second time this night, Roach rides to the rescue. Somehow he's on the bar, standing, behind the Diana Ross girl. He tugs down his zipper. I hear whoops and cheers. The girl turns. I can't see what Roach has just exposed; the girl's wig is blocking my view. Plus, I'm so drunk I can't project my vision past a foot and a half. But whatever Roach is displaying to the crowd, it is creating a sensation.

"Where you get *that*, boy?"

"That ain't real!"

"Kill that snake!"

I get one look at Roach's cock (which I have never beheld before) and I gotta say I feel a little like cheering too. What a schlong! It looks like a policeman's billy club if a billy club could pulsate and had an incandescent scarlet knob on the end.

The Supremes girl has turned completely toward Roach now. She's doing something to him with both hands. The crowd is going out of its mind.

For no more than half a second, a look passes from Roach to me, over the Diana Ross girl's right shoulder. The look says, "I'm paying you back for what I did with your wife. After tonight, you and me are quits."

Now Roach and the Supremes Girl start getting it on. He's 130 pounds, she's 230. They're like a train wreck rolling down the track and I'm on my back directly in their path.

Somehow the Scary Girl is at my shoulder. She's helping me off the bar. I feel boundless gratitude, but I'm also about to lose my lunch. The Scary Girl sees it in my eyes. She jinks clear just as my insides convulse.

Somehow I find the men's room.

Johnny Schwantz stands in the corner beside the urinals, getting a pipe job from another dude. A clutch of guys is spiking up in a stall. I heave into a sink. From the club's main room ascends roar upon roar of hilarity and approbation. The whole building is rocking.

The last thing I remember is Jackie Q in the alley, holding me upright beside the band's '71 Dodge van while pressing a wad of greenbacks (three hundred bucks when I count it later) into my shirt pocket. "Brother," he says, "this is Club Inferno's greatest night of entertainment since James Brown and The Famous Flames in '67. Come back any time."

Two codas to this adventure:

One, as I'm puking into the sink while Johnny Schwantz is getting his joint copped against the wall six feet to my right, I suddenly realize what I need to solve the ending of my book. The whole thing comes to me in one all-encompassing flash. I know with blinding urgency that I must race home at once and get it all down on paper before I forget it.

Which I do, working in an adrenaline rush till ten the next morning with Teaspoon curled up peacefully on the tabletop with his back against the left side of the typewriter while the carriage shuttles back and forth over his head.

Two, at 10:30 the next morning, as I'm staggering out into the dazzling daylight heading to the Guantanamera Bodega to get a coffee and a bagel, a '72 Chevelle with spinner hubcaps pulls up and stops alongside the line of parked cars in front of my building. The passenger door opens and out steps the Scary Girl, still in black, still with her black eyes, nails, and lipstick, still looking sensational.

She walks past me into the building without a word or a glance, as though she had never seen me in her life.

12.

Joey

I have an ex-girlfriend named Joey. She's a cop. I met her when she was a storyboard artist in the bullpen at Grey Advertising, my first job, when Tracy and I were still together. Joey's last name is Collins. She was just a friend then. One morning she and I were standing in line for coffee and bialys at work when she casually mentioned that she had been accepted at the academy. I congratulated her; I thought she meant an art academy.

"Fuck that. I'm gonna be a cop."

Now Joey and I are banging the snow off our shoes and trouser legs, entering the Tunnel Diner on Twelfth Avenue. Joey's shift ends at the same time mine does.

We sit. We order coffee and breakfast. It's one thirty in the morning with Brenda Lee's "Rockin' Around the Christmas Tree" piping from the overhead speakers. I tell Joey about the Turk and my job shadowing his old lady. "Can I get in trouble for this?"

"Not with me."

Joey is an Irish Catholic from Gerritsen Beach in Brooklyn. Her father was a cop too. He's retired now. Joey has two brothers who are firemen and a raft of cousins who work for the PD and the Sanitation Department. The whole family is on the Civil Service payroll one way or another.

"I'm serious, Joey. Do I have to know anything about privacy laws or surveillance statutes? Do I need a license to do this stuff?"

"Yes, yes, and yes," Joey says. "But does anybody give a shit?"

Joey was a really good storyboard artist and I'm sure she's a good cop too. She gets out her notebook and asks me a bunch of questions about the Turk. I tell her about the Russian and about the mysterious underground tank at the taxi company. I tell her about Bablik and his brother being indicted in the drywall scandal.

The likely way this job could turn into trouble, Joey says, is if the Turk or his wife or the Russian are mixed up in something seriously criminal. "The NYPD won't come after you, but these creeps might."

Joey says she'll dig around a little. If she comes up with something, she'll let me know.

The waitress brings our eggs and hash browns.

"Still seeing the girl with the hair?"

"Nicolette? She cut it all off."

"No shit. How's she look?"

"Great."

I ask Joey what she's up to.

"The streets, man. I love 'em."

"You don't miss the ad biz?"

"Are you shittin' me?"

Joey looks hot in her uniform. The only thing sexier to me than a lesbian is a woman with a gun.

"Oh no," she says, wagging her finger.

Outside I try to give her a kiss. She ducks away. "I'm not fucking you in the back seat of your taxicab. I might slip and break my leg on all those used condoms on the floorboard."

Joey turns and slides behind the wheel of her police car. She looks great with that .38 on her hip.

"Stick with the girl with the hair!" Joey calls. "I'll get back to you on that other stuff."

13.

Chemistry

Two nights later I'm back at Gotham Cab. The Turk still hasn't paid me. It's been almost three weeks. I've left half a dozen messages on his service and with the hack manager. Now, finally, the Turk is here and calling me into his office.

I climb the stairs and wait outside the steel door with the camera peep. I've worked myself into a healthy state of outrage by the time the Turk buzzes me in, but as soon as I see him, on his feet and distraught about something, behind his huge fortress-like desk with the .45 out in the open, it strikes me that I feel for the guy. I like him. He's been good about my time. As I said, on nights when he knows Abby will be with him or staying home, he leaves a note with my service. I drive the cab that night for fares.

So what if Bablik has stiffed me so far? At least tonight he's paying up.

But the Turk, it turns out, has no intention of coughing up my back pay. In fact he's pissed off. Pissed off *at me*.

"You parked your cab in my private spot last night. Three hours before your shift ended."

I admit this.

The Turk is pacing. His face is red.

It's true, last night driving my taxi I picked up a girl outside the Bookmasters on Columbus Circle. She was going to an address near Co-op City, not far from the cab company.

By her looks, I thought the girl was a lesbian. She had the hair.
I'm always attracted to lesbians. Invariably I mistake them for
straight. More than one night I've been at a party or someplace,
chasing some semi-butch-y chick all evening long, only to stumble
upon her in a corner at closing time with her tongue six inches
down the throat of another woman.

We get to talking, this girl and me. She's from Hungary. Her
name is Mika Lukic. She's got a doctorate in Chemistry from the
old country, but over here until she gets US papers she can only
work as a lab technician. In fact she's on her way to her job right
now. She's leaning forward in the cab with her elbows over the
back of the front seat.

"Ever do it with anybody in this cab?"

"You mean in the taxi itself?"

"Yeah. Here. In the back seat."

We're on the Hutchinson River Parkway, approaching Gun Hill
Road. Lights and traffic everywhere.

Mika leans forward a little farther. "I don't have to be at work
for another forty minutes."

Now it's two nights later. I'm in the Turk's office. He's pacing,
getting more agitated with every stride.

"You parked your cab in my spot cause you were shtupping
some broad."

The Turk warns me not to lie. Kingie saw everything. He tells
me that shorting my shift by three hours takes money out of his
pocket. I'm cheating him.

"Why'd you bring a dame back here to the garage?"

"Because it's safe."

Bablik fixes me with a look.

"You were eating her pussy, weren't you?"

I mumble something.

"That's disgusting! In the back seat of one of my cabs!"

The Turk has stopped pacing now. He faces me.

"You're Charlie Moses' nephew! You went to college! What are doing banging these skanks?"

"I wouldn't call 'em skanks."

"When you bang a skank, you're a skank. What college d'you go to? Harvard?"

"Duke."

"Never heard of it. Look, you're like a son to me. Stop with these skanks. Show some respect for yourself!"

As I'm leaving to start my shift (Bablik forgives me after another five minutes of impassioned admonishment—and even comes up with a couple of hundred bucks of my arrears, peeling it in twenties off a wad that he extracts from his right-hand trouser pocket), I notice an eighteen-wheel tanker truck with

SHELL OIL

on the side pulling in under the lights to the fueling area beside the garage. A line of cabs is waiting to gas up at the two north-side pumps adjacent to the underground tank. The Shell truck comes in on the south side. It parks beyond the taxis, on the concrete hardstand above the second tank, the one Tito said was "where Bablik makes all his dough."

For a second I don't think anything of this, like I dismissed Tito's remark when he first made it. Then something makes me perk up. I cross to my cab, which is parked on the street since I filled up when I first got to the garage. The Shell driver has dismounted from his truck. He's got his wrench and his heavy gloves. He crosses to the underground tank and kneels to open the cap.

On the side of his truck, beneath *Shell Oil*, are the words

INDUSTRIAL AND COMMERCIAL FUEL SERVICE.

Only "Industrial" is spelled wrong. It says "Industiral."

Book Three

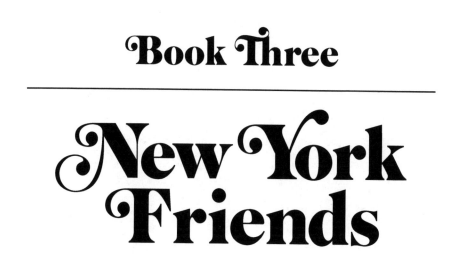

New York
Friends

14.

New York Friends

Jake is talking about bringing me back to the agency for two weeks of freelance. Y&R is pitching Burger King. The job would pay $250 a week, which would definitely help fill my rice bowl, and it'd be regular hours so I could keep working with Tito at night.

I'd have my old office back, Jake says—a cubicle actually; the agency hasn't hired anyone to replace me. That'd be aces, as I'd get my favorite IBM Selectric typewriter, which Jakes says has not been removed, not to mention unlimited carbon paper, white-out (the tape kind that I like, which I can't afford at home) plus free xeroxing in the copy room.

But the best part is I'd get a temporary ID that would entitle me to use the office on weekends to do my real work. I don't know why but I'd much rather write in the office than at home. Weekends are golden at Y&R. The place is empty. The Creative Department has two floors, each one a full block square. It takes five minutes to walk one lap. The place is warm; there's plenty of light. There's all the paper you need and good clean bathrooms with high-quality, soft toilet paper.

Y&R is at 285 Madison Avenue, two blocks from Grand Central and one long block from the Public Library. There's a hooker in every doorway as you approach. I like it. It gives the neighborhood color.

My habit on weekends is to go in really early, seven thirty when the streets are empty. I stop at the Acropolis Coffee Shop on the corner of Vanderbilt and 43rd for a bialy with cream cheese and a coffee, which I take in a to-go bag to eat upstairs in my office. I spread the meal out over my desk with the paper wrappers and napkins, the packets of sugar, the little plastic knife and the coffee stirrers. I can work all day both days and never get tired. I accomplish prodigies in a weekend. If this freelance gig comes through from Jake, I'll knock off the book by the last week in December, a week before Tracy gets here. I'll owe Jake big-time.

Jake and I are New York friends. This is a good thing and a bad thing. In the city, you can be close to somebody, share secrets, do stuff together that you've never done with anybody ever, but when crunch time comes, you look around and your pal is AWOL.

I've never had conversations of the depth and intensity that I have with Jake. We stay up all night. I feel like I'm vibrating at ten thousand cycles a minute. We talk about women, we talk about money, we talk about the state of the democracy, the future of the world. We rehearse books we want to write, movies we intend to make and visions of the selves we're going to be. We drop all bullshit. We speak from the heart. And this is not one night. It's five, six times a month. We work ourselves into a state.

One night we decided to move to Kyoto. Fuck advertising. Fuck New York. We're gonna enter a Zen monastery.

Another night we decided to join the French Foreign Legion.

"This is no shit," Jake said. "We're gonna do it."

"Fuck yeah, bro!"

I can't tell you how convinced we were (or at least I was) that this was totally for real. "Did you know," says Jake, "that you can't join the Foreign Legion under your own name? You have to adopt a nom de guerre."

"Get the fuck outa here."

"You trade in your entire identity. You take on a completely new self." Wow.

Another time we were going to climb Annapurna. We were sailing to Tahiti. I would get so worked up I'd go home and couldn't sleep a wink. The next day at work I'd march straight into Jake's office (he's my boss, remember) ready to confirm and commit.

"Stretch, do you have the copy on that Johnson & Johnson trade ad?"

At that time, Jake was one of maybe a dozen young Creative Directors who were riding rocket ships to Superstar City. He was on Hot Twenty lists in *Ad Age*. You read his name in the columns. What am I thinking: he's gonna bail from the Big Time to trek the Mountains of the Moon with me?

Except Jake's other side, his ascetic half, is just as real as his New York winner side. He's been studying at the Dai Bosatsu Zendo since he was fourteen (he's twenty-nine now). This place is hard core. No heat in the winter, no A/C in the summer. Jake's hero is a monk named Brady. No one knows where Brady lives. No one has ever heard him speak. But he's in the zendo, Jake says, at four in the morning sweeping up and he's still there when the last light is doused. When Jake talks about Brady, his whole body changes. He becomes another person.

I love that. That's the Jake I want him to be. I want to be that person myself. I went to Jake's one night in January last year. He was on the roof, barefoot. I had to slap him across the face just to bring him back to Planet Earth.

Jake goes on bike rides, solo, that start Friday night at the office. He takes off with a jug of Gatorade and a few tubes of energy gel. When he comes in Monday morning, he hasn't been home or shaved or bathed and he hasn't changed clothes.

We read Gary Snyder. We read Gurdjieff and Ouspensky. We read Peter Matthiessen. One time Jake talked me into going with him to a sesshin upstate. A sesshin is zazen meditation seven days in a row, all day. No talking. No eye contact. Two grapes and an Ak-mak hippie cracker for lunch. I bailed after twenty-four hours. Jake? The man sat like the Dalai Lama. You could detonate a bomb next to him. He was in deep. His focus was incredible.

Another time he took me up to a town near West Point to do a "hill run." We parked the car at the base of some mountain, changed into shorts and running shoes and started up the trail. Jake was out of sight within ninety seconds, tearing like a man possessed. There was nothing for me to do but go back to the car and wait. I sat there for five hours. Jake just ran and ran.

No friend has ever backed me in the real world like Jake. I applied for work originally with Jake's boss, Ricky Vaughn, a bona fide ad legend, back when Jake was Ricky's #1 rising star. All I did was walk past Jake's office on my way to interview with Ricky. (I had just come back to New York after three years in England and on the American road; my portfolio was on 3X5 cards in a manila envelope.) I never even saw Jake as I passed. Jake had never met me, had no idea who I was or where I was coming from. When I left Ricky Vaughn's office, Jake went in and said, "Hire that guy."

I can't talk to anyone else about the shit I talk to Jake about. But New York friends are like friends in the movie industry or the music biz. They're not really friends. You link up with someone because you're working together for the moment or you're on the same trajectory temporarily with women or money or whatever. But when that trajectory alters, all bets are off.

New York friends are about competition. Under optimum conditions, Jake would take a bullet for me and I'd do the same for him. But in altered circumstances, he'd leave me twisting. I hate to say it but I'd probably do the same to him.

15.
Glen Island Casino

I'm thinking about Jake and listening to Tito.

"Ya think I don't know Bablik thinks I'm a schmuck? To him I'm a two-bit mook that he hires for muscle and nothing else. He brings a kid like you in on my job. Why? 'Cause I'm not good enough to walk into the Plaza Hotel? I'm gonna get spotted for a bum?"

We're in the cab, Tito and me, parked and freezing our asses off in the weeds alongside a dirt trail east of Weyman Avenue and Shore Road that leads down to the causeway for Glen Island. I understand Tito's feelings toward the Turk. I'd be pissed off too if I were him. Yet at the same time, for me anyway, Bablik is a more authentic soul than just about anybody I know. Am I crazy to think this? Clearly the Turk is a crook and probably a lot worse. But I like the guy. He's in the shit. He's suffering.

"Fuck him," says Tito. "What time is it?"

It's one thirty. Tito and I have been following Abby since nine. We got on her tail at University Village, where she exited her apartment, hailed a cab and took it to Gleason's Boxing Gym on West 30th off Eighth, a block south of Madison Square Garden. There she connected with the Russian and his bodyguards in the Chrysler Imperial and a '72 Ford Fairlane and drove up Broadway to Gallagher's Steakhouse on West 52nd. Tito and I loitered outside for two hours (with me going in twice just be sure the party hadn't ducked out the back), let Abby go when she emerged alone and was picked up by the

Fairlane (which headed south down Broadway, no doubt to take her home to Washington Square), then waited another hour on the chance that the Russian and his goons had further business this night and would reappear.

They did. Tito and I followed them up the Henry Hudson, over the Cross-Bronx, onto the Hutch and up to Orchard Beach and Shore Road, where the Imperial's gunsight taillights turned toward the water into an unlit region of canals and sloughs choked with wild fennel and swamp grass. During the evening Tito has killed one pint of apricot brandy and is well into the second. I've inhaled a noseful myself. It's antifreeze. You need it, just to keep your blood from turning to ice.

I've got the cab idling for the heater but it's still arctic in the front seat and this sodden swampland isn't helping. "What the fuck are they doing out there?" says Tito.

The Russian and his gorillas have stashed the Imperial in a turn-out among the cattails and gone forward toward the shoreline on foot. I want to follow but Tito says it's too risky. If the Russian or Ivanov or Ponytail spot the cab with a company name that's recognizably Bablik's (every taxi in NYC is incorporated individually for insurance purposes and each one has a different company name, but all of the Turk's have GOTHAM CAB stenciled on the side as well), they'll suspect something immediately. If we're not in the car, they may lay for us when we come back. In the cab at least we can run away.

Tito gestures toward a dark structure across the inlet. A '30s-style edifice sprawls just east of the causeway. "That used to be Glen Island Casino. Ever hear of Tommy Dorsey?" He starts humming "In the Mood."

"That's Glenn Miller."

"Couples used to come here for the dancing. Big bands. You wore a suit and tie. You shined your shoes."

The clock on the dash says one thirty-three. It's about twenty degrees outside and forty in. Back at Gallagher's I was telling Tito about the article I found at the library, the one about Bablik being named Man of the Year by the Israeli Army.

"Yeah, he told me about it twenty times. When's the date? Three weeks from now?"

Tito takes a snort and offers me the pint. I wave it off.

"The Turk," he says, "is gonna get a medal from Robert Moses himself. Know what that means? It means he'll be a Big Jew. Why? Because Robert Moses is the Biggest Jew of all."

Tito explains to me who Robert Moses is. Lifetime chairman of the Port Authority of New York and New Jersey. Built the Triborough Bridge, the Throgs Neck, the Verrazano. Built the UN.

"That's as big of a Jew as it gets. And the Turk's gonna get his award handed to him by Robert Moses himself."

I'm actually related to Robert Moses. He's my Mom and Charlie's cousin. I've never met him though. I decide not to say anything to Tito. It might sound like I'm showing off.

"Now," Tito says, "Bablik is a Little Jew. No one knows who the fuck he is. But three weeks from now, he'll be a Big Jew. Jew of the Year."

Tito raises the pint.

"Here's to our employer. May he get what's coming to him."

Tito is just tilting his head back when a dark form appears outside his window. I feel a shadow fall across mine. My door is jerked open from outside. Powerful hands haul me into the freezing air. Something hits me, hard, across the temple. A face as broad as a bear's thrusts itself in front of my eyeballs.

"Who the fuck are you?" the face demands.

"Me? I'm nobody."

16.

Busted

In every private eye flick, there's a scene where the bad guys beat the crap out of the hapless dick.

That's exactly what happens now, except the main freight of the thrashing comes down not on me, but on Tito. The Russian bear has released me. I've just been hammered in the solar plexus by Ivanov; I'm doubled over, gasping for oxygen, with my assailant torqueing me sideways against the driver's door of the cab so that when I start puking I won't splatter his wingtip shoes. Out of the side of my eye I see two sinister profiles, one of which belongs to the Russian, the other being the Ponytail Guy, dragging Tito's 250-plus pounds out of the passenger door and body-slamming him forward to the front of the cab. The two men open the hood and raise it high. Together they jam Tito face first into the engine block and slam the hood onto the back of his neck as hard as they can. Once. Twice. The metal frame bends and buckles.

"Hey, hey, hey!" I'm half shouting, half gagging.

Ivanov pops me hard across the ear. I feel warm blood on my neck and face.

"What the fuck!"

I'm thinking (this is how dumb I am) that if I can only explain to these neck-breakers who Tito and I are and what we're doing, they will understand and we can all be friends and even get a laugh out of it. I can't believe they're this serious about the situation. In my mind I'm reeling off the story: some crazy guy who owns a cab company hired us, we're just a couple of idiots, we'll stop what we're doing, we promise.

Ivanov drills me again in the space between my heart and my ribcage. I'm on my knees now in the frozen mud. Around the corner of the cab I can see Ponytail reach down to the muck and pick up a cinderblock or part of one (it's broken). The Russian hauls Tito upright. Ponytail wallops Tito across the temple with the cinderblock. It's a sickening sound. They drop Tito face down into the frost.

I'm being pulled to my feet now. Suddenly Ponytail appears. He grabs me by the collar. "Gimme this fucker," he says to Ivanov. "You're going way too easy on him." He punches me once in the gut, which knocks the wind out of me completely, then hammers me furiously between the shoulder blades as I double over. I'm thinking, These sonsofbitches have gotta start interrogating us (or me at least, since I'm the only one still conscious) pretty soon. That's the whole point of this demonstration, isn't it?

But apparently that item is not on the Russian's agenda. The thought occurs to me that they intend to kill us. An image of Tracy flashes before me. I want to tell her I love her as my last words. Ivanov has taken me back from the Ponytail Guy now. He drags me upright. I have just enough breath to confront his partner.

"Hey, man," I wheeze to Ponytail. "What's your problem?"

"You," he says. "You're my problem."

He hauls me away from Ivanov, seizes me by the collar with both hands and head-butts me so hard it feels like a lightning bolt just blasted me right between the eyes. The greasy sweat from Ponytail's long dark hair slings into my face. My thought is, "Good, this means they're not going to kill us."

And in fact the beating stops. The Russian lurches forward, flush before my face. I can see his ruddy pate shining in the spillover from the dome light in the cab.

"Tell your boss ..."

The Russian has to catch his breath. He's been working so hard in the past ninety seconds. "Tell your boss that there's plenty more where this came from."

My last thought, before I crash face first into the icy muck, with Tito's upturned shoes and trouser bottoms visible to me on the ground on the other side of the cab, is that the Russian speaks with hardly any accent, other than Brooklynese. The Russian is as American as apple pie.

17.

Salesian Hospital

I phone the Turk from the emergency room at Salesian Hospital on the Boston Post Road in New Rochelle. In those days, as I said, there was no such thing as voicemail or answering machines. Bablik has an answering service. An actual operator comes on the line.

During the beating, I had managed to maintain my own half-assed version of presence of mind. I'd been outraged and frantic but not actually scared. Now in the aftermath I'm shaking all over. It takes me two hands to get the coin into the slot and four tries to dial the number.

The operator comes on. I identify myself and tell her I'm an employee of Mr. Bablik. "Tell Mr. Bablik that I'm here at Salesian Hospital in New Rochelle. Three guys just beat the hell out of me and my partner."

The great thing about answering services is, if the message is urgent enough, the operator can phone the client on her own initiative and get the word to him on the spot.

"Time right now," I continue, "is two fifty in the morning. Please inform Mr. Bablik that if he isn't at Salesian in twenty minutes, my next call is to the NYPD."

Tito has been worked over pretty good. Both eyes are black and swollen shut; his mouth is a well of blood. Somehow he's lost one shoe and his winter coat.

I'm telling the nurse at the counter that Tito is an ex-cop and a Roman Catholic. Salesian is a Catholic hospital. The nurse, who's wearing a crucifix as big as a pork sausage, couldn't give less of a shit. She's more concerned with the Christmas tree that two maintenance guys are decorating in the corner by the candy machine. I've never been to Salesian before; I didn't even know the hospital existed. I chanced to spot an ambulance on the way and trailed it here. The emergency room is L-shaped, with the entrance off the Post Road funneling you directly to an intake station, then the treatment rooms and surgery and the hospital itself off to the right. I couldn't carry Tito in myself. I had to leave him in the cab and run in to get help. It took ten minutes. Tito still hasn't been seen by anybody. He's slumped in a plastic chair with his gashed head leaning against the wall. A black kid no older than twelve is being wheeled past on a gurney bleeding so copiously that a trail of crimson is spilling under the carriage's wheels, leaving a smear on the floor. A Puerto Rican couple, at least sixty, is screaming at each other in Spanish. Next to them a guy with no shirt is reading *Good Housekeeping*.

"Insurance card."

"What?"

"Does your friend have medical insurance?"

Two male medics are attempting to get Tito onto his feet. He's so heavy they can't lift him. There's no sense of urgency whatsoever.

"Do *you* have insurance? We can use your card."

Me? Insurance?

Two hours later I'm still in the waiting area. The medics have wheeled Tito into the hospital. No one will tell me how he is or what they're doing to him. Instead I'm the one answering questions. What is Tito's last name? Where does he live? Does he have a wife? A family? Is he an American citizen? Who is responsible for making medical decisions on his behalf?

I answer "I don't know" a hundred times. I spend an hour in the parking lot, straightening out the hood of the taxi from where it got bent beating on Tito's head. The Turk has not phoned or shown up. Finally a cop comes in. I accost him. He's blond and thin and looks like he's eleven years old. "Three guys just beat the crap out of me and my friend, can you help me?"

"Where'd it happen?"

I tell him.

"That's Bronx 49th Precinct." He indicates the pin on his own collar—NRPD, which I assume means New Rochelle—and points south down the Post Road. "The station house is on Eastchester Road. They'll take your report."

Another hour passes. A nun in a black habit has me fill out a four-page intake form. I've never lied more in my life. I scribble a fake name and address and a bogus Social Security and phone number. Where is my wallet? "The attackers stole it." No one asks about the cab, which is in the lot outside now, probably being impounded by the NYPD, not for purposes of evidence but to charge me five hundred bucks to get it back. A nurse appears and asks me to read the sign on the wall. It's some kind of test to see if I have a concussion.

"What wall?"

She tells me not to be a wise guy.

What has become of my normal All-American clean-cut-ness? The nurse and the nun clearly know I'm feeding them a yard of bullshit. They don't care. I am accepted as another denizen of the urban netherworld, the scum of the earth just like every other derelict dope-dealing mugger, murderer, and wife beater in here. I assimilate this partly with a sense of relief (it takes a lot of pressure off) and partly with a distant, self-reflective regret.

A black lady whose son has been shot offers me a donut. She has a box of a dozen from Dunkin Donuts up the street. The sky is starting to get light. Now I'm the one reading *Good Housekeeping*. No one will tell me anything about Tito. Still not a peep from Bablik.

The article in *Good Housekeeping* is about cloth diapers vs. disposables. Apparently there are good points to be made on both sides. I decide if I had a baby I'd go with cloth. Yeah, the laundering wastes water and creates pollution, but it's probably less harmful to the planet in the long run than the expense for paper and plastic in disposables, not to mention the landfill problem or cutting down all those trees. I'm congratulating myself on the ethics of this decision when a shadow falls across the magazine. I look up.

Abby stands there. "Have you given them your real name?"

I stare. I've never seen Mrs. B. this close. "No."

"Well," she says. "We can be grateful for that."

Mrs. Bablik hands me a lit Marlboro and indicates a black sedan outside at the curb.

"Wait for me in that Cadillac. I'll be back in five minutes."

18.

Empire Diner

"Well, your friend's going to live. Thanks in part to you."

Mrs. Bablik has led me back to Manhattan, trailing her Caddy, to the Empire Diner on Tenth Avenue and 22nd Street. The place is a glossy, retro-style burger joint favored by artists and hipsters. It's seven thirty in the morning. Every table is occupied. Counter too.

Abby has taken not five minutes at Salesian but an hour and a half. Through the glass doors I could see her working with the nurses at the intake station. They were sticking forms in front of her and she was signing them.

Afterward, in the Cadillac, I introduce myself.

Abby: "I know who you are."

Mrs. B. is visibly shaken by the report of the injuries to Tito, not to mention the sight of my own busted-up face. She swears to me she's not cheating on her husband. Bablik was lying when he hired me.

"I can only assume," she says, "that that's what he told you."

The reason Bablik wants to learn the Russian's whereabouts is he intends to kill him. They're in business together. Who is the Russian? He's dangerous, says Abby, very dangerous. Both men are crazy.

At the Empire Diner she orders a bagel with a shmeer and coffee. I get bacon and eggs. I'm starving. My skull feels like it's splitting down the middle. I can't focus out of my left eye and the right one is not much better.

"How are you feeling? You look terrible."

"I'm okay."

"That eye. Did someone look at that eye?"

"How did you know to come to the hospital?"

"You phoned my husband's service."

I ask Abby, in earnest, what she found out from the doctors about Tito.

"He's got a dislocated jaw and a possible concussion. Also several of his ribs might be cracked. But he's stable. His family's on their way to the hospital now."

"Thank you for stepping up for him."

"You're welcome."

Mrs. Bablik is hot. She's wearing a midriff-cut leather jacket with black stovepipe jeans tucked into the same high boots she had on when I tailed her into the Terminal Bar. Her honey-colored hair, which is teased up into a sort of bouffant, is covered by a silk scarf knotted into a kerchief. She undoes this now and tucks it into her purse. She applies lipstick using a compact mirror.

Mrs. B. is what … fifty? More than twenty years older than me. She's fifty but she's smokin' hot.

"What do you do for a living? I mean when you're not shadowing someone."

"Trust me. I'm not shadowing anyone ever again."

Our food comes.

We both eat without speaking. You can tell when you're with someone if they're anxious to get the encounter over with. For whatever reason, Abby is not. I realize I'm not either. I wish my stomach would settle and my head would stop throbbing. About Mrs. B. I'm starting to get that crazy feeling I had when I first met Tracy. Like I want to protect her. This is ridiculous of course. I know it, but there it is.

"My husband never called you back at the hospital, did he? Do you know why?"

"Because he's an asshole?"

She asks me if it's true that I'm Charlie Moses' nephew. Apparently she knows my uncle via his friendship with Bablik. I tell her that my mother is Charlie's sister. Charlie is my uncle.

"So your mother's maiden name is Moses?"

Abby finishes a quarter of her bagel and pushes the plate aside. She tamps a Marlboro against a gold thumb-roll lighter. "You mind?"

I don't.

Mrs. B. lights up, leaving a scarlet lipstick blot on the cigarette filter. She turns her head away courteously and exhales a silky, feminine plume.

"Does it hurt?"

"What?"

"Your face."

The phrase "like a motherfucker" comes to mind. But Mrs. B. is a lady.

Me: "Little bit."

Abby pushes the pack of smokes across the table to me. I take one. She lights it for me with the gold lighter. The waitress comes and warms up her coffee. Abby indicates her plate; the waitress takes it. Abby waits till the waitress has gone.

"My husband, in case this is not apparent to you, is not a man of virtue. I understand him. I care for him. But he's a dangerous individual. He's capable of everything and more than what those men did to you tonight."

She studies me to see if I have any idea what she's talking about.

"Do you know why Marvin hired you for this preposterous undertaking? I mean you specifically and no other?"

Before I can answer, she says, "For your name."

"My name?"

"Do you know who Robert Moses is?"

I do.

"You're what? His second cousin? His grand-nephew?"

"I don't know. I've never met him."

"My husband wanted you because you're related to Robert Moses, and Robert Moses is the most important man in New York and the dignitary who's going to give Marvin the Man of the Year award twenty days from now."

I don't get it. What does my being related to Robert Moses have to do with the Turk hiring me to tail his old lady? The surveillance job was a ruse?

"You represent something to him. You can't see it, can you? You don't know what I'm talking about."

The check arrives. Mrs. B. reaches for it. I stop her. I pay with a ten, which covers both our tabs with five bucks left over. As Abby protests and tries again to pick up the tab, a thought hits me.

At the restaurant in Brighton Beach, when Mrs. B. was sitting in the front booth with the Russian, he paid the bill—with a credit card. How could I have forgotten that? I think: I could go back to the restaurant tomorrow, give the cashier a bullshit story and maybe get a look at the receipt.

That would give me the Russian's name, maybe even his address.

The waitress makes the five dollars change from a sheaf of singles she keeps in the front pocket of her apron. I leave it all on the table.

Abby: "Are you trying to impress me?"

"I know what it's like to work for tips."

There's this about beautiful women. They've always been beautiful. They were beautiful girls and before that they were beautiful babies. They know their power and they know how to turn it on when they need to.

Mrs. B. does this now with majestic subtlety. Her hand trembles slightly, her eyes go a little scared-y. I know what she's doing. I'm a sucker for it just the same. She knows it.

Abby: "I need you to do something for me. I know you've had it with this surveillance business and you don't want any part of it. I don't blame you. You'd be crazy to feel any other way. But I'll pay you five hundred dollars now and a thousand more if you succeed. But you have to do what I need within the next twenty days, and the sooner the better."

She tells me she wants me to find her husband.

Blood is crusting under the bandage over my left ear. My head feels like a wad of bubble gum. Can I be hearing Mrs. B. right?

"Find your husband? He's living in the apartment with you. I know because he's been phoning me each night for three weeks, telling me which evenings you'll be going out and which evenings you're staying in."

Abby glances to the booths in front of and behind us, then to the seats nearest to us at the counter. She turns back to me.

"Marvin moved out of the apartment in October. I haven't seen him in six weeks."

19.
Visitors

I get home to find yellow tape across my apartment door, or the vacant space where my door used to be. POLICE LINE DO NOT CROSS. The door itself is off its hinges, hanging halfway into the hall. The building's super is there, whose name I don't know, along with a delivery guy from the Guantanamera Bodega on the corner.

My first thought is for Teaspoon. I dash into the apartment with my heart hammering.

"Where's my cat?"

"What cat?" says the super.

I'm out the back window now, onto the fire escape, above the two flights of steel stairs that descend to the rear courtyard. For ninety seconds, I whistle and call Teaspoon's name. The block-long space below me is three inches deep in snow. Trees are bare. I can see everything.

No Teaspoon.

"Yo, homes!" calls the super. "Get back in here. The cops are coming."

It's twenty degrees outside. Almost certainly Teaspoon has fled on his own. He'll hole up someplace and come back when the coast is clear. That's what I'm telling myself anyway.

But my heart won't stop pounding.

"Get back inside, man. You'll freeze your ass."

I climb back in.

The super and the bodega guy are rubbernecking around the apartment like it's a wreck on the highway. The super tells me what time the cops came and what time they left and that they said they'd be back in a few minutes. Apparently the break-in happened around four in the morning.

Super: "Looks like they really fucked up the place, bro."

Me: "That's the way it always looks."

The kitchen drawers have been pulled out and strewn. The fridge door is open. The bed and its mattress have been overturned, along with the bookcases and the cardboard boxes I keep my clothes in. But my writing table, typewriter and chair are still in place.

The super is eyeing the forty-seven boxes in the back room.

Super: "What you up to in here, man?"

He picks up a Death Warmed Over T-shirt.

Me: "Is this my apartment?"

Super: "Okay. I'm leaving."

The Scary Girl from next door has come out into the hall. She moves into the frame of the doorway, barefoot in a housecoat but still wearing black lipstick. I ask her if she's seen Teaspoon. She doesn't answer, which is normal behavior for her. This is why she's scary.

"It's amazing," she says, indicating her own apartment just a few feet away. "For all this damage, the intruders hardly made a sound."

I'm thinking I've gotta get down into the rear courtyard, go door to door asking people if they've seen my cat. Do I have a photo of Teaspoon? As I'm thinking this, the buzzer rings from downstairs. Before I can move, the super hits the button. "Yeah?"

Voice from speaker: "Who is this?"

It's Nicolette. I buzz her in.

I apologize to the super for what I said before. I'm upset. My cat is missing. I didn't mean to be rude. He and the Bodega Guy have made themselves completely at home in the apartment. So has the Scary Girl. The Bodega Guy, who apparently was just making a delivery on the hall, takes off. I explain to the super that I manage a band. The T-shirts are a marketing item to promote the band's music and their appearances. I show him the name DEATH WARMED OVER on the front of the T-shirts and explain that that's the band's name.

I hear the elevator doors open in the hallway. Nicolette appears.

Me (to super): "What size you wear?"

From the doorway Nicolette takes in the carnage. Her look to me says, 1) Does this have anything to do with those gangsters? and 2) You can move in with me if you want.

I wave her in. I tell her Teaspoon is missing. She gives me a kiss and a squeeze. Then she sees my beat-up face.

"It *is* those gangsters!"

I hand the super two XLs for himself and a couple of smalls for his kids.

I'm standing in the doorway of my back room now. My manuscript is intact. The typewriter is still in place.

Two uniformed patrolmen have appeared in the door.

Cop #1 (to me): "This your place?"

He comes in followed by his partner.

Suddenly behind the cops appears Tracy.

What the fuck?

My wife is wearing heels and a business suit, with a St. Laurent shoulder bag and her hair in a Barbara Stanwyck up-do like she wore in the final scene of *Missizombie*.

With one glance Tracy takes in me and my bandaged face, the super, the death's-head T-shirts, the wreckage of the apartment, Nicolette, and the Scary Girl, who instantly susses her out as a former or current spouse and lasers her with radioactive jealousy.

Tracy stands five-eleven in her stilettos. She looks sensational. "Sorry not to buzz. I came up with the police."

She steps in with a smile.

"I brought our Dissolution of Marriage papers from the lawyer," she says to me. "Is this a bad time?"

Book Four

What The
Fuck

20.
Whatthefuck

"I thought your ex-old lady wasn't coming into town for another two weeks," says Nicolette.

"Her plans changed, I guess."

It's two in the morning. Nicolette and I are at a table at the White Horse Tavern. I have given her a fuller but still sketchy version of my involvement with Bablik and Abby and the background to the beat-up last night. Nicolette insists on accompanying me when I go to check on Tito.

"Am I going to check on Tito?"

"Yes, you are. And you're bringing flowers."

I have passed the entire day, since noon, scouring the neighborhood for Teaspoon. Nicolette has worked with me the whole time, drawing up and xeroxing LOST CAT signs (with description and photo) and posting them on every lamppost between West Fourth Street and the Chelsea piers.

My main search area has been the rear courtyard—the block-long open space between the buildings on Fifteenth Street and Fourteenth. What a world! I had no idea.

"Yeah, I seen him," says the owner of the Chinese takeout diagonally across from my rear apartment window when I show him a photo of Teaspoon. "He comes in the back door every night at 11:30 sharp. He's very polite. The cook gives him some fish guts and a saucer of milk."

Teaspoon was in last night at his usual time, says the owner. That's no help, since the break-in of my apartment happened past midnight. I leave my number. "Please call if you see anything. I'll buy thirty dinners."

I hit Ray's Pizza next. Teaspoon has a girlfriend, says one of the delivery boys.

"They come around together some nights. Actually he's got three or four girlfriends. Unless he's gay. Who can tell these days?"

Teaspoon has enemies. At the Portuguese restaurant the owner's wife fixes me with a glower when I flash my cat's mug shot. "That beast picks a fight with my cat every night. I've called Animal Control on him twice. He's a menace! I'll have him put away if I catch him. You keep that wild animal away from here!"

Now at the White Horse, I tell Nicolette I've figured out how Teaspoon makes his way to her apartment without getting run over in traffic, or at least I have a best guess. "He goes out the front door of the Szechuan takeout, cuts down to Jackson Square, then takes Horatio Street to Hudson. He only has to cross Eighth once. It's not that dangerous."

What I don't tell Nicolette is that sometime past midnight tonight, returning onto Fifteenth Street, I spotted the Ponytail Guy following me. When I turned and yelled out to him, he ran away.

Was it really Ponytail? Am I being paranoid? Could the guy have been only an innocent passerby? So what if he took off running? I'd run too if some freaked-out character started shouting, "Hey! You!" and chased me across traffic at twenty minutes after twelve.

But it was Ponytail. I know it. The sight of him one block from my home has changed everything for me. I no longer believe my cat has escaped and is safe on his own.

I believe the Russian took him. Or worse.

"What are you gonna do now?" Nicolette asks.

"Sleep for two hours. Then go back out looking for Teaspoon."

"I mean in your life."

"You mean am I gonna stop with the Russian? How can I? He's got my cat—or he knows what happened to him."

Nicolette orders a third Scotch. I've never seen her drunk before. She's worried about me. I'm deeply touched and grateful. Except now I'm worried about her.

Nicolette wants me to stay with her in her apartment. It's not safe in my place, she says. But I have to stay home in case Teaspoon comes back. Besides, I tell Nicolette, it's too dangerous *for her* if I move into her place. I would never forgive myself if anything happened to her.

At the same time, Tracy has volunteered to put me up in a room in the hotel with her movie crew. The place has 24-hour security, she says. I'll be safe. Whoever tore up my apartment will have no way of knowing I went there.

"You're sleeping with her, right?"

"Tracy? She won't even shake my hand."

"The other one. Black Lipstick."

I mumble something.

"Since how long?"

"I honestly can't remember."

Nicolette gives me a look. "You're beyond hope. I don't know why I continue to hang out with you."

Tracy is not in town to return to Columbia Law School. She's here to make a movie (as she informed me at my apartment after the super and the cops and the Scary Girl and Nicolette had left) but not as an actress. She's producing now.

"Co-producing actually, but who's quibbling? I'm so happy to be on the right side of the camera for once."

When Tracy and I were first married, she was the sweetest, least material person you could imagine. And she was absolutely sincere in everything she said and did. That was why I loved her. Now she has become such a different person that it's hard for me to even remember the girl she once was. And it's my fault. I did this to her.

Tracy has mastered the art of the mixed message. She does it to

torment me, though she would never cop to it, ever. What do I mean
by mixed messages? She insists this afternoon that I sign the divorce
papers (which I refuse to do, citing my state of trauma and claiming
the need for a few days to clear my head). And though she fixes me
with a look of simmering ire, she immediately offers to take me in,
free, and give me a room at the Burgundy Hotel on West Broadway
off Canal (I've never heard of the place but she swears it's very clean
and respectable) at which she and the production have rented three
floors as lodging for cast and crew, editing suites, etc. No, she and I
will not be in the same room. In fact, Tracy explains, she probably
won't see me except in passing for the entire three weeks of the shoot
since she has early calls every morning except for the night shoots
when she'll be sleeping all day or trying to. But she and I will be on
the same floor, only a few doors apart, so maybe we'll have a chance
to spend a little time together.

That's what I mean by mixed messages.

I thank Nicolette, now at the White Horse, for posting the dozens of LOST CAT signs and for offering to put me up and just for
sticking by me through all this insanity.

The White Horse is the bar that Dylan Thomas used to hang out
in. It's on the corner of Hudson and Eleventh. There's a two-person
table next to an old cast-iron radiator under a giant photo of the
author. That's the one Nicolette and I are sitting at.

It's two thirty. We have both switched to coffee. I take mine with
six aspirin. Nicolette is looking at me with a sober expression.

"You're going to be a wonderful writer someday."

I turn away.

"You are. If I had money, I'd buy stock in you. You're going nowhere but to the top."

"You're the one," I say and I mean it. Nicolette is a real artist. You
can feel it in everything she says and does.

"Straight to the top if you don't kill yourself first."

Nicolette informs me that I'm operating, however, by a very

fraught philosophy. "I've been studying you. I've got you figured out." She asks me if I want to know what my philosophy is.

I don't.

"You have a comprehensive world view," Nicolette says. "An authentic *Weltanschauung*. It colors and defines everything you do, and it can be expressed in a single word."

Nicolette scrawls on a coaster and passes it across to me.

WHATTHEFUCK

"That's it. That's your philosophy in one word."

Nicolette has great teeth. Big white Chiclets that light up her face when she smiles.

"You live this philosophy in both of its conventional meanings. One, 'Whatthefuck?' as in, 'Why not?' Why not leap into bed with any slut who slows down long enough for you to stick your dick into her? Why not say yes to any cockamamie and probably illegal scheme that gets put in front of you by any obviously-out-of-his-mind maniac? And two, Whatthefuck in the sense of an exclamation of surprise. As in, 'Hey, whatthefuck happened? I just got run over by a truck. Wherethefuck did *that* come from?'"

I take exception to this.

"That's not true, Nicolette, and you know it. Next to you, I'm the hardest-working person in this neighborhood. Have I been busting my ass at that typewriter for the past four years (with absolutely zilch to show for it, by the way) while simultaneously turning my nose up at no opportunity for employment, no matter how menial or non-remunerative?"

"You work hard, darling, but you work stupid. And you should not be taking six aspirin with a cup of black coffee."

Nicolette wants to go see Tito.

"It's two thirty in the morning."

"He's hurt. He's alone in the hospital."

"You don't even know him."

She stands. "Are we going or not?"

By the time Nicolette and I get halfway to the subway stop at Christopher Street-Sheridan Square, I've convinced her to return home and let Tito sleep. We walk toward her place up Bleecker and across Eleventh. She's insisting now that I tell her everything, in detail, about the Turk and Abby and the Russian and what I've been doing at night for the past three weeks.

"I can't."

"Why not?"

I indicate my beat-up face. "Because these guys are crazy. I don't want you involved."

"I'm already involved. I care about you."

I hate it when people say things like that to me. The worst part is that Nicolette really means it.

I stop and take both her shoulders in my hands. We're on the sidewalk outside Petite Patisserie.

"Listen, Nicolette. You've got a future. Don't screw it up."

21.
Catch of the Sea

My uncle has come into the city specifically to see me. He never does this, so I know I'm in trouble. When he sees the purple welts above my left eye, he seizes me roughly by the arm.

"What's the matter with you? I told you to stay away from that sonofabitch!"

Charlie demands that I tell him everything that has transpired relating to my employment with Bablik, specifically who turned my face into chopped steak and why.

The Turk, it turns out, has phoned Charlie, inviting him and my aunt Peg to the upcoming awards banquet—the IDF Man of the Year event. (They can't come because they're touring colleges with their daughter, my cousin Pat, who'll be graduating from high school in June.) Apparently when Charlie began querying Bablik about me, Mr. B.'s evasive answers set off alarm bells. Charlie then phoned my apartment and reached the building's super, who told him about the break-in, etc.

Now here we are, my uncle and me, sitting in a white-on-white booth at an upscale seafood joint called Fay & Allen's Catch of the Sea on 72nd and Third next to the Trans-Lux movie theater. It's eleven in the morning; the restaurant won't be open for hours. But Charlie knows the owner. The Brazilian busboys have unlocked the door and even brought us coffees and a basket of dinner rolls and butter.

I give Charlie the Reader's Digest version of the past few weeks, leaving out the part about Teaspoon, which apparently the super has failed to impart to him. I apologize to Charlie for not keeping him informed. I acknowledge my recklessness. I swear I will extricate myself from the situation.

My uncle doesn't believe me.

"What's wrong with you? How can you meet a guy like Bablik and not see that he's a criminal? If I didn't know better, I'd swear you think he's your friend!"

Charlie tells me about Bablik's brother Lou, the one the Turk owns the four other cab companies with.

"He's a gangster, a straight-up Jewish racketeer like Meyer Lansky. I knew him in North Africa. This kid beat it out of Lithuania in '39 one step ahead of the Gestapo. He made his way, God knows how, to Budapest and Geneva and finally, sixteen years old, reached Bablik in Tunisia, when Bablik was a sergeant with me in II Corps under George Patton."

The Turk's brother, Charlie tells me, was the outside man for all the stuff Bablik stole from the army. He came to the States with Bablik after the war and he's only gotten more dangerous since then.

"This is who you're in business with when you're in business with Bablik. So please," Charlie says, "get out of this business."

One of the busboys appears. He sets down a bottle of Remy Martin and two tulip glasses. Charlie nods thanks. The busboy acknowledges and moves off. My uncle turns back to me.

"You communicate with Bablik how?"

Charlie wants to make sure there's nothing in writing, no piece of paper with my name on it.

I tell him about the surveillance log. But my name isn't on it, it's not in my handwriting, and besides I've never given it to Bablik. "Get rid of it anyway," orders my uncle.

He pours me a brandy and one for himself.

"Why are you doing this? Money?"

He assures me if I need cash I can come to him.

"What's it really about? Your ex-old lady?"

"She's not ex yet."

"You need cash for her? To prove what?"

Charlie sips his Remy. I sip mine.

"Still writing that book?"

"Yeah."

"Same one?"

"New one."

"What happened with the other one?"

"Nothing."

We finish our drinks. Charlie leaves two fives on the table.

There's crusty snow underfoot when we step outside. A sharp wind makes my uncle turn up his collar. He lights a Pall Mall behind cupped hands, using his Army Zippo.

"Just so we're clear on Bablik. You're finito with him. *Capisce?*"

My uncle sets a hand on my shoulder. He pulls me close for a brief but emotional embrace.

I hate to say it but I'm already thinking, If Bablik's brother is indeed a big-time gangster, maybe I can enlist him to help track down the Russian.

22.

A Love Pat

Tito looks better than I thought he would.

"You okay, Tito? The Russian hasn't been here, has he?"

"What?"

"He hit my place, turned it upside down. And he stole my fucking cat—or killed him."

"What? What are you talking about?"

Leaving Charlie, I have taken the Lexington Avenue Line from 77th to Canal Street in Chinatown and walked the rest of the way to the secure lot adjacent to the Burgundy. I pick up the cab (I've been parking it there, taking Tracy up on her offer) and drive to New Rochelle, to Salesian Hospital. It's just after lunch, a bright, blustery December 21st with prop Christmas presents under the tree by the candy machine and a kid-drawn Baby Jesus and Three Wise Men mural bedecking the wall. A candy-striper in a Santa hat directs me to Tito's room on the third floor.

"What are you talking about, your cat?"

"The Russian took him."

"Calm down, kid. Why would he do that?"

"Who knows why anyone does anything? That guy with the ponytail was tailing me. Last night."

Tito sits, propped on pillows amid a welter of get-well cards and Mylar balloons. I expected him to be half-dead. He looks like he could stand up and walk out.

I slip a pint of apricot brandy beneath Tito's sheets. I ask him about Ivanov, the Russian's bodyguard whose plates Tito ran at the DMV. I want his address. Tito refuses to give it to me. Tito tells me I'm into way deeper shit than I realize and he won't be a party to me risking my ass by getting in any deeper.

We talk. He gives me the orange juice left over from his breakfast tray. He tells me to keep my voice down; his wife could walk in at any moment. She's down in the hospital chapel now, praying.

I press Tito on the Russian. "You were on this job long before me, Tito. Is there anything you can tell me that might help? What's the Russian's name? I gotta find him."

"Kid, I've told you everything."

"What about that neighborhood? Little Russia. Could he live there?"

Tito asks me if I've heard from Bablik. I tell him my uncle has, but I haven't.

"Tito, help me. Please. I gotta find this fucking Russian."

Tito indicates an oversized bouquet of chrysanthemums beside the bed. The note is from Bablik. Tito tells me that Mrs. B. has intervened in his behalf on the medical insurance front. "The Turk made sure I'm covered."

Okay, okay.

I start to calm down a little.

"Listen to me, kid. The guys who worked us over the other night? If they had really wanted to hurt us, we'd both be face down in the river right now. This," he indicates his bandages, "was a love pat."

Yeah, yeah. I see Tito's trying to deflect me.

"What about that tank? The underground tank at Gotham Cab."

"Forget that."

"You told me that was how the Turk made all his money."

Tito groans and turns his face away.

"What's in that tank? What does it mean? Is it connected to the Russian? Is it connected to Bablik's brother?"

"Stay away from that tank. You hear me? Right now, you don't know nothing. They got no reason to fuck with you."

"But what if that tank would lead me to the Russian?"

"Are you listening to me? Stay away from that tank. Stop asking questions and stop trying to find the Russian."

"I can't stop. He's got my fucking cat!"

I run into Tito's wife in the hall, coming back from the chapel. Her face is puffy from crying. I've only met her one time, when I dropped Tito at home a couple of weeks ago, but she recognizes me at once.

"Oh my God! Look what they did to you!"

I give her a semi-hug and assure her that my face looks worse than it actually is. I remark on how well Tito is doing. An orderly rolls a patient past in a wheelchair. On the wall behind Tito's wife is a ten-foot-long glitter-drawn banner:

HARK THE HAROLD ANGELS SING

Mrs. Cerrone presses her palms together. "It's God's will," she says. "I told my husband to keep away from these animals."

"No," I say. "He looks good. He's gonna be out soon, maybe tomorrow."

"I light candles but what good does it do? God sees everything. You gotta pay for what you done."

23.
Tank Number Two

My mind is made up. I'm getting to the bottom of this business with the underground tank. I don't even know why, except that Tito is so insistent that I keep my nose out of it that it makes me even more determined to find out what's going on.

But first, I decide, I'm gonna revisit the Russian restaurant in Brighton Beach, the one that Tito and I tailed Abby to.

It's Sunday the 23rd. I have slept around the clock, trying to recover from the previous three ZZZ-less nights.

I wake up this morning with a memory-flash of Mrs. B. sitting across from me at the Empire Diner. In my mind's eye, I'm seeing her reach into her purse for her American Express card, intending to pick up the check. She did the same thing with the Russian at the restaurant in Brighton Beach. I remember vividly because I was watching through Tito's binoculars from our cab parked across the street, a few spaces up, and I thought, That's a woman with class, who reaches for the tab. And the Russian responded just like I did at the Empire Diner. He snatched the check and paid it himself. I remember him handing a credit card to the waitress.

I've parked the cab the last two nights in the secured lot of the Hotel Burgundy, on West Broadway just north of Canal, where the production vehicles and stunt cars for Tracy's movie are parked. I pick it up now, ten thirty on a bitterly cold, two-days-till-Christmas morning. No suspicious characters have been around, says the lot attendant when I ask. He hands me my keys. I tip him two bucks, what I'd make in half an hour driving a hack, and another two for the night man.

"This a fake cab for the movie?"

"No, it's real."

"Why ain't you using it?"

I point to my face. "This is real too."

"Hey," he says, "Merry Christmas!"

I get to Cafe Dacha, the Russian restaurant in Brighton Beach, at twelve fifteen, smack in the middle of holiday-madness brunch. Take-out bags are stacked three-deep at the register. Plates of piroshki and blini pancakes are sailing out of the kitchen. The girl cashier barely glances up as I struggle in through the crush.

"Reservation?"

"No."

"The wait's an hour. Oh my God, what happened to you?"

Actually I don't look half as bad as I did yesterday.

"Some guys beat me up. In fact they were here at this restaurant, three of 'em, about two weeks ago. They sat at that booth right there up front."

The manager appears, smelling trouble. He's got takeout bags in both arms with checks stapled to the tops. Behind me, four women who look exactly like Mrs. Khrushchev are searching for their names, shoving fives and tens at the cashier. The owner starts shouldering me away from the register. We're busy, pal. You gonna stand here all day?

I've worked at half a dozen restaurants and I know this: the only thing that matters to an owner when a person walks in the door is that they order something. So I do. I point to the Dumpling Special, flash two fingers, and add a second order for a couple of kebab plates to go. I put a ten on the counter and stick another in the owner's shirt pocket.

I tell him I'm looking for a credit card receipt from two weeks ago.

"Please," he says. "I don't want no trouble."

But three minutes later he's back from the office with a fuzzy photocopy of an Amex card printout.

The name on the card:

YEHUDA BABLIK

Me: "That's not the one."

Owner: "Whaddaya talkin' about? You said two weeks ago."

He points to the date. "That's the one. I remember taking the order."

Belly dance music screeches from two overhead speakers. The half-Jewish, half-Commie crowd presses around the register, elbowing in and swimming out in the jet stream of Siberian air that howls through each time the front door opens. I'm trying to remember. Abby didn't pay that night. I know it. Or did she? Am I losing my mind?

But this is obviously her card. Her husband's.

Yehuda must be the Turk's real first name.

A busboy appears with my four takeout bags; he squeezes them onto the counter alongside a dozen others. "You can't eat 'em standing here," says the owner, pushing me into the crush migrating toward the exit. The cashier gives me a wave. "Feel better!"

Outside I'm muttering to myself. "Stretch, you are one fucked-up detective. You just blew twenty bucks and you didn't learn a goddamn thing."

Wait.

A phone booth.

I squeeze in, lugging my four takeout bags, and wrestle the chained-down phone book open to the I's.

Ivanov, Ivanov, Ivanov—

What the fuck.

There are four pages of Ivanovs. Fifty percent are named Dimitri.

Dimitri Ivanov is apparently the Joe Smith of Russia.

What am I gonna do?

My plan, as best as I can formulate one, is to drive to Gotham Cab and find out everything I can about Tank Number Two. But wedging my bounty of brown-bagged goodies back into the cab, the lamb-on-a-stick smells pretty tasty. I wind up driving to the location in Queens where Tracy is shooting her movie today. I contribute the takeout to the crew. I'm a sport.

Short version: I don't get to Gotham Cab till ten that night. Sunday is a dead evening in the taxi business. The hack manager's office is dark; there's only one light on in the garage. My mechanic friend Kingie is out back when I pull in.

"Man, am I glad to see you! The Turk is looking for you."

"That's great, cause I'm looking for him."

"He left me three messages. He wants you to phone him right away. Says to tell you he's sorry he didn't call you at the hospital. Whoa, bro … what happened to your face?"

"That's why I was in the hospital."

Kingie is from Tennessee. His full name is Alvin York King. How he wound up in the Bronx I have no idea, but he's a good guy and, apparently, the only employee at Gotham Cab that the Turk actually trusts.

"I seen the Turk serious before," says Kingie, "but never like this. You gotta call him. I got his secret number. He don't give this out to nobody."

I tell Kingie I need to gas up. I'm parked on the street. He tells me to pull my cab in and use the pumps. As he's saying this, a tanker truck turns in off Southern Boulevard, just like the one I saw a couple of weeks ago with *SHELL OIL* on the side and "Industrial" misspelled below.

"Lemme help this guy set up," says Kingie. "Then I'll get you the Turk's number from the office."

I get my cab and pull in alongside the first underground tank, the one with the gasoline pumps that we drivers fill up from. A key opens the lock on the nozzle. Tank Number Two squats adjacent, beneath a concrete pad on a black, winter-sodden mound just above the river.

The tanker driver has climbed down and is opening the intake at the top of the tank. He's wearing rubber boots, a smock, and thick rubberized gloves.

"Watch yourself," says Kingie as I approach the tank. "Don't let none of that shit get on you."

"Why? What's in it?"

"You don't wanna know."

He heads over to help the driver. I fill my own tank, scribble the gallon total along with my initials on the clipboard sheet that dangles on a chain from the top of the pump, then replace the nozzle and secure it with the padlock. Kingie is still busy with the tanker truck, so I re-park my cab on the street and kill five minutes having a smoke. When I cross back to Tank Number Two, Kingie is signing some kind of manifest and handing it back to the tanker driver.

I eyeball the guy as he climbs back into his cab. He's a hard, Slavic-looking character, about thirty, dressed in dirty overalls and an even dirtier newsboy cap.

"Hey!" I call up to him. "How you like working for Shell Oil?"

The clutch makes a shuddering sound as the driver shifts into first. I hear the hiss of the air brakes releasing.

"Pays good," he says.

The truck exits the lot and pulls out onto the lane that leads to Southern Boulevard. Kingie has crossed to a maintenance shed just upslope from the tanks. He's tugging on a pair of rubber overboots. "Wanna know about this second tank?" He grabs a pair of gloves for himself and tosses another pair to me. "C'mon. Gimme a hand."

We cross to the overgrown slope just above the river. Signs say

NO DUMPING

and

NO SWIMMING
NO FISHING
NO WADING

"I wouldn't tell you none of this," Kingie says, "if you and the Turk wasn't so tight."

Rising from a pumping station on the slope is a hand valve, like the steering wheel of a car and about the same size, beneath a weather cover. A few feet to the side, the surface of an unlined overflow basin about four feet square glistens black and greasy in the lights from the shop. Kingie sets both gloved hands on the valve and turns it open. "Every time I do this, three twenty-dollar bills show up in my pay envelope."

For about ten seconds I hear and smell nothing. Then, very quietly, a flow of liquid begins to gurgle underground. Phew. What a stink!

"What is it?"

"Restaurant grease, industrial solvents, toxic shit, who the fuck knows?"

Kingie indicates the slope between the tank and the river. Gravity feed, he says. No outfall pipe. The stuff goes straight into the ground and from there into the river. "So if there's trouble, the Turk can claim it's a leak. He don't know nothing."

Kingie says this tank takes four or five loads a week, thirty-two hundred gallons, thirty thousand pounds. And this is just one tank. "The Turk and his brother got four other cab companies. Two more in the Bronx, one in Brooklyn, one on Staten Island." Every one of them, Kingie says, sits on a river or a bay.

I ask him how long he's been doing this.

He says twenty-two years.

Kingie straightens and turns toward the river. I can hear the seepage clearly now and even feel the slope trembling slightly beneath my feet.

"Back then when we started," Kingie says, "nobody gave a shit about this stuff. You didn't need no underground tank. We used to pull the trucks right up to the water's edge. Now you got the EPA, Department of Sanitation, inspectors snooping around …"

He remembers that he has the Turk's private number for me.

"Keep an eye on this valve for me, will ya? If this black shit rises above that line, shut it off. And watch yourself, don't touch nothing without them gloves on."

He strides away toward the office.

I'm thinking: "Stretch, you gotta be outa your freaking mind." But as soon as Kingie bolts, I scrounge through the trash on the hillside, grab a discarded gallon milk jug and dip it into the brew in the overflow basin. Glug glug, the container fills with noxious sludge. I seal the top and scurry to my cab, set the jug carefully in the trunk, wedged between the spare tire and the jack kit so it won't tip over. I close the trunk and hurry back to where Kingie left me.

He returns with the Turk's phone number, scrawled in pencil on a Bablik Bros. message slip. "This is for the Turk's place in the country," he says. "Don't show it to nobody and don't tell nobody who you got it from."

I ask Kingie about Bablik's brother Lou. Does he have a number?

"Right there." Kingie's forefinger taps the message slip, an address in Marine Park, Brooklyn. "That's the cab company headquarters. But call the Turk first!"

I promise I will.

"Good. The Turk really wants to talk to you. He likes you, man."

As I'm backing out to leave, Kingie strides alongside my window. "What kinda job you doing for the Turk anyway?"

"Tailing his old lady."

Kingie laughs and points upslope toward Tank Number Two.

"She's hip to all this. She's the one who found the contractor that put in that tank."

Book Five

The Knowledge

24.

Peter

I stop at a pay phone on the corner of Southern Boulevard and West-chester Avenue and call Mika, the Hungarian girl I met in the cab who works as a chemist. Will she analyze a sample for me? Turns out she's heading in to work right now. "But the lab is crazy busy," she says. "Can you come by my place tomorrow morning? I'll take the sample in from home."

Mika lives in a loft above a Goodwill Store on Eleventh Avenue in Manhattan. I'm waiting outside the next morning an hour early. I watch her mount the steps from the subway (she hasn't seen me yet) with her butch haircut and Doc Marten boots and tromp toward me up the snowy sidewalk. Mika outweighs me by twenty pounds, but I've got the insatiable hots for her. I'm groping her under her army jacket before we even get into the stairwell. We wind up bouncing off the walls of her bedroom for most of the morning, with the gallon container of toxic goo parked on her kitchen counter. When we finish Mika conks out, flat on her back, snoring like a truck driver.

I leave a note, tiptoe out, and head to the Burgundy to work.

I gotta get some pages done.

Gotta get the book ready for Marty.

The hotel is empty when I walk in around noon—or at least the floors that Tracy's movie has reserved for cast and crew. There's a two-man detail in the lobby in police-blue waterproofs with SECURITY on the back and a solitary girl P.A. at a desk in the first room on the third floor (whose door is open, with a hand-written sign affixed: PRODUCTION OFFICE) wearing a TISCH SCHOOL OF THE ARTS sweatshirt, with a breakdown board behind her and an industrial coffee urn with cups and plastic spoons, sugar and creamer, and a spread of bagels and Danishes, granola bars, M&Ms, apples, oranges and bananas on a long table against the wall. The P.A. is manning a console of three phones, no doubt juggling various crises between the crew on location in Fort Greene, Brooklyn and whatever insanity is being generated back in L.A., despite it being the day before Christmas, with budget overages, casting emergencies, etc. I fill a paper plate with donuts, grab a coffee, and head down to my room to get to work.

I may be an unpublished writer (and I may remain unpublished as long as I live) but one thing I know how to do is work. The new ending I came up with a few days ago has solved the climax. But the changes have screwed up the middle. I've got to go back and fix at least half a dozen setups. No problem. I can knock the bastard off with two all-nighters and a morning. I'll have the manuscript to Marty seventy-two hours from now.

Where did I learn self-discipline? From my greatest friend ever, Peter Mayne.

I'm trying to remember where I first met Peter. It was in New York in '69 sometime. Tracy and I were still together. Peter was writing music for advertising jingles. I was working at Grey Advertising then. My boss hired Peter for a Kent cigarette commercial. All I know is I liked him immediately. Peter had come over from England six months earlier, alone after a divorce, knowing nobody. He had two years at Oxford and one before that at LSE, the London School of Economics, where he was friends with Mick Jagger. Peter was a classically-trained pianist who also knew how to rock. He left for L.A. not long after I met him. He was doing session work out there and hating it. When Tracy and I split, she bolted for Los Angeles to stay with her father and I followed, trying to get her back. I stayed with Peter in his apartment on Crescent Heights and then later house-sat a one-room cabin he had subleased in Laurel Canyon. By then he had fled Tinseltown and was working on a cattle ranch in a place called Arroyo Seco, about three hundred miles north near Greenfield off Highway 101.

Peter was a type that is produced only by England. He could ride, he could shoot; he traveled the globe without fear, without money, and without hesitation. As a photographer he had covered wars in Kenya, Iraq, and Oman for the BBC. He had driven eighteen-wheelers from Frankfurt to Baghdad. He had skills that I never knew existed. Peter did not buy shoes; he made them. He built guitars from scratch. He knew carpentry, electricity, and auto mechanics. He was the greatest croquet player I ever saw.

I was in Santa Cruz when Peter was working on the cattle ranch; I was putting on my second or third full-court press to get back together with Tracy, having driven up from SoCal to surprise her on the set of a horror flick she had a part in, in the redwoods around La Honda. After my first unannounced on-location pop-in, the security guys put up a notice with my photo:

KEEP THIS ASSHOLE OFF THE SET

I had no money for gas back to L.A. so I wound up working in a beach umbrella rental stand at Cowell's Beach, the surfing spot. I was still there two weeks later when Peter showed up, having hitchhiked from Arroyo Seco looking for me. He had had his fill of the States, he declared, and was flying home to England. He would pay my way if I fancied coming with.

Our plan was to write songs. Peter would compose the music; I would supply the lyrics. "You're the verbal sort," Peter said.

Was he serious? I knew nothing about music or the recording business. But Peter, it turned out, was chums with every limey bluesman, R&B freak, and rock 'n roller in London. In addition, his sister Jemima had recently vacated her flat in Chiswick, moving with her husband to Tanzania and leaving the digs to Peter rent-free. I had no idea how flush Peter's family was, but on the third Monday of each month the post arrived with a cheque from his solicitor for 140 quid, a flaming fortune in 1970. "What's mine is yours," Peter said and he meant it.

Peter was the first person I had ever known who possessed self-discipline. I had read of this virtue before but had never actually met anyone who implemented it. The experience changed me in every way.

Come sleet, hail, or the Apocalypse, Peter was awake, shaved and bathed by a quarter past five. Meditation: forty-five minutes. Yoga: another forty-five. Nor were these candy-ass, mind-wandering, corpse-pose-lying snooze sessions, but major-league, full-focus, banks-of-the-Ganges workouts, complete with ujjayi pranayama, "breath of fire," string in the nose, the whole nine yards (or meters, as they would say in the UK).

By seven Peter was preparing breakfast for himself and me and whatever wayward band members, session players, sound engineers, not to mention assorted displaced heiresses, visitors from Kenya or Rhodesia, or just general lost souls happened to have washed up on his doorstep overnight. Again, this was no piker's repast, but farmer's eggs that still had hen-shit and straw stuck to their shells (Peter rode his Triumph Bonneville out into the countryside every Sunday morning to acquire directly from the source fresh bacon and sausage, raw oats and honey, potatoes straight out of the ground), toast grilled "on the irons" in the oven, fried tomatoes, beans, and for himself India tea whitened with Carnation condensed milk and five sugars. Or he fasted.

At meal's end, no later than "half eight," Peter retired to the studio, i.e., his room, and locked the door behind him. By nine he was at the keyboard doing scales and exercises. He had a Hammond B3 organ that he ran through a Marshall amp "to make it dirty and nasty" and a Fender Rhodes electric piano that he wired to the sequence generator of an Arp 2500 (this was before presets, when you had to calibrate every setting by hand), until he traded up to a 2600 that he got from Rick Wakeman of Yes, who had wrecked Peter's sister's E-Jag and felt guilty about it. How did he keep from driving the neighbors batty? Headphone tech was Stone Age in those days, so Peter padded his room with blankets stuffed in every doorjamb and mattresses set upright against the doors.

Peter ran. He swam. He rode. He would rent horses in Hyde Park and be gone all day. He journaled from seven to seven thirty every evening. And we wrote music all night.

My plan was to have a hit and get Tracy back. I would prove to her that I was not a bum and a loser.

The music scene at that time in England was post-everything. The Beatles had broken up, Woodstock had come and gone. Altamont had wreaked its havoc. The Who had done *Tommy* and moved on. Serious drugs had entered the picture. Bands were forming and splitting up like atoms. The Yardbirds, Cream, Blind Faith, Derek and the Dominos. You couldn't tell who Eric Clapton was playing with from one fortnight to the next, or Jeff Beck or Jimmy Page or Steve Winwood or John Paul Jones. *Led Zeppelin IV* was selling strong but everyone agreed that the great days were over. *Melody Maker* had an article every week mourning the demise of rock and roll.

Peter saw this as an opportunity. "The next wave is forming. I dunno what the fuck it is, but you and I are gonna catch it and ride it home."

First of course we needed money. No problem, declared Peter. In those days, when heroin and cocaine had become mother's milk to every freak with a Fender Stratocaster and a wah-wah pedal, groups were forever scrambling to keep the full package onstage and in the studio. Peter was on the keyboard go-to list right below Nicky Hopkins because he was clean, he was dependable, and he had the chops. He worked session gigs at Olympic Studios and Abbey Road and half a dozen other houses. He filled in for bands on tour in Britain and the continent.

I booked him. Our company was called Bob's Yer Uncle, Ltd. This was my first exposure to the world of session and gig pimping. I knew nothing. I had no contacts. But I had an American accent, which still possessed novelty in those days, and my partner was Peter. Within a month I had three hundred names in my Rolodex. I'd ring up and say, "Hi, it's Stretch." No one turned down my call.

London too was where I found Teaspoon—at midnight, beside the kerb in Cheyne Walk in the Embankment. My cat was a Yank from Minute One. He looked American; he meowed in American. I never for a moment thought of him as a Brit.

You may think reading this, "How could any freelance team peddle material in an era when it was a matter of honor that every band write its own songs?" But the reality of the music biz is that everybody is always looking for material. Everybody. Always. Finished songs are the least of it. Bands are looking for licks, for riffs, for guitar lines, and, more than anything, for concepts—not just for individual tunes, but for albums and shows and even tours. The market was nuts at the primary level and absolutely insane at the secondary, with the wannabes, the almost-theres, and even the no-hopers, who were ravenous for material and would besiege you shamelessly if you had produced even one promising hook or bass line.

As globe-girdling a phenomenon as rock and roll was in those days, the community of musicians in London remained incestuously small. Everybody knew everybody. The myth was that these rockers were up-from-the-gutter types. In fact most were solidly middle class, with mums who still did their laundry and dads who'd spot them twenty till payday, and no few came from the pure Empire cream, I mean Eton, Harrow, top of the pops. The rich sods and the university-educated, who were everywhere in the business, though they concealed their intelligence with the same diligence with which they disguised their gentle-born accents (except in circumstances where they needed them), had their own network that went back to childhood. Peter shared grammar school and public school roots not just with band members but also with managers, lawyers, studio producers from the Kinks, Pink Floyd, Humble Pie. As a photographer he worked fashion shoots at Mary Quant's shop on King's Road for Andrew Oldham. He had a gardening trowel that was a gift from Bill Wyman. Peter's younger sister Edwina's first b.f. was Glyn Johns' brother Andy.

Beyond music and drugs, two threads united the scene: ambition and sex. Half the males in the city were living off women then. The lasses toiled as shop girls or in factories or served as domestic help; the guys played nights in dives and mooched off their mistresses like vampires. Women would do your laundry, cook your meals, put you up in their flats, then lend you ten bob on payday and never remember to ask for it back. Despite having been technically single for almost two years, I was still trying to stay true to Tracy. But in the city at that time, Thomas Aquinas himself could not have retained his virtue. All a bloke had to do was emerge from the side door at Olympic Studios or Abbey Road and some saucy little tart would swoop you up and take you home. And these were nice girls! All they wanted was to be part of the scene, which was all you wanted too.

Chasing girls in those days, money meant nothing and looks counted for even less. If you could play an instrument or just load one onto a lorry, you could score with beauties who wouldn't have given you a toss of their manes in an alternative incarnation. And if you were willing to slide a few notches down the food chain, you could have a different twist every night and sometimes two or three in a twenty-four-hour period.

Through the first spring and summer Peter had one girlfriend, a dazzling six-foot white blues singer named Tawny Trelawney, whose father was the Minister of the Exchequer in South Africa. I never brought home a girl who passed muster with Tawny.

Tawny: "My Gawd, man, where d'you find these Iron Curtain wenches?"

Me: "What's wrong with Urva (or Petra or Irina)?"

"Hygiene for one."

"They're clean!"

"Indeed. Especially the crop of alfalfa under their arms."

Tawny and I shared one passion however. We both lived to protect Peter.

I got Peter work and I went with him on the job to be sure nobody screwed him over. I made him eat. I insisted that he sleep. I took every phone call. I wouldn't let him sign anything. I had no work permit of course, so rivals were constantly threatening to turn me in to the Visa Bureau. I didn't care. My role was to keep the predators away from my friend. In a room full of sharks, I parked myself at Peter's shoulder and never let him out of my sight. Everything went through me. I blocked his door. I shielded his time. I protected his creativity.

I revered Peter. He was who I wanted to be. I was in awe of his work ethic and his level of aspiration. In Peter's universe no effort short of maximum would be tolerated. No product shy of extraordinary would be permitted to see the light of day.

I studied him. I copied everything he did. I was Peter's guardian but I was his acolyte as well.

I had taken Peter's schedule as my own. Dawn found me inverted in sirsasana (standing-on-your-head pose). I hiked with Peter. I meditated with him. Midnight to four I was banging out lyrics on my Smith-Corona with Teaspoon curled up happily beneath the shuttling carriage. I loved it. I felt like I was living with the Dalai Lama.

We were working. We had money. But Peter was chafing more and more at having to take session gigs. He was fed up with peddling lines and concepts to bands that were out there doing what he knew he could do better. "I'm twenty-seven years old. I didn't fuck off from hearth and home to render other buggers' licks or drop tapes into the post slots of bleeders I could outplay when I was thirteen."

A breakthrough was required. Our game had to be taken to the next level. Peter and I needed something original, something creative, something completely our own.

25.

The Knowledge

We came up with an idea. To this day I don't know which one of us blurted it first.

The idea was "The Knowledge."

We knew at once that we would never sell this to anybody. We would keep it for ourselves. "This is yours and mine, bugler!" declared Peter.

The Knowledge would be a concept album like *Sgt. Pepper* or *Tommy* or *The Dark Side of the Moon*. We would write it ourselves and produce it ourselves, even build a group around Peter and perform it ourselves.

What was *The Knowledge*? The idea was sparked by a friend of Peter's, a starving bass player also named Peter but whom we called Gill (his last name was Fothergill), who had moved in with us in Chiswick.

Gill was studying to be a London cab driver. In the city then, and to this day as well, you cannot get a taxi license until you have committed to memory every twisted, crazy-quilt lane and alley in the maze of 20,000 streets that comprises the ancient capital, and until you have passed a state-administered examination (often called "the hardest in the world") to prove it.

This street-by-street mastery was called The Knowledge.

Gill had been studying for two years and still knew only half the city. He spent days pedaling his bicycle from Earls Court to Eaton Place, from Hammersmith to the East End, jotting notes and scribbling maps. Gill's bibles were the *London A-Z* ("Z" pronounced "zed") and his collection of Blue Books. These worksheets, supplied by the city once your taxi application had been accepted, laid out the dozens of runs upon which an applicant might be tested. "Calling a run" meant reciting the street-by-street route between Point X and Point Y.

Here's one I still have from one of Gill's Blue Books–Thornhill Square, N1 to Queen Square, WC1:

L/By	Matilda Street
R	Copenhagen Street
L	Caledonian Road
L	Killick Street
L	Pentonville Road
R	Lorenzo Street

and on through seven more such turns, through King's Cross Road and Gray's Inn Road, finally coming out of Great Ormond Street to face Queen Square. On top of that, you, the applicant, had to be able to call out points of interest along the way (in case that was how your passenger directed you), e.g., on this run the October Gallery in Old Gloucester Street, the Holborn Grange Hotel at 130 Theobalds Road, and the Art Workers Guild at 6 Queen Square.

And this is just one of scores of runs that the aspiring cabbie had to tattoo on his brain. "The city's like life," declared Gill. "You can never master it, but you've got no option but to try."

That was it.

That was the idea.

But our album, Peter's and mine, would take the metaphor to the next level. "The Knowledge", in our lexicon, would not be of a physical locale but of a realm of the imagination–the City of Life, with levels ascending and descending across time and space.

The City was the world and we, all of humanity, were tasked from birth to acquire The Knowledge that would let us live in it. That was the external metaphor. But on a deeper level the city was our own soul, our unique identity, our gifts, our fears, our hero's journey, even our previous lives and future incarnations, The Knowledge of which we were all seeking as well.

Peter and I set to work. No days off, no holidays. Our schedule was to sleep or toil for lucre all day, then labor in the studio, i.e., Peter's room, all night, batting around ideas for concept, story, musical themes, individual songs.

Were we crazy? Was this a fool's errand? Could we possibly pull it off?

We started working five hours a day. This became seven, nine, twelve. Eighteen songs was our goal for the album. By fall we had twenty-two. But only two passed muster with Peter and he wasn't 100 percent certain about either. I started getting nervous. Even Teaspoon was showing signs. He upped the daily dosage of affection he lavished on Peter. But Peter had become possessed.

He had stopped taking session gigs. He no longer did fill-ins. He insisted that I cease promoting him. I was uneasy about this. Money was money. We needed it. But when Peter became obsessed with something, economics went out the window.

He had a board on the wall that he called "Hit or Shit." It measured our progress according to a timetable held inside his skull. One week in October we had a breakthrough. We got two songs that were keepers and one major musical theme. Champagne! We had passed out of "S" and into "H."

Our efforts redoubled. We had a protagonist now—an aspiring taxi driver, our innocent, our hero. We added a mentor, a villain, a love interest. We had a trickster character and a spirit guide. The City itself had become a character, part monster and part savior. Each day the project acquired grander dimensions. We had Act One, Act Two, Act Three. We had a theme, we had a climax. So deeply was Peter into the work that he barely protested when Tawny bolted, declaring that he had gone "off the trolley," not to say "completely barmy," nor did either he or I take more than the scantiest notice when what Peter called a "right to-do" with his family put an end to the monthly cheques from his banker, or when on one wet, blowy evening two tailored representatives of his parents' solicitor appeared at No. 27 High Street (his sister's digs in Chiswick) and refused to depart until Peter and I had vacated.

Musically Peter was pushing the symphony (he was thinking in those terms now) into dimensions that only he could access. There were synth gods in England at that time. Keith Emerson for one; he could build a Moog Modular ten feet tall and as complicated as the phone system of a small city. Guys like Emerson and Rick Wakeman of Yes were making sounds that had never been heard in heaven or Earth. That was what Peter was after. He wanted his music for *The Knowledge* to merge with the intellectual concept. A + B = Z, with Z equating to pure primal emotion.

What's a concept? *Sympathy for the Devil* is a concept; *The Wall* is a concept; *Aqualung* is a concept.

Peter demanded unity. A dominant theme that worked lyrically, musically, conceptually. I was onboard heart and soul. *The Knowledge* was gonna wail. It was gonna shred.

There was only one problem. When you start working in concepts, you're compelled to follow your ideas to their logical extremes. This meant getting into some seriously heavy shit.

God.

Mortality.

The meaning of life.

Constructing *The Knowledge*, Peter and I were asking nothing less than What Is Life About? How the fuck did *we* know? We're asking questions about the nature of consciousness, the limits of the senses. We're talking about flow, the Zone, ecstasy and nirvana and transcendence. The unaided intellect can't reach the level required to take on such mysteries. We needed help. What else but the ingestion of substances banned under Her Majesty's statutes and ordinances?

We started with peyote, moved on to psilocybin, then mescaline and after that LSD. It was research. R&D. What *was The Knowledge* anyway? What was inner Knowledge? We read R.D. Laing, C.G. Jung, Fritz Perls. We did Gestalt therapy. We did Primal Scream. Our reading list became deeper and more abstract. We plumbed Nietzsche and Kant, Marx and Hegel. We pored through Sartre, Schopenhauer, and Wittgenstein; devoured Kierkegaard and Heidegger and Knut Hamsun.

Meanwhile Peter's morning sessions of yoga and meditation had taken on an unexpected dimension. It was clear to us that we were neophytes in the sphere of the mystical. Adepts possessed of true inner discipline could go in deep and not come out with their personal identities dissolved or their consciousnesses vaporized. But who knew anybody like that? The freaks we were hanging with just wanted to get high.

We had to go deeper. We began studying quantum physics. Heisenberg. The uncertainty principle. Einstein, Schrodinger, Niels Bohr. We spent nights at Oxford with Peter's old tutor and other geniuses. Of course they were as stoned as we were. Can there really be a particle at one end of the universe that alters instantaneously in concord with its twin, ten gazillion light years away on the other side of the cosmos? And what does it all mean?

Winter was approaching. We were broke. Should I be worried? Peter began selling his instruments. He parted with his Gibson Les Paul and two Stratocasters. The Fender Rhodes went to the hock shop, followed by his Arp 2600. This was like selling your baby. We were down to one second-hand Minimoog. No matter. Peter could make it sing.

Where could we stay? Friends shone through. One mate got us two weeks in his father-in-law's flat in Shepherd's Bush. We house-sat another chum's digs in Knightsbridge. We piano-sat. We pet-sat. The penniless were squatting then in abandoned apartments all over the city. These were called "sit-downs" or "lay-bys." As December broke, Peter and I carted our few remaining possessions into one on Rowan Road in Hammersmith near the tube station. I had found a daytime job teaching American accents to actors. I worked for an agency called Yanks and Wanks. The office would send me out hourly to film or theater locations or, on occasion, for a week at a time. I rode the underground all over London and took buses or trains as far north as Scotland. If you're looking for a job that gets you more poon than Elvis Presley, find employment that puts you in day-long proximity with actresses who are desperate to find work or who have found work and are frantic to keep it.

But women were the least of my preoccupations or Peter's. Humans may be capable of self-delusion but animals are not. Teaspoon understood the emergency. He took to parking himself directly in front of my face, springing up onto the kitchen table, say, while I was having my tea, or standing on my chest as I lay on my back in bed, to transmit a feline distress signal at full volume. "Stretch!" it said. "This is getting crazy. Do something!"

I urged Peter to take work. Against his wishes I booked gigs for him. He refused them with fury. Would he ring up his family for help, or at least phone his solicitor? "Strangle me first."

One night he and I got into an actual fistfight. We were rolling around on the linoleum at sub-zero Centigrade with Teaspoon looking on from the mantel with an expression that said, "These are the idiots I'm depending on for my kibble?"

In the aftermath I succeeded at last in convincing Peter to integrate work-for-hire into our greater creative schedule. Sanity must prevail. But two mornings after this accommodation an article in *Rockabilly* reported that not one but three London bands were working on concept albums disturbingly like ours. One was even calling theirs by the same name.

We plunged more frantically into work. Gill was long gone now. I had been fired from Yanks and Wanks. Friends had ceased ringing up.

Just like our protagonist, the aspiring taxi driver seeking to master The Knowledge, Peter and I were locked in battle with the City. The City was our antagonist and we ourselves had become our own worst enemy.

By January we had been writing for nine months without a break.

We were out of London now, putting up in an abandoned row house (along with half a dozen wayward families) in a town called Slough, west of Heathrow off the M4. Trains to the airport rumbled past, meters away. No place in the world is colder than England in winter. I was literally gathering firewood in the brambles alongside the tracks.

The crazy part was that we were able to work. We shared food and spirits with our neighbors. We lived like communists. One of the squatters had worked as an electrician. He managed to poach us all into a power line. We had light. We had wattage for the synth. We scrounged cigarettes and wine. And we kept hammering on the album. I was as into it as Peter. Even Teaspoon had gotten with the program. He supported himself. He prowled. He hunted. His coat was as thick as a grizzly's.

One day I'm in the attic bedroom trying to tap the heater (in British the "electric fire") into a working power line. I can hear Peter below in the front room hanging clothes. Do you know what a creel is? It's the Andy Capp version of a dryer—a wooden frame that you hang just-laundered underwear and shirts on to air-dry. A creel is big. It's heavy. You load it at eye level, then haul it up, by a stout line looped through a pulley affixed to a heavy-duty hook, to the ceiling (the warmest part of the room), and tie the line off to a cleat on the wall. When your clothes are dry you lower the creel and take 'em off.

That's what Peter is doing. I can hear him cursing, struggling with the creel, when suddenly the floor under my soles buckles and heaves. For a second I think it's an earthquake, or maybe some kind of structural failure in the house. Then I hear the creel crashing. What the fuck? Did it fall onto Peter? I'm on my feet, banging down the stairs as fast as I can.

I hit the landing, turn the corner into the front room, and run teeth-first into one of Peter's boots. He's in the air, swinging wildly, suspended from the hook in the ceiling that holds the creel.

"Peter!"

I see a rope around his neck. The fingers of his left hand are wedged under this noose, struggling frantically to tug it free. I seize him by both feet, my palms forming stirrups under the soles of his boots, trying desperately to lift him (I'm thinking he must have accidentally entangled himself), to take his weight off the rope that's crushing his Adam's apple.

Voices are calling from downstairs and from the flats on both sides. I'm simultaneously taking the Lord's name in vain and crying out to heaven to help. The ceiling in the front room is at least twelve feet high. Peter is dangling from a hook strong enough to hang a side of beef on, screwed into a beam as stout as a railway tie.

Suddenly the rope snaps. Peter crashes. The fall is not like in the movies where a person seems to descend to earth in slow motion. This is a flat-ass drop. Peter's body plummets dead weight; his head smashes onto the floor like a bomb. I fall too, tangled up in his limbs. Splinters of the creel blow sideways like an exploding grenade.

Fists are pounding on the door. I'm on my knees over Peter now, tearing a noose made of double-twined clothesline off his throat and heaving sodden shirts and trousers and the wreckage of the creel off him. I'm shouting to him and calling out to the neighbors as loudly as I can.

A Pakistani family is squatting in the flat below us. Their twin boys, Ari and Bal, ten years old, highball in. Harry the baker from next door follows, with his wife Viv and grown daughter Edna. In thirty seconds we've got six or seven people filling the hall and piling into the room.

I'm lifting Peter, with my left arm under his back, my right hand supporting his head. I know in one second that his neck has snapped. I'm cradling him and shouting his name.

My friend is inert.

"He's pissed himself," Ari says, pointing at the front of Peter's trousers.

Teaspoon is watching from atop the fridge. He's the only calm person in the room. I've dragged Peter clear of the wreckage now. His eyes are open and empty. A lurid welt rings his neck. I shake him again. I call his name over and over. The father of the Pakistani clan is a doctor in his own country. He works here at the chemist—the pharmacy—four blocks down the street.

Ari's pointing at Peter's jeans and crying that he smells feces.

"Ari, get your fucking father!" I kick at him. "Get him now!" The lad bolts for the doorway. I can hear his footsteps pounding away down the stairs.

26.
The Heath

Peter's chest is flat. I can't find a pulse. I'm thinking, His airway's crushed, we've got to get oxygen to his brain. I pump his chest. Nothing happens. Harry tries. The kettle is whistling on the stove. I grab it, pour boiling water over Peter's finger. No response. His hand. Nothing.

"He's fucking sodded off."

"What?"

"Did he waste himself?"

"No!"

"Well, he's brown bread and no joke."

I can't believe it. Peter is not dead. And if he is, he certainly didn't do it intentionally. There must be another explanation.

An accident.

He mounted the mantel to hang clothes and his foot slipped.

Now I'm smelling shit too. The front of Peter's pants is soaking wet.

Bal: "He's fucking croaked, man. He hung himself."

"He didn't!"

All mental faculties have deserted me. I'm unable to summon a cogent thought. I believe now that Peter's physical functions have ceased. But that doesn't mean he's dead. Can we revive him? Who can we call? What can we do?

"Mate! Mate ..." Harry has seized me by the shoulders. I realize I'm pumping Peter's chest so violently I'm nearly cracking his ribcage. "Easy, brother. You're doing more harm than good ..."

Ten minutes later Ari comes clomping back up the stairs followed by his out-of-breath father. In the interim Virginia, Harry's mum, has rung the paramedics. No reply yet. I have become possessed by the need to preserve Peter's dignity. I've dug up a pair of golf rain trousers and manhandled them over his shoes and slacks.

Ari's Dad, Dr. Gee, without even kneeling, pronounces Peter dead.

"Pupils fixed and dilated." He bends and closes Peter's eyes. "Who've you called?"

"The medics," says Edna.

"Bloody useless. They won't show till Easter." Dr. Gee says he'll call the morgue from the chemist's. "They'll send out the meat wagon. Who'll sign for the corpse?"

I've quite lost my mind by this stage. No fucking civil service lorry is going to zip Peter into a body bag, write him up as a suicide and haul him away.

I have a plan. A better plan.

Home.

I'll take Peter home. To his family.

I enlist Harry and Bal. We haul Peter down to the alley and wedge him into Peter's Morris Minor. The scene is like a Monty Python movie. The Morris' tires are the size of lawn mower wheels. We can't get Peter into the front seat so we fold him into the boot, which is just the back with the rear seats folded down. We have to haul out Peter's golf clubs and spiked shoes to make room.

"Are you sure about this, mate?" says Harry. "D'you even know where his people live?"

"Leeds. Bingley. Somewhere."

No, I don't know where Peter's family live. I've never been there, never met them, have no address. All I know is the place is called the Heath. I'll ask when I get there. Someone will know.

"It's quarter to one now," Harry and Ari are saying. "Daylight's gone by half four. It's five hours to Leeds on the M1."

Edna (in tears): "Why did he kill himself? A beautiful boy with everything to live for!"

I'm behind the wheel now, trying to crank the Morris. Nothing. "Bloody hell!"

"The battery's bought it."

I hear sirens. The paramedics. Their truck rolls past on the High Street and keeps going. "It's a squat," declares Viv, referring to our home. "The wankers can't find the address."

I'm out of the car now, more frantic than ever.

There's Peter's Bonnie.

"I'll take the bike."

My glance darts from Peter's corpse to his Triumph Bonneville, which is parked under the half-eave that shelters the driveway.

"Well," says Dr. Gee to his twins. "Help him."

There's this about the Brits (and I include Pakistani immigrants in that category): the loonier the idea, the more readily and enthusiastically they embrace it.

No one protests. No one tells me I'm mad. Like a pit crew at Indy, our gang manhandles Peter's corpse out of the Mini. Other neighbors have gathered. "Make sure the bloody bike starts," declares a wizened vet of about eighty, clad in a threadbare Air Warden's overcoat, who has materialized in the alley and assumed a posture of command. Bal and his sister return from the house with my field jacket, gloves, and two helmets. Together we wrestle Peter onto the rear of the seat. Ari uses electrician's tape to secure Peter's boots to the bike's foot pegs.

It's no small thing lifting a dead body. Peter goes about 175, with probably another fifteen pounds in coat, boots, and helmet. "The bugger must weigh twelve stone," says Harry.

The old sweat in the Air Warden coat has looted a length of rubberized laundry line from a neighbor's yard. "Lash the pair together about the midsection," he orders. The crew obeys. Harry tapes Peter's wrists together, wrapped around my waist. The same duct tape is used to secure Peter's helmet to mine, in tandem, his faceplate flush to my rear shell.

"Wait!" cries Dr. Gee, tapping my visor. "You can't turn your head."

I'm on the bike now. You don't start a Bonnie with a push button, at least not in those days. You have to toe the bike into neutral, open the fuel valve to get a flow into the carburetors, then crack the manual choke on the handlebar. Now punch down hard with your boot on the kickstarter, staying ready to release the choke as soon as the engine fires so you don't flood the carbs. It's freezing this day so I keep the flow open, jiggling it wide to narrow for the fifteen seconds the engine takes to clear its throat and get a rhythm going.

It works. The bike is running. I toe it into gear. We can hear the paramedics' klaxon returning along the High Street. "You realize," says Dr. Gee, "that this is positively mad?"

He tells me I won't be able to turn my head with Peter's helmet taped to mine. I say there's no alternative. He insists I'll be unable to maintain my balance with Peter's dead weight lashed to me. I won't get to the first street corner without spilling. "What if you roll over on the M1? You'll be under some lorry's tyres in moments."

"No, I can handle it." Peter's weight feels solid on the seat. "I'll get the hang as I go."

Road distance from London to Leeds is 195 miles. Take the M25 to the M1. The M1 is a wide, fast, multi-lane motorway. All I have to do is get on it and I'll be all right.

In ten minutes I'm past Uxbridge and Stoke Poges, following signs for

THE NORTH.

A Triumph 650 is a serious bike. It's heavy and fast with only minimum room for the #2 rider. I can feel Peter's body shift ominously rearward, pulling me with him when I accelerate even slightly. Leaning into a turn, his weight heels over with mine; it takes all my strength to get us both back. Twice I almost drop the Bonnie before we get onto the flat of the motorway. I'm talking to Peter. "Sit up straight, fucker. Stop mucking about!" I'm furious at him. "This is the end of *The Knowledge*. And we were so close!"

Somehow I've forgotten my gloves. I didn't take them from Bal's sister when she brought them out. This is serious, as the temperature on the lorry park signs when we pass reads -1 degree Celsius (30 degrees F).

Daylight: I've got four hours max. Worse, I see thunderheads approaching out of the east. Before we pass the exit for Bletchley on the A421, it's pissing right proper.

I still don't believe Peter's dead. I refuse absolutely to accept that he's a suicide. I keep talking to him. "Wake up, man. Tell me it's all some ghoulish prank and you're having a great laugh that we've taken it so seriously."

As I'm thinking this, I glance at the fuel indicator. 1/4. Fuck. I'll have to stop at a lorry park or a transport cafe (pronounced KAFF). I should do it now, but I can't face it. My hands have retracted inside the sleeves of my field jacket. It has become clear to me that I've made a terrible mistake embarking on this journey. Each truck and panel van that passes drenches me in road spray. The bike has no windscreen or even a deflector. The only thing that's keeping my visor halfway clear is the wind, which is howling at 105 kph up my sleeves. I can no longer feel any part of my hands.

You enter a state of mind. Survival mode. Your job now is to endure. There can be no stopping. No turning back. No one you can phone, no one who can help, no one who will even understand. You've begun and there is no alternative but to finish.

We pass Harlow and Cambridge. One hour. Two. The Bonnie's tank is on fumes now. I take the roundabout at Peterborough and follow the signs for a BP lorry park. The sun has set; it's still raining. My hands are frozen bricks. I pull into a brightly-lit stop full of minis, microbuses, and caravans.

The fuel cap on a Triumph is centered atop the tank, between my legs. I'm beside a pump now, holding the bike upright with my knees (both lower extremities are numb from the calves down), trying not to let Peter's weight shift and still reach the pump and the nozzle. People are staring. Why do these blokes have their helmets duct-taped together? Why are Bloke #2's boots taped to the rider's pegs?

I stretch for the fuel nozzle.

Peter's weight shifts.

We roll violently to port.

This time it *is* slow motion. I'm bracing against the fuel pump with my numb left hand. My left foot, equally sensationless, struggles for purchase on the icy pavement, pushing against Peter's weight and the bike's.

Over we go.

I hear the duct tape tear. Peter's head inside the helmet crashes into the tarmac with a mighty crack. His whole body comes loose from mine, from the laundry line round our waists, and spills rearward. Both his feet are still taped to the pegs.

"Oh my Gawd!"

Motorists swarm. Half a dozen cluster over Peter. "You all right, mate?" Another troop has collected around me. What little fuel remains in the tank is now spilling onto the pavement. At least four bystanders are holding lit cigarettes. I'm begging people to help get the bike up. I manage to rip one of Peter's boots free. Hands pull him off the Bonnie. We right the cycle.

I have now entered a zone of mental hell beyond any I knew existed. I'm expecting to be arrested, charged, imprisoned, if not beaten to death by the mob right here under the halogen lights.

"This one's dead," declares one fellow.

"The other one's his mate."

I confirm this. I'm trying to get my friend home, I say. How far are we from Bingley?

"Bingley? Haven't you heard? The motorway's closed."

There's a phrase in England: "shining through." It's what the Brits did during the blitz.

Now here under the lights, they do it again for Peter and me.

Within five I've got a full tank and ten fresh quid stuffed into my pockets. A mum and daughter have brought me a cup of hot soup. A bloke in a camper says he'll escort me to the Leeds go-round and another in a Vauxhall wagon will follow so no one runs over Peter and me from behind.

By ten, we've found the stone gate (unmarked of course) to the Heath, Peter's family's ancestral digs. My benefactors are waving me forward. So long! Good luck! I start through the gate, onto the unlit drive. Fifty feet. A hundred. My hands and feet are frozen so solid I'm afraid to shift out of first gear.

The lane keeps going. Two hundred meters. Four. A half mile. What the fuck. I've shifted up to fourth, doing fifty per, and there's no sign of house or host.

I'm on the moors. It's Heathcliff country. I see animal eyeballs in the bike's high beam. Is this some kind of sheep road? Am I lost in a Bronte Sisters' novel?

Can all this acreage belong to Peter's family?

Lights! A compound. I trundle up behind the bike's anemic headlamp. There's an open-sided barn, tractors, a farm truck, sheds stacked with firewood. Hounds are baying. I stop. Clearly this is not the main house. I don't dare get off the bike for fear of toppling. I rev the engine till a face appears in a window.

"Help!"

The keeper emerges. "What's this then?" An electric torch shines point-blank in my eyes. "Raise your plate. Let's have you!"

I push my visor up with the stump that used to be my right hand. The keeper's wife has come out now. I'm trying to speak but my jaw has entered rigor mortis. I can feel Peter's weight listing to starboard. The missus catches the keeling form. She shoves up the face plate.

"Jesus Gawd! It's Master Peter!"

I remember practically nothing from the rest of the night. Somehow the keeper and his sons have carried Peter and me inside. I recall a conference held over Peter's body, which has been set down, upright on the sofa, still swaddled in boots and coat. How did Master Peter die? Frozen to death from the motorcycle ride? What's this rope burn round his neck? The keeper is shaking me by the shoulders. Has the young master taken his own life? Do I realize I've had a corpse on the seat behind me?

What do we do now? Peter's mother and father are asleep in the Big House. We can't take him up there like this!

I remember a bath. The keeper's wife and younger son are lifting me from under my shoulders. "Don't make it too warm, you'll shock his heart!" I'm immersed in liquid at about 40 degrees Fahrenheit. Out in the kitchen Peter's clothes are being swapped out to make him more presentable ...

Was it that day or the next when I was summoned into the parents' presence? It may have been more than forty-eight hours. I remember trying to shave with the keeper's straight razor. A jacket, shirt, and sweater have been sent down for me from the manor house.

The interview takes place in the sitting room, or one of several sitting rooms, fronting onto the south lawn. Winter sun lights the forecourt. The fireplace, which is roaring yet produces not the slightest diminution of the hyperborean temperature in the room, is voluminous enough for a six-foot man to walk into and not muss his hair. Peter's father, a striking gentleman of about seventy, sits upright in an electric wheelchair, clad entirely in white, in what I can only assume is the uniform of an admiral in the Royal Navy. His breast dazzles with a panoply of medals. He neither moves nor speaks. His wife, who may or may not be Peter's mother (I understand no more than one word in three throughout the conversation), conducts the interview.

Peter's remains have been interred already. The memorial service was held yesterday; the family has come and gone.

Peter's parents never ask my name, though apparently they have it, as my wallet with driver's license, which I had thought lost, has been returned to me along with the jacket, shirt, and sweater sent down to the keeper's cottage.

No questions are put to me about Peter's life in London or the cause or circumstances of his demise, though again I sense that this intelligence has been obtained, somehow, by agents of the family over the preceding forty-eight hours.

From my chair in the sitting room, I can see a distance up and down the adjacent hallways. Upon the walls hang a number of oil portraits, apparently of family forebears. Many are in military uniform. My sense of Peter's people's grief is that it is compassed within this annal and that the seemliness of his death, or the lack thereof, is a factor of minimal significance.

Peter was born into the land, into the family. He has pursued his destiny as a constituent of both. He has come home, now, as have all others before him and as will all in the future.

I ask if I might be granted permission to visit Peter's grave.

"Of course. You were his friend. You brought him home."

In parting the lady hands me a cheque on the Back of England for five hundred pounds along with her husband's personal card, scribbling her own number on the back. "Should you ever require anything ..."

The coda to this saga comes ten days later. I have bought a ticket home on Icelandic Airlines and have rung up to arrange passage for Teaspoon. Can I bring him onboard in a cat carrier or will he be transported with the baggage?

"I'm so sorry," says the agent. "You can't take an animal out of the country. Your pet must be quarantined."

I go down in person to the airline office. I'm confident that the issue can be sorted out. The agent, quite a cute little blonde in fact, informs me that I'll have to arrange for Teaspoon's sequestration in a holding kennel in England for six months. If the animal has not been cleared by the end of that time, she says, the department will dispatch it.

"You mean dispatch him to me in New York?"

"I mean dispatch it."

The girl vouchsafes me the look one would proffer to the village moron.

"To heaven," she says.

I'm generally a pretty temperate fellow. But this is too fucking much. I explode. I go through the agent and her supervisor and her supervisor's supervisor, becoming more irate with each. I'm threatening to call the *Daily Mail*, to bomb the Tower of London, to camp out before the palace of the Queen.

Suddenly I remember Peter's dad's card.

"Wait a minute. Lemme make one call."

The supervisor's supervisor demands to know whom I intend to ring. I pass him the card.

"Where did you get this?"

The man stands and exits, taking the card with him. The walls of his office are glass; I can see him cross a common space and enter a larger office, also glass-enclosed. Supervisor #1 is there, speaking to Supervisor #3. Supervisor #2 enters. He shows the card. A call is made. The three supervisors confer. #1 points across the common space toward me.

Supervisor #2 returns to the office in which I'm waiting, accompanied by Supervisor #3. I stand. Supervisor #3 shakes my hand. He informs me that the quarantine protocol has been waived. My animal will be permitted to leave the country. "There will be a fee however."

"How much?"

"Two hundred forty pounds." Five hundred and seventy-five bucks.

"And my cat comes with me on the plane?"

"Indeed."

I write the cheque. A secretary appears from the office of the third supervisor. She sets a freshly-executed document on the desk. My name has been typed in near the top, along with the airline, flight

number, and so forth. Supervisor #3 checks these items for correct-
ness with me, then signs the form at the bottom. I sign too.

A single unfilled space remains.

"Your cat's name, sir?"

"Teaspoon."

I spell it for him. He fills in the blank and hands me the document.

"Good luck then, sir, and Godspeed."

And that's how I got my cat home to New York, courtesy of my
dear friends, Vice Admiral and Mrs. Lionel Mayne.

Book Six

Aesthetic Distance

27.
An Evening At Elaine's

The first thing I did when I got back to New York was to phone Roach. I wanted him to help me finish some songs I had been working on with Peter. Roach had a band then called the Spyders. I did a little booking and promoting for them, just trying to scrape up enough cash to get out of Dodge. Three years later when Roach put together the group that would become Death Warmed Over, it fell out naturally that I'd come back and be their manager.

The thirty-four months in between comprised my period on the American road. I wanted to put Peter's end, England, and the quixotic questing after Art as far behind me as possible. Couldn't I just be a blue-collar guy and live a simple life?

I worked as an oilfield roustabout in Plaquemines Parish, Louisiana; I picked fruit in Washington State; I taught school in Dallas. In Kentucky I worked in a mental hospital and a body-and-fender shop. In North Carolina I took a tractor-trailer course and wound up driving eighteen-wheelers out of Durham, North Carolina, and later Seaside, California. For two years I listened to country music and nothing else. It helped.

My Smith-Corona stayed with me and so did Teaspoon. He had his spot in my Chevy van, atop the bed by the rear window. You always wonder–how much does an animal understand? Can a cat feel grief? Does he know that Peter died? Can nature's creatures even conceive of death?

All I know is I couldn't have gotten through that time without Teaspoon. He was my friend and ally, 100% true one hundred percent of the time. Nor was he, as some animals can be, a clinging parasitic moocher, dependent on his owner for survival. Teaspoon was his own man always, a born traveler and hunter, an outdoor cat who could survive anywhere and take care of himself under all conditions. He was with me when I finished my first novel and my second and he was with me when I finally came home to New York and moved into the apartment on Fifteenth Street that had the staircase that went down into the rear courtyard so that Teaspoon could remain an independent operator, free to live his own life. It was the least I could do for my best friend in the world after Peter.

Now here I am, Christmas Eve, back in that apartment after the Russian and his goons have turned it upside down, trying to write. I've phoned the Turk at the number Kingie gave me, but the recording says the number has been disconnected. I've left a dozen messages for Abby. "I need to reach the Russian. VERY IMPORTANT. Can you tell me his number? Put me in touch?"

No response from Mr. B.

Nothing from Mrs.

I sit at my writing table in my back room. The window is cracked open in case Teaspoon returns. It's midnight and freezing. I initiate my routine. I make a cup of coffee, set it on the right side of the typewriter, and say my prayer to the Muse. This would normally be Teaspoon's cue. He would see me standing in a reverent posture with my eyes closed and my hands clasped behind my back, reciting, "O Divine Poesy, goddess daughter of Zeus," and he would know it's time for us to get to work. He'd hop up onto the writing table and take his post on the left side of the typewriter, curled up, with the carriage shuttling back and forth over his head.

Only Teaspoon isn't here now. Where he would be is just an empty space.

For the first time the thought truly hits me that this episode may not have a happy ending. Where is my cat? Has something terrible happened to him? I have to confront the possibility that I may never see him again.

I get in two hours of work. I'm making progress. I've fixed about half of the middle. It fits now with my new ending. But I can feel the out-of-tune-ness of the sentences even as my keystrokes hammer them onto the page. They're sour. They're discordant. Everything feels undercooked and overthought.

In the morning I phone Marty and tell him I need more time. He's getting frantic. "How close are you?"

"Pretty close."

"Pretty close is good enough. Gimme the pages now."

I can't. I tell him to hang on.

It's Christmas Day. I work through it. I work all day on the twenty-sixth. Marty is leaving me one- and two-word messages now. "When?" "How soon?" "Hurry."

The twenty-seventh, a call comes from Abby.

She has found her husband.

Bablik has returned home. He's back in the apartment at University Village. Mrs. B. apologizes to me for not responding to my messages. Bablik is sorry too. He meant to phone me but things have been too crazy.

The news, Abby says, is all good. She and the Turk have resolved their misunderstanding. Better still, an accommodation has been reached between Bablik and the Russian. Peace is at hand.

Mrs. B. insists that I keep the five hundred she has advanced me. She'll write a check for half of the other thousand, even though I have contributed nothing to the Turk's reconciliation with the Russian. It's good karma, Abby says. She says I have been lucky for her.

I tell her I have to talk to her. "About the Russian. I need you to put me in touch with him right away."

"I can't," she says. "Things are still too shaky."

Instead she invites me to join her and Bablik tomorrow night at a charity fundraiser at Elaine's, the watering hole of the rich and famous on 88th and Second. Norman Mailer will be there, Abby says, and Woody Allen and Truman Capote. John and Yoko too, if we're lucky.

"We'll talk then, I promise. Come on, we've had enough *tsuris*. Let's get drunk and be somebody!"

Tomorrow. I hate this. How can I wait a whole day?

To keep myself sane, I invite Tracy to the affair. I know she'll say yes and I know why. It has nothing to do with any desire to be with me. Rather, the event at Elaine's will put a high-glam finishing touch to her 18-hour-a-day toil-athon in the Big Apple. Producing a movie on location is killer work, and 99% of that labor is thankless and devoid of glamour. Tracy is exhausted. She's been busting her butt with no R&R and zero moments in the spotlight. This night will change that. A high-profile evening with the glitterati will serve as the climax and validation of Tracy's time in the city. She can count the occasion as a chance to mingle professionally. And she can doll herself up and make a splash.

We're in a cab now, bouncing and rattling up First Avenue. It's 9:30 at night. Tracy is recounting the various emergencies she's had to deal with on the movie. She's animated and funny. She looks gorgeous. But the more she shines, the worse I feel.

When Tracy and I were first married, we were *with each other* down to our bones. I don't mean just time. I mean everything. If you've been lucky enough to have that in your life, you know there's nothing better.

Now in the cab, banging over potholes amid a river of illuminated TAXI signs and red brake lights, that happy time has receded so completely I can't recall that it ever existed. Tracy is wearing Chanel Number Whatever. But the fragrance is not for me or for us. It's for her. My wife inhabits space on her own now—an independent contractor, wary and seasoned and tough as dirt—and this transformation is one million percent my fault.

I was the one who betrayed our vows to each other. I was the one who broke faith. Specifics? What difference does it make whether I slept with her sister or her best friend or the nun who prepped her for her First Communion? And the worst part is I did it out of cowardice. Because I didn't have the guts to finish the book that Tracy had dropped out of law school to back me to write. Did I say that was the worst part? No, far crueler was watching Tracy's heart break. Watching her writhe and struggle, with no one to call on but herself, summoning her innermost resources to construct from scratch a self that could survive the blows her worthless husband had delivered upon her. But even that wasn't the cruelest component. More painful still were my attempts at salvage—the forgive-me moments, the I-can-change pleas, the excruciating nightlong talks that only drove my bride and me more deeply into despair. The silk had been torn and nothing could make it whole again.

I had robbed Tracy of everything she had dreamed of for herself and for us as a couple—children, grandchildren, the life we would build together, the prospect of growing old at each other's sides. And the damage didn't stop with me. How would Tracy trust anybody from now on? The next lover? A future husband? I have ruined her life. And nothing I can say or do can ever redeem that.

"How do you know these people?" Tracy asks now (meaning the Turk and Abby), peering ahead through the windshield as the cab makes the left out of 89th Street and turns south onto Second Avenue. A fire engine booms past, klaxon whooping, trailing a paramedic truck and two NYPD patrol cars.

"It's a long story."

I'm just starting to tell Tracy about Bablik and Mrs. B. when the cab brakes sharply, jinks right and nosedives to a stop half a car width out from the curb and a block north of Elaine's. A uniformed officer appears in the headlights, waving us to go round and turn away on 88th.

Tracy: "What's going on?"

Cab driver: "Somebody hit a hydrant."

Sure enough, we can see a geyser blasting thirty feet into the air from the sidewalk half a block ahead. Sheets begin drenching the cab. The driver turns on his wipers.

We pay and climb out, dodging the downpour. The sidewalk is jammed. We see news vans, emergency vehicles, tow trucks. A second fire engine and a chief's sedan weave through the press with more emergency vehicles arriving every second.

Tracy and I work our way forward through the crush. Two lanes of Second Avenue have been cordoned off. I see a '73 Coupe de Ville halfway up on the sidewalk with its right front bumper smashed into a power pole.

"It happened right in front of Elaine's," says Tracy.

We're close now. Partygoers are being escorted out of the restaurant. The Cadillac apparently has jumped the curb, decapitated a fire hydrant, and smashed into a utility pole. The NYFD is just now containing the damage.

Suddenly I see Abby.

She spots me and rushes forward. She's bleeding; her hair is wild. A sleeve has been torn off her jacket. Mascara streaks both cheeks.

She comes up and seizes me by both arms.

"They tried to kill Marvin!"

"What?"

Abby clutches me.

"He pushed me out of the way! He saved my life!"

Bystanders are clustering.

"What happened?"

I'm peering up and down the street, seeking sign of Bablik.

A young guy who looks like he could be a male model has emerged from the clutch of bystanders.

"A valet was at the wheel of the Caddy. He floored it just as this lady and her husband passed in front. If the power pole hadn't been there, he'd have cut the guy in half."

Two cops, a male and a female, have spotted Abby and are hurrying toward her. I sense that they were interrogating her but have lost her temporarily and now re-found her.

I'm holding Abby upright. "Where's Bablik now?"

"I don't know. I don't know!"

"He bolted," says the male model.

The two cops come up. The male addresses Mrs. Bablik by name. The female tries to tug Abby away from me. Abby pulls herself tighter into my arms.

"It's true what this lady says." The male model speaks not just to the cops, but to me, to Tracy, to the whole crowd. He's poised and articulate and his diction is impeccable. "The old guy saved her. He pushed her out of the way. But the Caddy was trying to hit *him*. You could see it. As soon as he knew the lady was safe, he took off."

Tracy's look to me says, "These are the people who invited us?"

But at the same time, to her credit, she's supporting Abby like a sister. Tracy's handkerchief daubs at Abby's mascara-smeared eyes; she struggles to tame Mrs. B.'s disheveled hair.

The male model is asking me who the old man was, meaning Bablik. I'm grilling him: "What happened to the valet?"

"He took off too. Like a rocket. In the opposite direction."

"What did he look like?"

"I dunno. Dark-haired. Tough. He had a ponytail."

Abby is now completely in my arms, sobbing into my chest.

"Marvin will think he was set up and double-crossed. We'll never find him now."

I can see Elaine Kaufman, the owner of the restaurant and hostess of the evening. She's on the sidewalk, a widebody woman in a flower-print muumuu, reassuring her clientele that the crisis has passed. The show will go on.

I pull Abby upright to face me. "Was he?"

"Was he what?"

"Set up and double-crossed?"

Finally the two cops succeed in extricating Abby. They tug her aside alongside a patrol car. Both have their notepads out.

Tracy's eyes meet mine. "Thanks," she says, "for a swell evening."

She's already stepping off the curb, raising her hand to hail a taxi. I tell her to wait, gimme twenty minutes. I'll take her home.

Tracy realizes there'll be no cabs amid this madness. She turns to walk toward 87th, to catch a taxi there. "I've got a 5:30 call tomorrow. I never should've said yes to this evening."

She glances back toward Abby, who is struggling to free herself from the cops and return to me.

"Besides," she says, "you've got an admirer."

28.

University Village

By the time I get her home to University Village, Abby has pulled herself together. The taxi we're in is a big, civilized Checker with abundant leg and headroom (unlike Gotham Cab's cramped-ass Dodge Coronets). Abby has repaired her hair and tucked her torn sleeve back into place. She fixes her mascara, reapplies lip gloss, shoots a spritz of perfume into her décolletage.

"How do I look?"

"You always look great."

My plan is to wait till Abby has recomposed herself, then hit her again for the Russian's address or at least his number. I still don't even know the guy's name! My hope is to extract this intel fast, preferably before I've dropped her off, so I can bolt immediately over to the Burgundy to catch up with Tracy. I've got to explain about tonight, at least a little, and apologize for wasting her evening. I know she'll be awake for at least another hour, prepping for tomorrow's shoot.

But the cabbie, instead of taking us around to the LaGuardia Place side of the 505 Tower where he can drop Abby a few feet from her door, turns off Second Avenue onto East Third/Great Jones, passes Broadway and Mercer, zigs one block south on LaGuardia, then turns left onto Bleecker. He pulls to the curb at the north end of the plaza fronting University Village.

"You're stopping here?"

I tell him he's still half a block from the 505 building—and seventy-five nasty, unlit yards from the lady's door.

The cabbie gives me a fuck-you shrug.

I lay into him. He's telling me if he stayed on LaGuardia he'd have had to drop us off on the wrong side of the street; we'd have had to cross traffic to get to our destination. If he has to cross Houston now and double back, it'll mean going five blocks out of his way. It'll cost me an extra buck. I'm telling him I'm not worried because *he's* the one who's gonna pay the freight for screwing us up in the first place. Suddenly I feel Abby's warm hand on my arm.

"Here will be fine, driver." And she passes the cabbie two bucks, about ten times what he deserves.

Inside the building Abby makes me ride the elevator with her up to her floor. She still seems so upset from the events at Elaine's that I'm feeling guilty about pressing her for the Russian's address and number. At her door I'm thinking maybe I should wait till tomorrow. I glance toward the elevator.

Abby: "Did I say you could go?"

Mrs. B. unlocks the door.

"Go in."

I obey. Abby follows.

"Close the door behind you."

I do.

"Lock it."

Mrs. B. deposits her keys and purse atop a console along the entry wall. All of her shakiness has vanished. I'm staring around at the Babliks' digs, whose interior I have never seen before—the Steinway grand, the floor-to-ceiling library wall, the double living rooms, and the panoramic view back over NYU and Washington Square Park.

"Make us a drink, will you? I'll be back in a minute."

Mrs. B. strides for the bedroom, or into a hallway that I imagine leads to the bedroom, tugging off the torn-sleeve dress.

I cross to the wet bar, trying to rally my will power. As hot as the lady is, a tumble in the sheets is definitely not on my agenda. Bablik's my boss. He loves this woman. Not to mention I gotta get outa here and catch up with my own wedded wife.

A row of silver-framed photos sits atop the piano. One immediately catches my eye. The pic is of the Turk in a tux, beaming at some gala. The man beside him can be none other than Moshe Dayan. Are you shitting me? An adjacent photo, also in a formal setting, is of Bablik, Mrs. B., and David Ben-Gurion.

Abby calls from the bedroom, "J&B, rocks."

I pour two.

Whatthefuck.

Sure enough, two hours later I'm standing naked and gooey in Mrs. B.'s same-size-as-my-entire-apartment bathroom, staring at my reflection in the wall-to-wall mirrors and asking myself, "Stretch, what kind of a schmuck are you?"

"Sweetheart, can you bring the tissues when you come back?"

Mrs. B. and I have already had two fights and one fuck. Fight #1 came when she re-appeared in a negligee to collect her J&B and I asked her about a third framed photo on top of the piano.

"That's Marvin in Tunisia, 1943," she said, indicating a black-and-white snapshot of a slender, dark-haired (and quite dashing) young soldier with a Ronald Colman mustache, in uniform, in the desert, posing beside two other G.I.s and a youth of about sixteen wearing civilian clothes. In the background is a military airstrip with several P-51 Mustang fighter planes visible. All four men are smiling and appear to be on top of the world.

"Who's the kid?" I ask.

"Who knows? A local boy probably."

Bullshit.

I recognize the youth. I've seen his eyes. I've seen them through binoculars from outside the Russian restaurant in Brighton Beach, and I've seen them up close in my face as he and his buddies beat the crap out of me and Tito in the cattails across from Glen Island Casino.

"Yehuda," I say.

I tell Abby about tailing her to the Brighton Beach restaurant. I tell her about going back and digging up the American Express receipt with "the Russian's" name on it.

"Yehuda Bablik. He's not Russian at all, is he? He's your husband's brother."

I'm remembering what my uncle Charlie told me about Bablik's brother, the "straight-up Jewish gangster like Meyer Lansky." And I'm recalling the newspaper clippings I pulled up at the public library: Bablik and "Lou" (née Yehuda) indicted in a drywall scandal, Bablik and his brother working hand in hand with the mob.

I tell Abby now that I don't care what beef Yehuda has with Bablik or Bablik has with Yehuda. It's none of my business. "But the Russian/Yehuda/Lou broke into my apartment and took something that's of extreme value to me, and I want it back."

I demand to know where Yehuda lives.

"It's in Brighton Beach somewhere, isn't it? Little Lithuania."

Abby slaps my face. She's in tears now, feigning dudgeon. She reels off a skein of imputations.

How much more do I know? Have I been to the police? Who else have I told? How dare I accuse her of lying? Of breaking the law!

"I'm tired," I tell her, "of getting fed independent lines of bullshit by you and your husband. Now, where is Yehuda? How can I reach him?"

"Reach him? Are you crazy? He just tried to kill Marvin!"

Next: the fuck. It keeps me around. Fight #2 comes after. I'm aware through all this that Mrs. B. has an objective. I don't know what it is but I know it involves me and I know I want nothing to do with it.

I'm back under the covers now though, having brought the tissues.

"That woman tonight. Was that your ex-wife?" Abby gives me a kiss. "You're a lot like Marvin, you know?"

She lights a Marlboro for herself and one for me. She pulls herself closer. I let her.

"Why do you think," Abby says, "I married a man who was obviously a criminal and obviously involved with other criminals? Do you imagine that I had no alternatives?"

She lays her head on my shoulder. Her right thigh lies across my left leg.

"I've had men promising me the moon since I was sixteen. But they were all so ... ordinary. I could project their ordinary lives into the ordinary future—and my own life with them if I said yes to their proposals.

"Marvin was different. He had such a hunger. He told me I would marry him the first night we met. Hear what I just said. He didn't ask me to marry him. He said I would marry him. He told me he would sleep with other women but, he said, 'I will always be true in my heart to you.'"

I lift an ashtray from the side table and set it on my chest. Abby flicks her ash into it.

"There's probably not a law in the land that Marvin hasn't broken. But, improbable as it sounds, he's the most moral man I know. He can recite the Books of Moses end to end, and all of Lear and Othello too. I've seen him in religious debates with rabbis and learned scholars. He shredded them. You wear a wedding ring. Why?"

Abby sits up, studying me. The apartment is dark, end to end; illumination comes only from the sky and the plaza below.

"I could make a real mess of you if I wanted to," she says. "If we fell in love, I mean. You go for me."

I do. I admit it.

"You're like Marvin. And I'm drawn to you in the same way I was to him."

In the morning Abby toasts bialys and brews a pot of Chock Full O' Nuts. She still won't give me Yehuda's address or number. We argue. It's clear I have no chance of winning. On a yellow pad she writes the addresses of the three properties that she and Bablik own, in northern Westchester, the Jersey shore, and Naples, Florida, plus her own family holdings in Kentucky and Colorado—all the places the Turk might use to hide out in. She writes me a check for a thousand dollars with the promise of five more if I find Marvin within the next two weeks.

I refuse it. I'm through with this shit.

"You don't even have to see him," Abby says. "Just get him to give up accepting that Man of the Year award. Understand? If he shows up, Lou will kill him."

I've been thinking about this all night.

"You were with Lou first, weren't you? Yehuda. You were with him before you went with Bablik."

"Take the check," Abby says.

I won't. "How would I find Bablik, even if I wanted to?"

The phone rings. Mrs. B. picks up the receiver. I stand and turn toward the door. Abby covers the mouthpiece with her hand and mimes to me: "Marvin."

"Yes," she says into the phone. Then again, "yes," and, "yes."

She holds out the phone.

"It's for you."

29.

Guard Hill Road

"Don't get me started on the subject of women, and particularly not on the subject of Abby."

This is Bablik. I have found him. It took no great detective work. He tells me where he is. He wants to see me. He wants to apologize to me.

The Turk is camping in the tack room of the stables on his horse property on Guard Hill Road in Bedford Hills. I'm in the cab he lent me. I've taken the FDR Drive north out of Manhattan, onto the Major Deegan and then the Bronx River. You're in the southern suburbs now—Pelham Manor, Mt. Vernon, Bronxville. Westchester County. To the east are the big-bucks towns with frontage on Long Island Sound—Larchmont, Rye, Mamaroneck, and the run of postcard villages that continues across the Connecticut border into even tonier enclaves like Greenwich, Darien, Cos Cob. "Leafy" would be the word if it were summertime. South of the Kensico Reservoir I turn onto 22 North, the Old Post Road, taking it through Armonk, where IBM is, then past the tiny hamlet of Banksville and north to Bedford Village. A few miles east lies Pound Ridge and, north a little farther, South Salem, the far suburbs, beyond normal commuter distance. Keep left on 22 through the village of Bedford. You pass a street called Tarleton Road. Guard Hill Road is the next left.

Properties are big up here, ten acres, twenty, much more. You're driving past real horse farms. Distance from Times Square is about fifty miles. It's gorgeous. Colonial-style houses, some dating back to the 1700s, are visible, one every half-mile or so, set back hundreds of feet from the road behind stone fences that look like they've been in place since Peter Stuyvesant. Up here the towns are so rich they don't even pave the roads. My cab's rump-sprung suspension rattles over a washboard surface under packed snow. On both sides of Guard Hill Road sprawl rolling pastures, white now, with fifty-acre stands of winter maple and elm along the skyline. Mailboxes have no names and no numbers. The postman knows, and nobody else needs to.

Guard Hill Road is one of the secret Edens of the seriously rich. There's no gated entry, no guardhouse. You just can't find the place if you don't know where to look. I'm driving down a lane with three-hundred-year-old oaks and sugar maples on both sides. The Turk lives here? A horse pasture of at least twenty acres extends on the right. Bablik has instructed me to pass a sign for Sycamore Farm, then start looking for a narrow drive on the left between white-painted stones.

There.

I turn.

There's a downed maple blocking the road. I pull to the side and get out. Have I passed the turnoff? How could the Turk have gotten in?

Down a long, snow-covered slope I see an equestrian compound—a big Colonial-style house with a guest cottage, barns and a horse ring, stables, a spring house.

Suddenly from the base of the slope: a gunshot.

Hunters? I peer. Across a quarter-mile of snowfield, a figure is waving.

Bablik.

The Turk signals me to come down the road. I get back in the cab, jink around the fallen maple. A few hundred yards downslope, there he is, tromping forward on foot, carrying an AK-47 with a thirty-round banana clip. You could ambush a platoon with that thing. I roll down the window.

"Are we in Vietnam?"

The Turk directs me to a narrow wooden bridge over a winter stream, only inches deep, with a drivable carpet of rocks and fallen limbs. He hops into the front seat beside me.

"Did you bring the coffee?"

Bablik has asked me to get him three pounds of Chock Full O' Nuts plus raisin bran, bagels, skim milk, sugar, and a dozen eggs.

"Go on, go on!"

We're driving in the actual stream now.

"Keep going, keep going!"

About two hundred yards in, the Turk points me to an even narrower dirt track. The cab bucks up out of the creek. Bablik springs down, carrying the AK. He's sixty years old but he's nimble as a jackrabbit. Within seconds he is mounting back up the snowy slope we have just descended. I stop, park, and follow on foot.

At the crest of the rise is a low stone wall, protecting a vantage that looks back over the approach via Guard Hill Road. Bablik motions me to get down. On the ground: raw planks, horse blankets, a thermos, binos.

Me: "Can I smoke?"

Turk: "Are you out of your fucking mind?"

Twenty minutes later (enough time for anybody who followed me to show themselves and be spotted), the Turk and I have descended to the stables, which are wet and cold and empty and reeking of winter straw and forty years of horse piss. There's a wood-burning stove in the Turk's tack room but he won't light it because the smoke might give him away. Two electric space heaters fight the ten-degree cold.

The Turk is cooking an omelet on a hotplate. He's wearing Wellingtons over farmer's dungarees and a hound's-tooth jacket. He looks completely ridiculous. For the first time since I've known Bablik, he seems old to me.

I ask if he's okay.

"You mean after Elaine's?"

Yeah, he says, he's fine. He asks me about Abby. "You sleep with her yet?"

"What?"

Bablik laughs. "You're too honest to run fares off the meter, but that don't stop you from shtupping my old lady."

I start to babble something. The Turk lets me twist for an endless twenty seconds. Then he laughs and raps my shoulder.

"I phone my wife's apartment at nine in the morning, ask for you and get you. Whaddaya think I'm thinking?"

He tells me to relax, he's just busting my balls.

I tell him I've seen the photos on the piano, specifically the one from North Africa 1943.

"I know 'the Russian' is your brother. Why did you lie to me?"

The Turk serves the omelet. He slides it onto my plate, which is an old mess tin with US ARMY stamped on the metal, and cuts it in half with a Case pocketknife. He gives me the big half and slides the smaller onto a plate for himself.

The Turk apologizes for getting me involved in this business. "You're right, I did lie to you. I fed you a line of bullshit for my own selfish purposes." He apologizes for being the cause of my getting beaten up and my apartment being ransacked. He knows about Ponytail, he says. "The sonofabitch worked you over pretty good, I hear."

"And you still haven't paid me."

"I know. I'm sorry."

I apologize to him for sleeping with his wife.

The Turk waves it off. "You ain't the first and you won't be the last. I'm no angel neither."

He tells me he knew that if the occasion arose when Abby got me alone, she'd put a move on. He didn't expect me, or anyone, to resist.

"Women," he says.

The Turk gestures with one hand toward the outside, indicating the barns, the house, the property. "How much you think I shelled out for this kibbutz?"

He holds up ten fingers.

"Ten years. Every penny I made for ten years of my life. Why? For her."

The Turk takes his coffee white, the same way Peter in London took his tea. Two-thirds coffee, one-third Carnation condensed milk straight from the tin.

"A dame like Abby comes with a price tag. My accountant knows it down to the decimal point and so will the judge if and when the time comes when my bride decides to dump me. Wanna hear it? Twenty-two hundred a month for clothes and a car; another deuce for jewelry, gifts, contributions to charity and political causes; a grand and a half for memberships in clubs and philanthropic organizations, Lincoln Center, MOMA, the Whitney, the Guggenheim, whatever it takes to keep my bride swimming in the circles she needs to swim in; plus mortgages, taxes, upkeep on our other places in Naples and Cape May; her family's properties; not to mention beauty treatments, her hair, nails, cellulite, varicose veins; the odd facelift, boob job, tummy tuck. We're up to what, ten grand a month, twelve? Not counting the spa, the health club, Canyon Ranch at a thousand a week, trips to Paris, Christmas in the Bahamas.

"I ain't complaining," says the Turk. "This is the game. Pay to play. A woman like Abby demands it. You pay in money, you pay in time and attention, you pay in deference. You gotta act a certain way toward her. She's the lady, you're the slob.

"Why do I put up with it? I hate to say it but it's worth it. She's worth it. Without her I'm just another Yid from Yid Town. With her I can pick up the phone and call the mayor. I can talk shit with Lindsay or Morgenthau, even Robert Moses, at least for twenty seconds at a benefit for the Museum of Modern Art that I write a check to for ten large every February and for which I receive jack fucking squat.

"You pay," Bablik says. "You pay with your balls and you pay with pieces of your soul. Are you listening? You think I'm a schmuck, don't you?"

I don't. I'm waiting for the moment when I can grill him about his brother.

"Does Abby love me? Who the fuck knows? If I step off, there's fifty guys waiting in line to set her up ten times better than I ever did. Do I love her? It's worse than that. I worship her. Do I fuck around? Of course. You think you can have a woman like Abby and she'll sleep with you too?

"This place," he says, gesturing to the hills, the horse pastures, the Colonial estates up and down Guard Hill Road. "How many Jews you think live in this Shangri-La?"

He signs: goose egg.

"Know what CC&Rs are? Covenants, Conditions and Restrictions. 'I will not sell my property to a non-Caucasian or to any individual not of the Christian faith.' The wops and the Irish couldn't buy here twenty years ago. How did I crack the code? I wrote a check for twenty grand to St. Somefuckingbody, Episcopal Church in Pound Ridge. When I die I go to heaven as a goy."

He asks me if my uncle ever told me about the job he had when he was sixteen years old. "We worked together, Charlie and me, for a manufacturer of ladies' handbags. Our job was to waltz into department stores, pretending to be customers. We'd slip up to the handbag displays, pick up the competition's purses, and bend the metal clasps, just enough so they wouldn't close properly." Bablik laughs and shakes his head at the memory. "Times were tough. It was that or starve.

"Charlie got it right," the Turk says. "Your uncle hit the jackpot when he married Peggy and went straight. But the truth is if I found a woman like Peg, I wouldn't go for her. I'm suited to Abby. I deserve the shit she dishes out."

I assure Bablik that his wife loves him. "She was meeting with your brother trying to protect you. To get him to back off. I watched her with him. She wouldn't let him touch her, not even a finger on her arm."

I tell the Turk that Abby's final words to me, twelve hours ago, were a plea to somehow talk him out of accepting that Man of the Year award ten days from now. "Your wife is convinced that your brother will go after you if you show up. He'll kill you."

I'm studying Bablik intensely as I tell him this.

His expression never alters.

"Why do you care about me, kid? I've lied to you and taken advantage of you. Why did you even come up here?"

I have one answer: I'm desperate to reach Yehuda. But that's not the deeper truth, and I know it.

"Why is this award so important to you? It's in the paper for one day and then it's forgotten. Who cares? Who's gonna remember?"

I indicate the tack room, the barn. "And this hideout? It's a death trap! Your brother obviously knows the place. He'd be a moron not to send his guys. You were a soldier. This barn is blind on all four sides. A regiment could tramp through these woods and you wouldn't see or hear 'em till they were right on top of you."

I stop. The Turk is looking at me. "I'm touched by your concern, kid. I really am."

He reaches beneath the table and pulls up the AK-47. "Here," he says. "Come on."

"For your protection."

I'm staring at this ten-pound monster with its wooden stock, pistol grip, flash suppressor, and thirty-round clip. "Got anything less conspicuous? Like a bazooka?"

Bablik takes the weapon back with grave reluctance. "Too bad," he says. "You were this close to becoming a gangster."

I tell the Turk I've gotta reach his brother. The Turk swears he can't help. "What about your taxi companies?" I say. "He's gotta come in to an office."

Bablik laughs. "You think this guy actually works?"

"Where's he live? Little Lithuania? If I walk the neighborhood asking for ..."

"... you'll be dead before you speak to the third person."

Bablik studies me for a long moment.

"What'd my brother do to you?"

I won't answer.

"He took something of yours, didn't he? I know the sonofabitch. He loves to twist the knife."

I don't know why, but I refuse to tell Bablik about Teaspoon.

The Turk senses something anyway.

I can feel his wheels turning. He wants to help.

"You can't go into that neighborhood and start throwing my brother's name around. It's too dangerous. But there are other ways to find him, if it's that important to you."

My expression must answer for me.

"Does my brother still have that '62 Imperial? The one with the gunsight taillights?"

I tell him the car is registered to Ivanov now, though the other goon, the one with the ponytail, seems to do most of the driving.

Bablik considers this.

"How many twelve-year-old Chrysler Imperials," he asks, "do you think there are on the streets of Little Lithuania?"

Wow.

That's a great idea.

There's no driving out through the creek at night, so I stay over. In the morning Bablik walks me out to the road, wading the stream in his Wellies so he doesn't leave tracks in the snow. "Little Lithuania's only ten blocks square. You'll find that Imperial easily. But watch yourself, okay?"

I ask Bablik why his brother wants to kill him so badly. "What's the big issue between you two?"

"Issue? Life don't come down to issues. He wants to kill me because he wants to kill me."

Bablik draws up thoughtfully.

"Everyone commits a crime. You, me, everybody. From that day your life becomes about nothing but dealing with that crime. How do you handle the fact that you've done something that can never be undone? Deny it? Seek redemption? Do you try to justify your crime? Become a criminal? Do you demand punishment? Square it with God by making sure you pay for what you've done? The Jewish religion is about justice. You devout? Me neither. I'm not even circumcised."

The Turk squints around, scanning the bare-branch woods. His comb-over blows open in the wind. "I'm going to that award ceremony," he says. "It would mean the world if you'd come with me."

"Are you crazy? I'm not going and neither are you."

"Robert Moses is gonna name me Man of the Year."

"Who cares?"

I have never seen an expression like the one now on the Turk's face.

"I lied to you to get you to tail Abby. The job was a pretext. What I wanted was you. You're Robert Moses' grand-nephew. I wanted you to come with me to that award."

Is the Turk losing his mind? I tell him I don't even know Robert Moses. I've never met him. We're related, yeah, but I wouldn't recognize him if I tripped over him.

"I want you with me at that ceremony, kid. When I shake Robert Moses' hand, I want you beside me. I want you to shake his hand right after me."

"I won't. I won't be part of putting you at risk."

I'm searching Bablik's eyes, trying to understand what he's thinking. How did I get so involved with this crazy sonofabitch? Does he *want* to get killed?

"I understand," says the Turk. "It's on me. It's my fault."

"And you owe me seven hundred bucks. And Tito too."

"I'll get it to you, I promise. And Tito'll get his."

Bablik. He's shivering, bare-headed, in the frozen tundra of northern Westchester WASP Central, wearing a Paul Stuart topcoat over striped pajama bottoms with his feet sunk into rubberized farmer's boots and an NVA Commie automatic rifle in his right hand.

"You gotta get outa here," I say.

"I know."

I'm peering up and down the road. What am I gonna do with this guy?

"Listen," I hear my voice say. "I know a place you can hide. It might cost you a few hundred bucks, and I might have to twist a couple of arms to make it happen. But where I'm sending you, your brother'll never find you in a million years."

Bablik's expression is still hurt from me saying no to him about the Man of the Year award. He sweeps his comb-over back into place and turns toward me. "Yeah?" he says. "Where's that?"

30.

Gunsight Taillights

I'm on the phone to Roach. He's resisting.

"Who is this character anyway?"

"He's a criminal on the run from gangsters who are trying to murder him."

"Stop fucking around."

"He'll pay a grand for ten days. Cash. I'll waive my percentage. The band keeps it all."

I've booked Death Warmed Over into a four-stop, ten-day, year-end tour—two joints in Atlantic City, one in Ocean City, Maryland, and a fourth in Rehoboth Beach, Delaware. Believe it or not, people come to the shore in January. Nine out of ten clubs are shuttered for the season. The ones that still put out a bar and a band are packed every night. New Year's Eve is a gold rush. It's one of the best times of the year.

It takes me another ten minutes to convince Roach that Bablik will be all right hiding out with the band; he's not nuts; he's not a pain in the ass; everything will be cool.

Privately I'm a little nervous. I've convinced the Turk to leave his Kalashnikov, but he's still packing a nine-millimeter in his briefcase and a Walther PPK (the same weapon that Hitler used to blow his brains out in the bunker beneath the Reich Chancellery) in an ankle holster.

The final bone of contention between Roach and me is he wants me on the road with the band. "If we're gonna put up with this fucker, you're gonna suffer too."

"Out of the question. I gotta finish my book."

I don't tell him about Teaspoon for the same reason I didn't tell Bablik. He'll think I'm crazy.

Maybe I am. That's what I'm thinking now, in the cab two hours after hanging up from Roach, as I complete my second circuit of the streets of Little Lithuania, searching for a '62 Chrysler Imperial.

It's noon on a bright, blustery December 30. Frigid air blows off the bay. I have phoned Abby first thing this AM and told her I've got plans in the works that will stash her husband someplace safe. No, I won't tell her where. And I'm working on the Turk, I assure her, to change his mind about going to that banquet. Abby is effusive in her gratitude. "You stay safe too!"

The signature feature on all Chrysler Imperials since '55 is the taillights. "Gunsight" lights that ascend flamboyantly, all by themselves, above the tail fin. The sexiest year was '56. Those lights were spectacular. But even a '62 has globes that stand out from half a block away.

Still I've been up and down Neptune Avenue twice, taken a back-and-forth under the El at Brighton Beach Avenue, and made the run of the beach streets three times without success. Despite the Turk's warning I have stopped at two kosher delis and a newsstand and asked for Yehuda Bablik.

I spot a parking place now outside a candy store at the corner of Coney Island and Ocean View. What the fuck, I grab the spot and go in. The place is called Sol & Mimi's. It's a classic Brooklyn joint with an old-fashioned soda fountain and a fat guy in a paper cap doing the jerking, signs on the wall for chocolate and vanilla egg creams, Dots and Mary Janes and Bonomo's Turkish Taffy in the candy display, "It's-It" ice cream sandwiches in the freezer, and bottles of Yoo-hoo ("It's Yogi Berra's Favorite Drink") next to White Rock and Hoffman soft drinks in the upright cooler.

About a dozen locals populate the joint—kids and grownups with ruddy-cheeked Slavic faces. They're all bundled to the eyeballs in Red Square earflap hats and boots that look like they just stomped in from the Gulag. Should I query these Commies?

I'm just reaching for my Polaroid of Teaspoon, when I hear a car pull up outside and stop. Through the candy store's front windows, I see a long black sedan.

The vehicle has a bisected grille and an eagle hood ornament. Above the truncated fins rise two gunsight taillights.

Ponytail gets out.

He's alone, bareheaded, wearing a full-length leather coat with gloves, tailored trousers, and black lizard-skin boots.

He comes straight into the store and straight up to me.

"Where's Yehuda?" I say. When I'm scared, I get a little reckless. "I wanna talk to him."

Everyone in the store has backed away at least one pace. Ponytail turns to the ring of faces. His expression says, "Do you believe the ass on this guy?"

"Where's my cat?" I say.

"What?"

"My cat. Did you take my cat?"

"You're kidding me, right? What kinda dipshit has a cat? What are you, some fucking faggot?"

For the first time I notice a tattoo on Ponytail's neck, just below his left ear. It says NIXON.

"Did you take my cat or not?"

Ponytail shoves me in the chest. "I wish I had taken your cat, you hippie dirtbag. I'd have drowned it in the fucking river."

He shoves me again. Against all logic, I'm starting to get pissed off. I shove him back. "What the fuck's your problem, man? What did I ever do to you?"

"I hate people like you."

"Whaddaya mean 'people like me'?"

"People like you are ruining this fucking country. You're like cockroaches. Somebody should put his size twelve on top of all of you."

It seems absurd to say this, but Ponytail's words have hurt my feelings. He sees it. It brings him great pleasure.

"Wanna know what I did with your cat? Huh? Wanna know? I wrung its flea-infested neck with my bare hands." He makes the wring-a-neck gesture. "Then I cut its heart out and ate it raw."

He grabs the front of my jacket with both hands and spins me toward the door.

"Now get the fuck outa here before I do the same to you."

Should I turn and fight? Am I a coward for letting this gorilla push me around? Maybe, but I don't care. I've just learned a priceless item of intel.

Wherever my cat may be, whatever dangers he may be facing, for sure he is not in the hands of these gangsters.

31.

The Withering Glance
of the Goddess

By two I'm back in Manhattan. I stash my cab in the secure lot at the Burgundy, which is empty except for one craft services truck with a flat tire (Tracy and the production are on location at the Hunts Point Produce Market in the Bronx), head inside and settle upstairs in my cubby, trying once again to make the middle and the end of my book fit together.

It's agony.

Still, I'm suffused with hope from the confrontation in Little Lithuania. What Ponytail said about wringing Teaspoon's neck tells me without a doubt that neither he nor Yehuda has kidnapped my cat. Until Ponytail heard it from me in the candy store, they had no idea I even had a cat.

I work on the book for two hours, accomplishing nothing, then give up and call Roach from the production office. I've been leaving messages for him all day. Yes, he confirms, he has connected with Bablik. Yes, the band will take the Turk with them to Ocean City. I tell Roach to get Bablik's thousand bucks in cash and promise to join them as soon as I can get free.

I have to find some way to break through this block that's stopping me from working. Four more messages have come in from Marty. He wants the book yesterday.

I phone Jake and ask him if he'll lend me his ID so I can use my old office at Y&R at night and over the weekend. Jake says no problem. We make plans to meet for dinner. When Tracy returns to the Burgundy at five and asks if I want to grab a bite with her I say yes, forgetting that I've already made plans with Jake.

I wind up going to dinner with both of them. Jake and Tracy have never met. I began working with Jake two years after Tracy left for California. But he knows what she looks like. He's seen her, in the movies, in *Missizombie*.

We meet at Fratello's on West Fourth. Tracy has taken a cab up from Canal Street; Jake has walked the five blocks from Abingdon Square. We have a table-busting dinner of linguini and calamari with bottle after bottle of some kind of Chianti that Jake knows from his travels in Italy. Tracy is in fine form. Jake picks up the check. Throughout the evening I detect not the slightest indication of sexual chemistry between my semi-ex-wife and my best friend. When we finish, Tracy has me drop her off (I'm driving Bablik's cab) back at the Burgundy. She says she's exhausted and going straight to bed. I'm wide awake. I take the cab and turn uptown for Y&R, to the office, hoping to get in three or four more hours on the book.

But as I'm pulling away, I get a bad feeling.

I circle the block.

Sure enough, when I pass the hotel for the second time, there's Tracy emerging from the lobby with her gloved hand up, hailing a cab.

Five minutes later, I'm outside Jake's building, watching Tracy enter.

I can't describe the state this puts me into. So she's gonna fuck him. I know I haven't got a leg to stand on, considering my own faithless past, not to mention the present, but I'm still near-homicidal.

I double-park and stalk into the building. The doorman knows me. "Don't buzz Jake," I tell him. "I wanna surprise him."

I ring Jake's bell. His eyeball appears in the peep. When I enter, he's clutching a bottle of Valpolicella with his hand on a Hammacher Schlemmer cork extractor and the cork halfway out.

"Stretch, this isn't what it looks like."

Tracy enters from the living room. They're facing me over Jake's hand-hewn, five-thousand-dollar kitchen island.

I tell them to go ahead and do what they're gonna do. "I can't stop you. But just know that I know what a pair of assholes you are."

Tracy (to me): "Am I single?"

Me: "Not yet."

"Then sign my fucking divorce papers."

I jerk a thumb toward Jake. "And don't flatter yourself because you're nailing this sonofabitch. He'd fuck a snake if it'd hold still long enough."

"Right. Like you don't have your face up the skirt of every X-rated trollop between here and the Bowery."

"That's different."

"Really?"

Tracy fixes me with double lasers.

Me: "There it is, Jake. See it? The withering glance of the goddess."

Tracy: "Don't quote *The Philadelphia Story* to me, you fuck. I'm the one who turned you onto that movie."

"Me chasing women is different because I'm doing it for fun. I'm not spreading my legs for my husband's best friend for the sole purpose of breaking his balls, which you know you're doing and which you fucking love doing."

"Maybe I do," says Tracy, "but who got me started?"

Jake has moved closer to Tracy. She's not gonna leave and he's not gonna back off.

"Fuck you both and may you both rot in hell."

Ninety minutes later I look up and I'm climbing the steps to the plaza level of the World Trade Center. I've walked the whole way.

I understand how people murder other people. Your wife. Your husband. The worst part is I can't even hate Tracy. She's not to blame. I am.

What the fuck.

I hike down to South Ferry and ride over to Staten Island and back twice. The experience is not remotely like the Edna St. Vincent Millay poem.

The sun is up, people are stepping out for coffee (it's the morning of New Year's Eve) by the time I arrive on foot, exhausted, back at Abingdon Square to pick up my cab, which sits smack in the street, blocking two parked cars, with four citations stuck under its driver's side wiper.

Turning the corner from West Twelfth Street is Nicolette, in winter boots and a knit cap, coming from the Greek deli with takeout coffee and a bialy. She comes up shaking her head.

"I saw the wad of tickets when I passed. I thought, What witless bastard leaves his cab double-parked on the street all night?"

She tells me I look like hell and gives me a kiss. She says she's been reading my book, the second one, the one about Peter and England. She wants to talk about it.

"Come on," she says. "I'll buy you breakfast."

32.
Aesthetic Distance

Nicolette dumps her takeout coffee into a street-corner trashcan and tucks her bialy in its brown bag into her coat pocket. She respects the restaurant etiquette of order here if you're gonna sit here. We take a window booth in the Noho Star (we had to cruise for ten minutes to find a place to park the cab) at the corner of Bleecker and Lafayette.

The best thing about living in New York is cold, bright mornings like this, with snow on the ground while it's still white before it turns to slush, when you can camp for half an hour or an hour in a toasty cafe and watch girls in boots and winter hats tromp by on the sidewalk outside.

I'm feeling better now that I'm with Nicolette. She orders a Danish and a coffee; I go for bacon and eggs with grits and wheat toast. I'm hungry.

"I read your book," Nicolette says.

She's looking at me very seriously.

"Where were you last night? Where were you yesterday?"

It takes me a minute to remember.

"This is you," she says, looking straight at me.

She asks how long it's been since I slept. I can't remember that either. I start to tell her about Ponytail in the candy store.

"Stop. Don't say another word." She's staring at me in exasperation. "Can't you see?"

"See what?"

"Yourself."

The waitress brings Nicolette's coffee. I decide I better have one too. Nicolette waits till both cups have been poured and we're alone at our table by the window.

"You know I believe in you," she says. "You know I believe in your talent."

I'm waiting.

"But your book," she says, "is fucking excruciating."

For a second I think she's talking about the one I'm writing.

"The second one, the one about you and your friend Peter in England. Do you remember giving it to me? Six months ago? Sorry it took me so long. I was avoiding it because I was afraid it was gonna be what I was afraid it was gonna be—and it was."

The waitress returns with our plates. Nicolette smiles and thanks her.

She launches into what feels like a five-minute harangue on my Whatthefuck attitude and the insane, self-destructive way I live my life.

"You haven't turned pro at all. You're an amateur. Look at your life. It's wall-to-wall with distractions. The rock band. This nutty taxi guy. You're getting yourself beaten up for Christ's sake! And when you run out of distractions, you dash into the street looking for more. Anything to keep you from doing your work.

"Not that your book is bad," Nicolette says. "There's a lot of good stuff in it. But you're stuck in the same dead end that I was when I was painting small and dark. You're too close to the material. There's no aesthetic distance. That's why publishers keep turning it down. The book is more like somebody's journal than a real novel. It's unreadable.

"And your friend Peter? Wake up! Do you think it was an accident that he was swinging from a hook with a noose around his neck? You're scared. I get it. You're afraid you'll do the same thing if you push too far into the endgame of Art. But what else is there? For people like you and me, nothing. We're artists," Nicolette says. "This is our life. There's no white picket fence out there for you or for me, honey. There never was and there never will be."

Throughout Nicolette's monologue, pedestrians have been passing outside on the sidewalk. They've all seemed like a blur to me, just stuff in the background. Suddenly I find myself becoming aware of one individual.

The Scary Girl.

She stalks past, inches away, staring through the cafe window directly at me. Nicolette doesn't notice. This is happening behind her back.

"Finish your book! Stop fucking around! And don't tell me you can't do it without your cat. Write the sonofabitch!"

Nicolette notices the Danish on the plate before her. She takes one gigantic bite and washes it down with an even bigger gulp of coffee.

"And I'll tell you something else," Nicolette says. "Forget this fantasy about your ex-old lady, what's her name? Stacy? Lacy?"

"Tracy."

"She's not right for you and she never was. Stop blaming yourself for screwing around on her. You did it to save yourself. You blew up your marriage deliberately because you knew if you stayed in it you'd never be a writer. You'd never do what you were put on this Earth to do."

Wow.

Nicolette's words are hitting me like a sledgehammer. She's right. She's absolutely right. But at the same time she's imparting these dead-on determinations, the Scary Girl is hanging a 180 outside on the sidewalk and stalking back, directly toward our window.

Nicolette follows my eyes and turns around.

"Who is that? Your slutty neighbor? Black Lipstick?"

The Scary Girl comes right up to the window, straight to me. Her expression says, "Come outside, I want to speak to you."

I mime a response through the glass. I'm busy. I can't come out.

The Scary Girl turns and stomps off in the direction she first approached from. I see her stop a few feet up the sidewalk and tug a pad of paper and a Magic Marker from her shoulder bag. She sets the pad on the hood of a parked car, using the vehicle as a writing surface.

Nicolette has turned away from the window, back toward me.

"You're trying to publish this new book to prove to Stacy/Lacy/ Tracy that you're not a bum and a loser. It's way past that, sweetheart. You've made her into an icon, as if she possesses the magical power to pronounce absolution on you. Don't put that on her. It's not fair to her. And besides, you're the one whose opinion counts, not her. Forget her. This is about you only."

The Scary Girl comes up again, fixing me with another freighted look. Nicolette turns around to face her. "What the fuck," Nicolette mouths to her through the window, "is your problem?"

The Scary Girl doesn't blink. She presses the notepad paper flush against the glass, right in my face.

I'M PREGNANT

33.

Toxic Sludge

I get back to the Burgundy just as Tracy is coming in from her night with Jake. She's in yesterday's clothes with her hair matted into an ill-repaired bedhead; she has that JBF look and she knows it. She strides past me in the lobby without a word.

I'm completely freaked by the Scary Girl, whose name, I have finally succeeded in remembering, is Adriana Novotna. (What is it with me and women from east of the Iron Curtain?) On the sidewalk outside the Noho Star she and I have held our first conversation of greater than two hundred words.

Yes, she is pregnant.

Yes, it's by me (she has slept with no one else in the time period, she swears).

And yes, she wants to get married. Insists, in fact. She's Catholic. She refuses to raise the child alone when she knows who the father is. And there's no way in hell she's gonna terminate the pregnancy.

She loves me and is determined that I will be her husband. We will raise our child as a family and remain together till death do us part.

Nicolette looks on from my shoulder throughout this exchange. Her last words to me are, "This one's all yours, Cowboy."

What am I thinking? I can't think at all. I know only that I've gotta get my book finished and turned in to Marty. I'll worry about everything else later.

At the Burgundy. I make straight for the production office on the third floor. I need a black coffee, then I'll head to my cubby and get to work. But as soon as I step from the elevator, the P.A. with the Tisch School sweatshirt hails me. "I'm so glad you're here!"

She hands me four phone messages. Three are from Marty. The fourth is from Mika, the chemist from Hungary. On the slip is her name and nothing else.

"She didn't leave a number?"

"She didn't have to. She's right there."

Mika rises from a couch in the reception area.

She says, "I'm going to the police."

I haul her straight to my room.

Mika is furious with me over the toxic sludge I asked her to analyze.

"What kind of criminal activity are you mixed up in? I still haven't got my Immigration papers. I could get deported!"

It takes five minutes and two paper cups of Courvoisier, but eventually I get Mika calmed down.

She tells me she has tested the sludge.

I ask her if she has written a report.

"Are you shitting me? I dumped that slop the minute I saw what it was."

She says she has hidden everything from her supervisor. She had to falsify papers to account for her lab time and use of equipment.

The tested materials, Mika says, proved to be an admixture of industrial solvents, corrosives (including battery acid and chemical effluents), various types of poison including arsenic and strychnine, as well as copious amounts of grease-trap waste, presumably from restaurant kitchens. The only noxious element missing, she declares, is plutonium.

"This is the worst shit in the world to dump into a river. Whoever did this deserves the death penalty—and I don't believe in the death penalty. Oh, and one more thing. The solid matter in the sample? It's the remains of a human femur."

"What?"

"A leg bone. From a person. Whoever is doing this is not just dumping toxic waste, he's disposing of at least one human body."

Now it's *me* who needs a brandy. I make Mika go over everything one more time. A human bone? Is she certain? It couldn't be from a cow or a pig? Meat from a restaurant grease trap?

"My last job in Budapest," Mika says, "was in the city morgue."

I assure her that I'm not involved in the dumping of toxic waste or the unlawful disposal of human remains. In fact, until this minute I wasn't 100 percent certain that the material I gave her was even illegal, let alone contained parts of a human body.

Mika says she's done further research. "I checked out your cab company. I looked up the owner. Have you seen this?"

She hands me yesterday's *Daily News*, folded open to Jimmy Breslin's column.

JEW OF THE YEAR

Jimmy Breslin is the Pulitzer Prize-winning columnist and investigative journalist who specializes in street-level reporting from the point of view of the common man. He's always writing from Irish bars and blue-collar workplaces. I like him. I read his stuff every day. Breslin has written novels, had movies made; he even ran for President of the City Council a few years ago on a ticket with Norman Mailer, who was campaigning for mayor.

Yesterday's column is about Bablik.

As I'm scanning it, Mika is telling me she wants me to move in with her, to her place above the Goodwill Store on Eleventh Avenue. We'll spend New Year's Eve together. I'll be safe with her, she says. "You don't have to fuck me. I just want to know you're okay. I've got plenty of guns and my door is two inches thick."

I'm struggling to maintain focus on Breslin's column. It's good, as usual. Literate and funny and street smart.

Breslin starts by citing Bablik's upcoming Man of the Year award from Friends of the Israel Defense Forces. Who is this character anyway? Breslin asks. The reporter speculates on the worthiness for such an honor of an individual who, like a cheap hoodlum, prides himself on his street sobriquet, "the Turk." Where is he from? Not Turkey, according to the State Department. Russia? Poland? Lithuania?

What, Breslin further inquires, are we to make of this fellow who leads a high-glam lifestyle, supporting several homes and a very expensive wife, while making major contributions to Jewish causes and to the state of Israel despite the fact that his sole source of revenue appears to be a handful of cab companies whose vehicles are, according to documents obtained from the New York City Taxi and Limousine Commission, barely maintained to the city minimum and which have been cited for more safety and maintenance violations than those of any other taxi enterprise in the five boroughs.

Breslin further cites the drywall prosecutions of the late '60s and goes on to name a number of colorful Mob-related characters, the pleasure of whose company Mr. Bablik has enjoyed on a number of occasions, including shared vacation jaunts to Trinidad, the Virgin Islands, and his own beachfront condominium in Naples, Florida.

As I'm reading this I'm thinking, Why would Breslin write this? Why now? Could the Turk himself have planted it? Why? Is Yehuda behind it? To discredit Bablik? Why?

When I finish reading, Mika asks if I know how many people disappear each year in New York City. She says she has researched this too. In the past ten years: two state senators, four city commissioners, three Port Authority officials, and God knows how many hundreds of others from the ranks of organized crime, not to mention plain old civilians.

"You think this kinda shit doesn't happen? I'm from Hungary. People disappear all the time!"

Suddenly, a knock on the door. I practically jump out of my skin.

The door cracks open. Tracy sticks her head in.

"Oh, I'm sorry."

"No," says Mika. "I'm just leaving."

Mika stands. There's an awkward moment as I introduce her to Tracy and Tracy to her. Mika insists that I keep the Breslin article. She makes sure that I have her phone number and extracts a promise from me to call her about getting together this evening. She squeezes past Tracy and scurries off down the hall.

Tracy has put herself back together since I saw her in the lobby. She looks stylish and professional.

"Listen," she says. "I'm uncomfortable having you here after that scene last night at Jake's. I know you're in a bind and I won't ask you to leave right this second. But I'd appreciate it if you'd pack your stuff and be out of here within twenty-four hours."

34.
Live and Let Live

I move in with Joey, my former girlfriend who became a cop. It's New Year's Eve. Her shift ends at six, she says. She'll be home two hours after that.

I meet Nicolette for coffee and to wish her Happy New Year. I call Mika and tell her I'm on the lam. I spend all afternoon revisiting the courtyard businesses, the Portuguese patio restaurant, the Szechuan takeout, Ray's pizza, plus the supers and various tenants in every building fronting on Fifteenth Street, Fourteenth Street, Greenwich Avenue, Eighth Avenue, and Horatio Street, seeking news of a sighting of Teaspoon, however fleeting.

Nothing.

At five I fire up Bablik's cab and head for the Williamsburg Bridge. Joey's place is a first-floor apartment in a single-family house in Gerritsen Beach, Brooklyn. The two upstairs floors belong to her father. He's a cop too. Retired. Joey's dad lives there with his sister Arlene (Joey's mom died a few years ago) and their parents, Joey's grandparents.

"So," she says, indicating the purple welts still visible on the left side of my face. "You've been holding out on me."

"I didn't wanna put you on the spot."

I park the cab on the street and carry in my suitcase.

"I thought you were bringing your cat."

"He's missing."

"What?"

I tell Joey the short version. Joey's ethic is Warrior Irish. It's a point of honor with her (and everyone in her family), when a friend asks for help, to say yes without hesitation and never ask why. I, for my own reasons, want Joey to know. Over coffee in her kitchenette, I give her the full update on Bablik, the beat-up, the toxic waste, the human femur, even my encounter with Ponytail in the candy store.

"Let's go upstairs."

Joey's dad's name is Frank. He's a good guy; I've been out on his boat many, many Sundays when Joey and I were together.

He, Joey and I settle now in the kitchen. No, Frank is not going out for New Year's. No one on the block is. They're all staying home to watch the Knicks game.

Again, it's understood that Frank will cut off his arm before breathing a word of anything confidential that I (or anyone in trouble) might impart to him.

He listens to my deposition about the Turk, interrupting only once to ask, "Who's the ex-cop you tailed the wife with?"

I give him Tito's name.

Frank: "I know him."

Frank is a thirty-two-year vet, a Sergeant/field supervisor. This is no minor rank. Frank's salary when he retired was forty-six grand and change, more than double what I made at Y&R at my peak, and his real take-home after overtime was probably twice that again. Frank won't say how he knows Tito, except it's not from the force but from work that Tito has done on his own since he retired. Frank won't talk about that either.

Gerritsen Beach is an interesting neighborhood. It's on the water. Joey's street, Bartlett Place, backs up to a channel that links to Rockaway Inlet and the ocean. Every backyard on the block (and the facing street across the waterway) has a dock with a boat tied up to it. From Frank's kitchen table we can see winterized twenty-four- and thirty-footers, some moored, others hoisted in sling rigs above the frigid waterways.

What's my aim in talking to Frank? I'm thinking that if I can get

Bablik arrested, or even just placed under investigation, report of that would torpedo his Man of the Year award. That would prevent his brother from getting to him at the ceremony. Not to mention the heat would compel Yehuda to back off on going after Bablik in some other way, at least for the moment.

"What would happen," I ask Frank, "if I reported this stuff?"

"To who?"

"To you."

Frank shrugs and turns both palms up.

"I'm serious, Frank."

"So am I."

Frank tells me an officer would look like a fool if he tried to pursue something like this, even a sergeant or higher. "This has to come from downtown, and downtown don't give a shit." Frank dismisses the underground tank, the toxic dumping. "You think this is news? Your buddy Bablik's probably been working this racket for thirty years."

Frank says if a cop took a matter like this to his superiors, he'd be laughed out of the room, or worse.

"Why?" I ask. "Is it money? People being paid off?"

Frank asks if I want more coffee. A Danish? Entenmann's?

"Loot is the least of it," he says. "It's live and let live. This is the Big City. You can't raise a stink about shit like this. It's a career-ender. You're Serpico."

"What about the threat to Bablik? This is a potential homicide!"

"Call me when it's real."

We watch the first half of the Knicks game and kill the rest of the coffee cake. Frank pours brandy.

"Ask yourself this," he says. "What kinda person winds up with their bones in industrial solvent? It ain't the Pope and it ain't Bess Myerson. Whoever's in the river is there for a reason. And whoever put 'em there is saving the city a lot of money."

At the door Frank puts a hand on my shoulder. "Live and let live. That goes for you too."

Downstairs, Joey helps me set up sleeping quarters on her couch.

She apologizes for her dad speaking so bluntly. "But he's right. This is how the world works. It ain't the movies."

She and I watch the second half of the game, then switch over to Times Square to watch the ball drop.

"You're worried about your cat, aren't you?"

I tell her I'm thinking about going back to my place.

"Don't be crazy," Joey says. "These guys are dangerous. Besides, if anybody can survive on his own in this city, it's your cat."

She asks me if Teaspoon is still going up and down the staircase outside my rear window.

"He was."

"He's got an ID collar, right? With your name and number on it?"

"He does."

Teaspoon always liked Joey. I tell her that now. Next to Nicolette, she was his all-time fave.

"That cat is just like you," Joey says.

It's true. Teaspoon is not a killer tom. He can't intimidate anybody. He's clean-cut. He looks like the kind of cat that other bully-cats would pick on.

"He's fearless and he's resourceful," says Joey. "In this town that ain't a bad combo."

She assures me that Teaspoon is fine. He's lying low somewhere. That's what cats do. Maybe he's a little hungry, maybe a little scared. "But he's chill," Joey says. "And I'll tell you something else. That cat loves you. If there's a way in the world to get home to you, he'll make it."

Around twelve thirty I go out to the cab to bring in my type-writer. I gotta get back to work tomorrow. As I'm locking the trunk, I see Frank coming up the sidewalk, returning from walking his Irish setter, Sly.

"I been thinking about your situation," he says.

Frank's last word to me comes as I'm standing with the heavy typewriter in both hands, trying to open Joey's basement door.

"Your buddy Tito," he says. "Don't close both eyes around him."

Book Seven

Little Lithuania

35.
Live from Ocean City

In the end it's Tracy who saves the day with Adriana, the Scary Girl. Who else? I call her because I know if there's one person who can bring order out of an emotion-driven, freaked-out situation, it's Tracy.

"I'm not doing this for you," she says, "or even for that poor girl. I'm doing it for the child."

Tracy is a Catholic. The Sunday after New Year's she phones Adriana and invites her to Mass. They talk for hours afterward. Two days later she summons me. I meet the pair of them, with Adriana's blonde roommate, at four in the afternoon at the Elephant & Castle on Greenwich Avenue above Waverly Place.

Somehow Tracy has squeezed out of Adriana the admission that she "might have" had sex with someone in addition to me.

Five someones.

There's this about Tracy: she's at her best in a crisis. She's calm. She's rational. She's not hesitant to act, and when she acts she makes the right decision. When she proffers a point of view or lobbies for an outcome, there's no resisting her logic.

She and Adriana have ruled out an abortion. Adoption is possible. Adriana raising the baby herself could be an option as well. She acknowledges that one or two of her other boyfriends might make a respectable father.

Me, I'm groveling like a dog. What can I do to help? I mean it. I know I've screwed up. I'll do anything to make up for my heedlessness. I'll get a job. A real job. I'll support the baby.

All three women regard me balefully across our untouched elephantburgers. "Do you really want," Tracy asks Adriana, "to have this man in your life forever?"

Outside on the sidewalk my wife fixes me with a look that says, "You owe me big-time."

"And by the way," she adds out loud. "You are the Number One asshole I've ever known."

I drive straight back to Joey's in Brooklyn, work all night and all the next day, finally delivering the manuscript to Marty at his apartment on Madison and 40th at 4:23 PM eight days after New Year's.

Marty is ecstatic.

"No one," he says, "was in town through Christmas or the turn of the year anyway."

Here's how he checks the manuscript (which he has never read all the way through): he reads a paragraph on page 43, another on 167, a third on 276. "Great! I love it! We're off to the races, my boy! This is going to change your life!"

I meet Nicolette at Chumley's on Bedford Street between Grove and Barrow. We order cheeseburgers and fries with a double Scotch apiece and another on top of it. Nicolette doesn't want to hear a word about Tracy or the Scary Girl or Bablik or Abby or Yehuda.

The Six O'Clock News is playing on the TV above the bar. Typical midwinter stories: murders, police shootings, homeless people freezing to death on the streets. Suddenly this banner pops up:

SHOOTOUT IN OCEAN CITY

A female reporter, on site, speaks into camera:

A New York City rock band, perhaps too aptly named Death Warmed Over, was involved Thursday evening in a

shooting at a nightclub here in Ocean City. Gunfire erupted in a dressing room and spilled over into the adjacent dining area. No injuries were reported, but a witness stated that the band, or some unknown person associated with it, returned fire upon the attackers, who fled when alarms went off along the boardwalk.

I phone the band from a booth in the bar. Johnny picks up.
Schwantz: "You're just seeing this now? It happened last night!"
Me: "I've been busy."
"Well, your friend turns out to be a world-class sleazeball. He drew a whole fucking death squad. A bullet missed my head by six inches!"
I've never heard Schwantz so furious or so freaked.
"The guy pulls out a nine-millimeter and starts wailing. He almost killed us himself!"
"Where is he now?
"Where is he? Who the fuck knows? Who cares?"
Apparently Bablik has vanished into the night like he did at Elaine's.
"The only good news," says Schwantz, "is the phone is ringing off the hook with offers for the band."
Roach takes over the line. The guys are okay, he says. They're a little shook up but they'll survive. And, like Johnny said, the publicity from this thing has been gangbusters.
I hear Roach clear his throat.
"Listen, uh, Stretch ... how would you feel about maybe taking a hiatus from your, uh, efforts on behalf of the band?"
I can't believe it. Roach is firing me.
"Nothing personal, man. You know we love you. But the band ... the band wants to go in a different direction."

36.
A Cot and a Fridge

My next call is to my answering service. Four messages, all from Abby, all urgent.

I refuse to answer.

It's seven thirty at night. I've had six hours' sleep in the last four days. Haven't I done enough for these crazy people? I've lost my cat. I can't go home to my apartment. I have no job, no money. My wife, who is banging my best friend, believes I am even more of a bum and a loser than she did before. Now the band has dumped me. All because of Bablik. I would blame him for Adriana's pregnancy if I could think up a plausible scenario.

I'm not gonna call the Turk's old lady.

I'm not gonna look for him.

I'm gonna dump his taxi at Gotham Cab and drop out of this freak show once and for all.

By ten I have walked Nicolette safely home (for some reason she makes excuses and won't let me in) and am rolling up the FDR Drive heading for the Bronx when I remember that Bablik has a cot, a fridge, and a hotplate in his office at Gotham Cab.

By now I know the guy. He's there. The fucker is holed up in his office, I'm sure of it. He'll make his last stand behind that steel door and that bulletproof glass.

I keep going anyway, just to get rid of my cab. Maybe I'm wrong.

Maybe the Turk has fled the country. Maybe he's hiding out with Abby. Maybe his brother has already murdered him.

Sure enough, when I get to Gotham Cab, the Turk is there. He and Kingie emerge from the shadows beside the shop when I pull in and they recognize my taxi. The Turk is packing his AK-47.

Is he happy to see me? Fuck no. He grills me indignantly beside Tank Number Two. How did I know he was here? Have I betrayed him to his brother? Have I told anybody else? Have I ratted him out to the cops?

"I'm here to drop off your cab, Marvin. I'm quitting. And no, I didn't plant the story with Jimmy Breslin either."

Finally Bablik calms down. He apologizes for doubting my loyalty. He's a little paranoid, he says. He hasn't slept in a week. He's not thinking straight.

No, he says, his plan is not to hole up in his office. The Man of the Year banquet is ninety-six hours away. No force beneath heaven will stop the Turk from collecting his award. His brainstorm is to take one of his own cabs and hit the streets. He'll make himself a moving target. "I'll keep driving till the night of the ceremony. I'll sleep in the back seat. My feet will never touch dry land."

I'm not thinking too straight either. I can't tell if the Turk's plan is genius or insanity.

Suddenly on the approach road: headlights.

Bablik and Kingie snap to red alert. It's mid-shift; no cabs will be coming to the garage at this hour. No other traffic uses this dead-end street.

Three sets of lights pull in at the top of the hill. They're about a hundred feet above us. We're in the open with no cover except a few spindly winter trees.

Lemme tell you this and you can believe me:

There are few sights in the world scarier than vehicles stopping with their headlights zeroed in on you, their doors opening, and men getting out (in this case, six of them) and marching toward you with hostile intent.

Kingie bolts like a jackrabbit.

Bablik chambers a round in the AK.

The men keep advancing.

I recognize Yehuda, Ivanov, and Ponytail.

And at the far end of the line: Tito.

The Turk sees him too. He raises the Kalashnikov and pulls the trigger. The weapon recoils violently, kicking the muzzle straight up. Bablik winds up spraying the trees and the wires on the phone poles along the entry drive.

The mag clicks empty. We both turn and bolt toward my taxi.

There's a rear driveway on the south side of the shop. I take it with the Turk piling into the front seat beside me and the passenger door still open as my right foot flattens the accelerator into the floorboard. Bablik's cabs are so underpowered and so poorly maintained (not to mention they have a governor set at fifty-five) that it feels like we're dogpaddling through Elmer's Glue. In the side-view I see Yehuda and his posse scrambling to take up the pursuit.

In the movies a car chase is unfailingly depicted as a bumper-to-bumper speed fest, like a NASCAR race or the Indy 500. Now, lumbering down Southern Boulevard at 55 per, with the cab's Dodge Coronet 225-inch slant-6 screaming and blue smoke pouring from the exhaust as we run red light after red light, I realize that reality is far less fast and furious. Bablik has jettisoned his AK (he had only one clip). A nine-millimeter has taken its place, apparently the same weapon the Turk used in the shoot-out at Ocean City. He's in the back seat now, with both windows rolled down and a frigid gale howling in, peering back through the rear glass.

"Are they back there?"

"I can't see 'em."

"Where should I go?"

"How the fuck do I know?"

I hit the lane for the FDR and power south toward Manhattan. My one thought is, Get to someplace crowded, somewhere with cops. The FDR Drive runs flush along the East River from the top of Manhattan to the Battery at the bottom.

Headlights are in the rear-view.

"Is that them?"

The lights are gaining. I gotta get off the Drive. I take the 96th Street exit with all four tread-free tires slewing. The Turk is clambering forward over the seatback. He's up front now.

Bablik: "I know where to go."

"Where?"

"Do what I say."

My scheme so far is to run every red light that looks safe and turn on those that don't. Every civilian vehicle we can collect behind us is one more impediment to Yehuda and his chase team.

There's only one problem: our pursuers have three cars; we've only got one. I'm pumping the gas and the brakes like Gene Hackman in *The French Connection* but each time I come out of a street, one of Yehuda's vehicles is gaining.

"South!" Bablik is shouting. "Get south to Canal!"

I'm at 30th and Broadway, in heavy but fast-moving traffic, trying to pass a bus. Cabs and buses are natural enemies. I can see the driver's face in the big, square outboard mirror. It's a black woman. She sees me too, coming around her on the left. She sideslips toward me. The bus's flank with its advertising placard for rye bread

YOU DON'T HAVE TO BE JEWISH TO LOVE LEVY'S

looms in the right side of my windshield.

I swing the wheel hard right and slam sideways into the bus. "Hey!" the Turk shouts. He's worried about his cab. He can't see the two sets of headlights in the mirror, which are closing on us like Sidewinder missiles. The bus deviates not one millimeter from the collision; in fact it's turning even harder into me. The driver is shoving. We're metal to metal. I feel both my front tires start to skid.

The car behind is Ponytail's Imperial. He's so close now I can't see his headlights. The traffic signal ahead goes amber. I bury the gas, which produces about .001 degree of acceleration, while the impossibly loose suspension sends the Turk and me skittering laterally across the bench-type front seat. Ponytail's Imperial pulls alongside. I can see him at the wheel, grinning like a fiend and pointing at me. Ivanov powers down the passenger window. He's got a gun.

We're four blocks north of Madison Square Park where Broadway, which runs at an angle, crosses Fifth Avenue. The park itself runs from 26th to 23rd. Twenty-third is a major cross-town artery. It's wide. Two lanes each way. I'm thinking, Pass the park, cut hard left across from the Flatiron Building and wheel east onto 23rd. That'll give us three options on the far side of the park—left up Madison, straight on 23rd, or one long block and south or north on Park. I'm trying to remember if the streets run the way I think they do when the bus shoulders into me even harder. The cab skitters left into the Imperial. "Watch it!" The Turk is turned sideways in the passenger seat, shouting into my right ear. His right hand comes up before my eyes. I glimpse something metallic. He palms my forehead with his left hand and shoves my skull back into the headrest.

You know how loud guns sound in movies? Multiply that by ten and that's the howitzer shell that goes off now six inches from my face.

"What the fuck!"

The window explodes into my left ear. I'm blinded by the muzzle flash. Cordite smell fills the cab's interior. The Turk fires again, and again after that. I'm hurtling through the red light at 26th Street now. The bus is flush on my right. The Imperial has swerved left and is ricocheting off parked cars. At least I think that's the banging sound, although it could be gunshots coming in at us. The cab, as I said, is a '69 Dodge Coronet with no power brakes and no power steering. Its wheel is as big as a Peterbilt's. I heave it over with both hands, as hard left as I can. The taxi slaloms around the downtown apex of the park and hurtles left into 23rd Street, whose eastbound lanes are bumper-to-bumper and stopped. I'm in the leftmost, going the wrong way. This side is empty, thank God.

"Punch it!" the Turk shouts. I've already got the throttle wide open. We're going nowhere. I hear that horrible rubber thwack-thwack from under the front suspension. Here comes Ponytail's Imperial. I brake hard, sliding sidewise and stopping in the middle of the opposing two lanes.

The Turk bails right. I bail left. "Run, kid!" I have half a second to note both front tires shredded and steam pouring from under the hood. Bablik is waving to me to save myself. What am I supposed to do—stop and reason with Yehuda and Ponytail? I'm running beside him, the long block from Fifth past Madison to Park. The Turk is limping. At the corner a flash of yellow materializes and suddenly we're both diving into the back seat of a Checker cab and Bablik is barking instructions to the driver, who's a West Indian woman, and slinging twenty-dollar bills into the front seat. "Brighton Beach! Get south to Canal and take the bridge."

The driver floors it.

Turk (to me): "You hit?"

I have heard this line in a thousand movies but this is the first time anyone has delivered it to me in real life.

The Turk is peering back through the rear window. He's saying he thinks we lost 'em.

In Hollywood action flicks when someone has fired a gun, they tuck it away into a holster or their belt and go about their business with no bystanders sensing a thing. In real life, the stink of cordite is so overpowering everyone for half a block can smell it.

"Hey!" the female cabbie calls to Bablik over her shoulder. "You just shoot a gun?"

"Don't worry about it." The Turk assures her that he's a big tipper.

Bablik is grabbing his left foot now, blotting his ankle with his trouser leg.

"Hey! You back there! You bleedin' in my cab?"

"We're good," says the Turk. He has tucked the nine-millimeter into his waistband. He pulls out a handkerchief and hands it to me. "Get that glass outa your face."

"If you bleedin', I gotta pull over," says the Calypso cabbie.

"We're good," Bablik repeats. "My son here just had a little accident with a soda bottle."

The Turk takes one final look through the rear window to satisfy himself that no one's on our tail, then leans forward and hangs both elbows over the front seatback.

Turk (to cabbie): "This is a beautiful cab. Who you drive for?"

"Myself."

"Got your medallion, huh?"

"Me and Chase Manhattan."

The Turk congratulates the driver. He turns back to me. "See this? The only way a cabbie takes care of her hack is if she owns it herself."

For twenty minutes Bablik and the driver dish the dirt. We're across the bridge now, deep into Brooklyn.

I ask where we're going.

Turk: "You're going back to Manhattan." To the driver he says, "Take him after you drop me off."

Billboards for the New York Aquarium are appearing. I see an outdoor ad for Luna Park.

"Little Lithuania," says Bablik.

Bablik guides the driver through the same neighborhood I was in a few days ago searching for Ponytail's Imperial. It's a tidy enclave of one- and two-family houses. Newsstands and kosher markets appear on street corners. Signs on storefronts are in English, Hebrew, and Cyrillic.

Opposite an Orthodox church, the Turk tells the cabbie to pull over. "Take the kid back to Manhattan." He tosses more bills into the front seat. "Sorry," he says to the driver. "I leaked on your floor a little."

Bablik opens the door. In the light from the street lamp I see his left shoe. It's soaked, with dark liquid pooling.

I grab his arm and pull him back.

"You're going to a hospital!"

The Turk puts a hand on my shoulder and pushes me back into the cab. I'm peering up the dark vacant street when I hear car engines in the distance. Two sets of headlights slew around the corner behind us, coming this way. Another pair zoom from the side. We're spotlighted like escapees on the wire. Bablik pushes free of me and, with a groan, rises and steps out.

Ponytail's Imperial whips in front of the cab, blocking it. A Cadillac and a Ford Fairlane hem the taxi from the rear and the other flank. Dark forms surround the Turk. The door on my right is jerked open. It's Tito. He grabs me by the collar and hauls me out into the street.

37.

Jamaica Bay Watershed

Here is how brainwashed I am by movies.

As Tito (who seems to have recovered totally from the beat-up and his hospital stay) shoves me into the back seat of the Imperial, I have to bite my tongue to keep from spouting, "You ratted us out, you dirty bastard."

Tito doesn't even give me a look.

He and Ivanov jam Bablik into the other half of the backseat. Tito piles in on the far side. Ponytail is up front at the wheel. Ivanov scurries back to the passenger seat and slides in, twisting to face me in back. He indicates the rear door handle. "Don't even think about it."

No one says a word for the next ten minutes as the three-car convoy zips back out of Brighton Beach and onto the Belt Parkway and rolls east and north into the wetlands west of Kennedy Airport. Jamaica Bay stretches ahead and to the right. We're west of the glide path for JFK. We can hear the planes overhead and see the landing lights reflecting on the water.

Am I scared? Believe it or not—no. Two concerns occupy my mind. First, the Turk's bleeding foot, which I'm truly worried about. Second, the atmosphere inside the Imperial. Are Bablik and me about to be murdered? I put the odds at fifty-fifty. Yet the vibes in the car are decidedly (and this is the exact word) collegial. Against all logic I find myself feeling a bond with Ivanov. If he asked me for fifty bucks, I'd give it to him. I even feel affection for Ponytail. We're a unit. We share secrets in this car. The civilian world, the buses and trucks outside on the parkway, might as well be occupying a distant galaxy. I'm thinking, I have more in common with these man-killers than I do with anyone else I know. As for Bablik, he's like my father or my brother.

Insane as this sounds, I'm enjoying myself.

The convoy passes what used to be Floyd Bennett Field but is now a state park and turns right, toward the water, into a long dark lane between high cyclone fences topped with razor wire. Ponytail takes up the trail position behind the Caddy and the third car, the Ford Fairlane that Tito and I first encountered when it picked up Abby outside Gleason's Boxing Gym five weeks ago. The caravan advances through two gates, both of which the driver of the Fairlane has to stop for, get out and unlock. Wherever we are, there are no other lights and no other humans for at least a mile. The Fairlane stops to unlock one last gate. The procession enters a darkened industrial enclave smack on Jamaica Bay. Overhead, commercial jetliners continue descending into JFK.

Bablik and I are hauled from the Imperial. The Turk is limping. Ivanov clutches him under one arm. Ponytail manhandles me. We're hustled past fifty yards of chain-link fencing. A dark, box-like building looms ahead. There's a parking lot, empty now, and a shop with two tanker trucks, like the misspelled SHELL one, under a high, open-sided shelter.

Finally I spot Yehuda. He's up ahead, beside the Fairlane driver, wearing a gray topcoat and a fedora. We're in the boxy building now. It's brick-faced, one-story, like something the Coast Guard or the Parks Department would build. We pass office spaces, an open bullpen area with desks and typewriters and filing cabinets.

"In here," says Ivanov.

Bablik stubs his foot entering the office area. He groans.

"Shut up," says Ivanov. "Get in there."

38.
A Russian Proverb

I'm planted in a gray, army-surplus office chair. Ponytail has jammed me into the seat with his hands on both my shoulders. Bablik is body-slammed in the same fashion into the chair beside me. Blinds have been drawn. Light spills from desk lamps and overhead fluorescents.

Up front Yehuda and Tito are wrestling with a Mr. Coffee machine. Bablik's look to me says, Keep your mouth shut.

We're in some kind of office area. Government-issue-type desks, gunmetal-gray, squat on a floor of colorless linoleum. Partitions divide the space into cubicles. I can hear diesel trucks outside, coming and going. The stink of sewage permeates everything.

Ivanov brings foam cups. One of the men from the Fairlane contributes sugar packets, creamer, and stirrers. He sets these atop one of the desks. Two others, from the Cadillac I'm guessing, sit now, to the right of me and Bablik. Ponytail and the Fairlane driver remain behind us. On the bulletin board above the desks I note various schedules, EPA guideline statements, employee notices.

SAFETY IS OUR #1 PRIORITY

Plainly this is a working office. Tomorrow morning, clerks and secretaries will be in here making the place hum. Everything looks ordinary and aboveboard. On the desk beside me I note a photo cube with snapshots of an overweight wife and kids, a New York Mets coffee mug, stacks of blank government forms, a calendar, stapler, etc. The label on the box of forms closest to me says "Hygienic Disposal of Toxic Materials, EPA-397B-Z."

Tito and Ivanov bring the glass pot from the Mr. Coffee. A wall clock reads 2:23. Yehuda, replacing the filter and setting a second pot in place for the next brew, has already begun tormenting Bablik, demanding to hear his plans for four nights from now, meaning the Man of the Year banquet.

Bablik is trying to keep his bloody foot out of sight under the chair.

The office clearly is Bablik Brothers Central. Clients are who? Legitimate and illegitimate businesses citywide that want or need a way around the federal, state, and city fees for environmental treatment and disposal of corrosives, toxic waste, restaurant grease and so forth. Instead they have their noxious effluents hauled here to the Bablik Bros., who for a fee supply phony papers, provide and file all required government and agency documents and then dump the shit into the bay or harbor. Instead of $500 per tanker truck, I'm speculating, the customer pays what? One-fifty? It's win-win. A no-brainer.

And if you've got a stiff corpse to dispose of, the brothers can take care of that too.

Yehuda has crossed back to the desk in front of Bablik. He's stirring Cremora into the contents of his Styrofoam cup.

Me: "Can I say something?"

Yehuda turns toward me.

"Your brother's hurt. He needs a doctor."

I hear snickering from the side and behind.

The Turk addresses Yehuda. "The kid's not part of this. He drives a cab for me. He knows nothing. He's nobody."

Yehuda smiles. "Nobody but Robert Moses' great-nephew."

It strikes me afresh that the Russian is not a Russian, and the Turk is not a Turk.

"Robert Moses," says Yehuda. "The most powerful man in the

greatest city in the world. And my older brother is gonna get a medal pinned on him ..."

"It's not a medal ..."

Yehuda leans back against the desk, crossing his legs in front of him. With his right hand he indicates his brother.

"Whaddaya think of this guy, kid? A born businessman, wouldn't you say? You know what the definition of business is, don't you? Business is about anticipating needs. You identify a need and you fill it."

Yehuda indicates the office, the shop, the facility.

"We share a certain proprietary technology, my brother and I. The marketplace wants it. Demand keeps going up. So, my brother the businessman hatches a bright idea. 'Why limit our market to New York and New Jersey?' Why not expand to Kansas City, New Orleans, Los Angeles? Our services are needed out there too.

"My brother's brainstorm," says Yehuda, "is to franchise the operation. Take it national. He's a genius!"

Yehuda is pacing now. He stalks from stage-right to stage-left, across the boards in front of Bablik. He speaks, not to his brother but to his confederates and to me.

"But then the craziest thing happens. Out of the blue, some Big Jews phone up my brother. They want to honor him, give him an award. Not just any award. A big one. The biggest.

"Suddenly everything changes for my brother. This award becomes his whole life. It's so important to him that he begins to worry that these Big Jews might find out what kind of a man he really is. Then they might not give him this award.

"Me, I don't like this award at all. It's heat. It's unwanted publicity. It's gonna put a spotlight where I don't want no spotlight to go. I tell my brother to turn down this award. He refuses. So I make him an offer. I say, 'Brother, you can have this accolade you covet. I won't do nothing to stand in your way. But I want something from you in return.'"

Yehuda draws up in front of Bablik.

"I want the business. All of it."

Yehuda turns toward the others.

"I think that's a pretty reasonable proposition, don't you? But you know what my brother does? He tries to have me waxed. Believe that shit? My own brother! He hires this ex-policeman here to put me in the river."

Yehuda has crossed to Tito now. He stands behind him, setting a hand on one of Tito's shoulders.

"Fortunately this streetwise cop knows the score. He comes straight to me. Warns me. What do I do? I vanish. My new friend, the ex-policeman, carries on as if the game remains unchanged. He pretends to keep searching for me. Together we even stage a little Hollywood punch-out, just to keep things looking kosher. Whaddaya think of this, kid? Any of it ring a bell?"

Yehuda has crossed from Tito back to Bablik's side.

"Lemme see that foot of yours, brother."

Bablik looks up but doesn't move.

"The kid says you're hurt. Show me."

With effort Bablik scrapes his left foot across the linoleum into the light coming from the table lamps and the overhead fluorescents. Before anyone can move or think, Yehuda raises his own heavy shoe and stamps down with all his might onto his brother's bloody foot.

Bablik screams in agony, but Ponytail and the Fairlane driver seize him from behind and gag him with his own overcoat. Bablik's face goes scarlet. His eyes pop wide, the whites wild with pain.

Yehuda produces a nine-millimeter automatic, cocks the slide, and presses the muzzle to Bablik's temple. Choked from behind, the Turk can only gag and gurgle.

For myself it's all I can do to keep from shitting in my pants. I'm certain that Yehuda is about to blow Bablik's brains out and my own right after.

But Yehuda draws up. He backs away a step and lowers the weapon. "Pay attention, kid. Learn something."

Ponytail and the Fairlane driver release Bablik. Yehuda steps to the desk in front of his brother, takes up his former position leaning back against it.

The Turk's head and shoulders rock forward, nearly to the desktop. I turn to ask, Are you all right? Ponytail wallops me across the back of the head.

Bablik pulls himself upright with excruciating effort. He refuses to show pain. He stifles whatever sound threatens to burble from his throat.

Somehow the Turk composes himself. By force of will he manages to bring himself to a sitting posture, if not fully straight then as straight as the pain will let him. His face is still the color of blood. His breath comes in tight, strangled wheezes.

His brother regards him with icy respect.

"There are two kinds of Lithuanian Jews," Yehuda says to his confederates and to me. "Litvaks and Galitzianers. The Litvaks think the Galitzianers are pussies. The Galitzianers think the Litvaks are beasts. My brother, God bless him, is a Litvak."

He reaches with one hand to Bablik, wipes his comb-over back out of his eyes. He helps the Turk sit up.

"Did you know," Yehuda says to the men around him, "that this flush bastard, who lives among Gentiles and who dresses and acts as if he was born one of them, once beat a man to death with a shovel? In the old country. He was twelve. Before he came here to the land of milk and honey. Before he became a hero of Israel and a benefactor of the Jewish people. Tell them, brother. Tell them what good works you've done."

The Turk manages to straighten fully. "Either you will kill me," he says, "or you will not."

"The Yom Kippur War of 1973," says Yehuda. "Ten days in, the Jews run out of ammunition. Artillery shells. Bullets. The army of Israel is down to nothing. Does the US send help?" Yehuda snorts in derision. He indicates Bablik. "Here is who helped. This piece of shit you see before you. He knew who to call. He knew where the money was. He saved Israel. He did."

A look passes between the brothers. Secrets are in this look, and a depth of hatred I have never seen before or since.

"We won't tell them the full story, will we, brother? That would wring their hearts. Or maybe I should tell it only to your young friend here. Your young friend who is kin to Robert Moses."

"Enough, Yehuda."

"You saved the Jews of Israel, brother, but you didn't save me."

Yehuda orders his brother to stand. When Bablik can't, Yehuda motions to Tito to make him. Tito rises and crosses to Bablik, hauls him roughly to his feet. Ponytail does the same to me.

Before I know it, we're being hustled down a hallway and outside into the frozen yard. Across a stretch of pavement squats a big, shop-like building. A roll-up door ascends. We're pushed through. I see industrial-scale storage tanks and heavy-duty piping; my nostrils fill with a ferocious stench.

We're forced up a flight of steel stairs. Bablik has to be half-carried. We emerge onto an elevated platform. The floor under our feet is perforated grating. Beneath us, visible through the grate, runs a vehicle lane down which tanker trucks advance to be filled from above with the toxic brew they will dump into the bay and the river.

The master vat rises in the center of the space. It looks like a sewage treatment tank, sealed on top but still stinking. A tanker truck waits beneath to receive its load. From where we are, one floor above the truck, we can't see the pipe that drains the vat but clearly it's there; the valves and swing-arms are plainly visible.

Yehuda orders Bablik hauled forward. Ivanov activates a switch on a circuit panel. With a screech the upper seal on the toxic vat opens—two feet wide, three, four ...

I'm thinking, My God, they're gonna throw Bablik in!

At a nod from Yehuda, Ponytail shoves me forward too. I'm hauled up, between the brothers, so close I can see the chest-hairs sprouting from beneath Yehuda's collar.

In short terse phrases, Yehuda tells of his parents getting out of

Vilnius in '34, fleeing Stalin, anticipating the rise of Hitler. Mother and father made their way by rail to Berlin, then Marseilles, sailing first to Venezuela, then later to New Orleans. From there they reached Philadelphia, settling eventually in New York.

The parents had taken Marvin, who was fourteen and the eldest. They left behind in Lithuania, in the care of an aunt and uncle, both Yehuda and his sister Leah, who were eight and six.

By '36 Stalin had made escape to the West impossible. Then came the war. By '41 Lithuania was in Nazi hands. Yehuda fled to the forest, age fifteen, with his sister, who was then twelve. The rest of his family, seventy souls, was rounded up for the death camps.

Yehuda tells, now, of surviving for twenty-one months in the wilderness of Poland and Slovakia, where his sister perished, before making his way via Budapest to Rome and from there across the Mediterranean to North Africa, until finally, at Tozeur in Tunisia, reaching his brother Marvin, an American now, a supply sergeant serving in II Corps commanded by General George Patton.

"We went into business, my brother and me. He took the inside, I handled the outside. We worked with others, soldiers mostly but also Arabs and Tunisians and Libyan businessmen, stealing from the American army everything we could lay our hands on. Cigarettes and Scotch whisky, gasoline, ammunition, whole trucks, bulldozers, parts for airplanes, even ships. But we didn't give the proceeds to Israel, did we, brother? There was no Israel then. We kept the cash. We kept everything ..."

Bablik breaks in: "What's the point of this, Yehuda?"

"The point is your obituary, brother. For those of us who don't subscribe to *The New York Times*."

With a nod Yehuda orders Tito to haul Bablik onto the catwalk above the toxic tank.

The pistol reappears in Yehuda's hand.

"Get him out there, Tito, where we can all see him ..."

The Fairlane driver assists, pushing the Turk from behind.

My gaze darts from Yehuda's face to Bablik's. The brothers' eyes lock across no more than six feet of space.

"There's a Russian proverb," says Yehuda. "*Tot, kto predast moego vraga, predast menya.* 'He who will betray my enemy, will betray me.'"

With one shot he blows Tito's brains out.

The ex-cop drops like a marionette whose strings have been cut. His body in its trousers and overcoat plunges to the catwalk and tumbles like a bag of laundry over the lip and into the vat. I see the Fairlane driver spring backward, dodging the splash.

My heart has stopped. I can't catch my breath.

I feel a powerful hand beneath my armpit.

I'm being hauled toward the catwalk. Ponytail grips me. My knees have turned to oatmeal ...

"Enough!" cries Bablik. "Stop. I'll do what you say."

Ponytail doesn't stop. He shoves me before him, out to the spot where Tito stood. I see Yehuda raise the nine-millimeter.

"Enough, Yehuda. You win."

The younger brother turns to his elder.

"I'm sorry, Marvin. Did you say something?"

"I said stop. I'll do what you say."

"Let me hear you again, brother."

Yehuda compels Bablik to spell out the specifics of his surrender. "I'll give you the business, 100 percent, including the expansion nationally. I'll work the contacts and make it succeed but all profits go to you."

"And what, brother, if a disagreement should arise between us?"

"I'll do what you say."

"Let me hear you again."

"I'll do what you say."

It's over.

Yehuda lowers the pistol.

Ponytail and Ivanov load me and Bablik into the Imperial and pack us back to Manhattan across the Williamsburg Bridge. Except, as the vehicle descends to the exit at Delancey Street, we see ahead a sprawl of fire engines and police cars, emergency vehicles and Con Ed repair trucks. A power transformer has exploded, we'd learn later, starting a fire that has piled up traffic in all directions.

"Get out," says Ivanov.

Ponytail dumps the Turk and me in the crosswalk at Essex Street with Bablik's crushed arch nearly dropping him faint and no hope of escaping this hell except on foot. I'm supporting the Turk with an arm around his waist and one of his elbows around my shoulder. He hops on his one good foot. We stagger three blocks to Allen Street, where I get through to Abby from a pay phone. It takes her an hour to reach the fire scene and another forty-five minutes to locate Bablik and me in the crush. The Turk's face has gone dark as iron. By the time we reach St. Vincent's he's quaking in all four limbs. The hospital treats his foot and gives him a shot for his pain. Somehow Mrs. B. manages to get her husband a private room.

The sun is up now. I'm crashing hard. Abby looks like she has been through a war. I have told her everything that happened tonight, including the promise that Bablik has made to his brother.

"What," she asks her husband, "are you going to do?"

Bablik's face wears the same expression it wore four hours earlier at Jamaica Bay, when he sat up straight before his brother and would not give in to his pain.

"What am I gonna do?" the Turk says. "Not what I told that sonofabitch, that's for sure."

39.
Tracks

It's twenty-four hours later. I'm in my uncle's office. I have had no choice but to come clean. Bablik has phoned Charlie from the hospital, giving him a short version of the events with Yehuda and Tito. "Get your nephew out of this."

My uncle is livid with me. "I told you to steer clear of this bastard. Did I tell you? Did you promise me?"

I need a lawyer, Charlie says. He's on the phone, making calls. Furious as he is, my uncle is gratified that at least I've told him the full story, however belatedly.

A day and a half has elapsed since Tito was sent to Kingdom Come before my eyes. The first twenty-four hours were the worst. Now, approaching thirty-six, I'm beginning to be able to breathe again.

Charlie's office is in Stamford, Connecticut. His business, Doubl-Glo Paper Novelty, manufactures and sells Christmas tree ornaments. Thirty feet down the hall, the factory floor is mass-producing foam candy canes and inflatable Santas, tinsel and paper snow and aluminum-foil icicles.

Bablik himself has vanished. Charlie has no idea where he is. He has phoned all five of Bablik's offices and been given different stories by every one. He has phoned Abby to equal avail.

"Did I tell you to keep clear of this sonofabitch?" he says to me again. "Did I tell you that? And his brother's even worse!"

Nothing of what I've told Charlie about the events of last night has surprised him. He listens as I speak—jaw jutting, smoking and stubbing out Pall Mall after Pall Mall, shaking his head.

My uncle's final call is to a criminal attorney recommended by his own lawyer. Charlie scribbles a number and address on a scrap of Doubl-Glo stationery and passes it across the desk to me. I have an appointment, he tells me, with Aharon Abolnik first thing tomorrow.

"He's my fucked-up nephew," Charlie speaks into the receiver. "Take care of him, will ya?"

I wait in Charlie's office through the whole afternoon shift. He's in and out, taking care of his own business. In snatches he imparts intel from the past—what the young Yehuda was like in Tunisia and Libya and later in Italy. He describes various racketeering enterprises that Yehuda and Bablik have been involved in since coming home to the States. At one point Charlie tells me the story that Bablik recounted at Guard Hill Road, of Charlie's and the Turk's job working for a maker of ladies' purses as sixteen-year-olds in '34.

"We'd go into Macy's or Gimbels pretending to be customers. We'd hunt up competitors' handbags and when nobody was looking we'd bend the wire frames—just enough so the purses wouldn't close properly." He shakes his head, recalling. "I could've gone down the same road Bablik did. The only thing that stopped me was marrying Peggy."

The workday ends. Charlie insists on taking me to the train station himself. I've had a phone call on my service from my agent Marty. He has news about my book. He'll meet me at Grand Central as soon as I get in.

Charlie and I are ten minutes early at the Cos Cob station. Temperature is twenty degrees and dropping. We wait in his Buick in a light fall of snow.

My uncle has regained his equanimity. I can tell he's been running worst-case scenarios in his head. In them, Bablik gets killed, I'm murdered at his side; the story is all over the *News* and the *Post* and TV. Robert Moses becomes implicated. Our whole family goes down the tubes.

Now, at 5:22, Charlie seems to have convinced himself that such a calamity is not imminent, at least not within the next twenty-four hours. There's a chance that we can avert Armageddon.

My uncle has re-interrogated me about my modus operandi with Bablik. My name, I have assured him, is not on anything. I have signed nothing. I haven't even cashed a check (what money Bablik has paid me has been in cash.)

I have told Charlie the full story that Yehuda narrated two nights ago—about Lithuania, fleeing the Nazis, tracking down his brother with the US Army in North Africa. I tell Charlie I've seen photos in Bablik's New York apartment of the sixteen-year-old Yehuda with Bablik in '42 or '43.

"And you still didn't run like hell?"

I have no excuse.

"So," Charlie says, "my nephew is stupid but he's not a criminal."

I accept this.

We're friends again.

My uncle and I sit in silence in the Buick. I sense that he has something to tell me, something from the past that he has never revealed to anybody. He's asking himself should he open up. Is his nephew mature enough to listen and to understand?

"Bablik," Charlie says at last, "was a Technical Sergeant by the time of the second Battle of Monte Cassino in the summer of '44. Tech sergeant was a serious rank then. Every supply shipment in the division ran through him. It was July or August, I'm not sure which. I was home already, with this." Charlie elevates a balky right arm; he was shot through the shoulder sometime after Anzio. "I'm in the infirmary at Fort Riley, so what I'm about to tell you is second-hand, understand?"

Charlie stares straight ahead through the steamed-up windshield. My uncle has never spoken of the war to me or, I'm sure, to either of his sons, my cousins Dan and Bill. He has probably never said a word to Peggy either.

"A certain shipment came through. Impeller blades for the superchargers on P-51 Mustangs. You know what a Mustang is? It's a fighter plane. Bablik's brother was part of this scheme, along with some other supply guys from Division and from Fifteenth Air Force.

"Bablik made the shipment disappear. Why? So that the manufacturer got an emergency contract to repair the existing superchargers on-site. I don't know what the Turk's cut was, but it was a fortune."

Charlie pauses. For a moment we both think we hear the commuter train coming. Clearly, beneath his calm, my uncle is still irate with me. The last thing in the world he wants to do is tell me this shit, or even to think about it.

He explains that the tempo of the bombing of Germany and occupied France and Poland was ramping up heavily in that summer of '44.

"Bombers can't fly missions unescorted. They need fighter cover. There were mechanical issues with the engines of the P-51s. You know what a supercharger is, right? It jams extra oxygen and fuel into the cylinders. A fighter plane has to have a supercharger at altitude because the air is thin. That's what the shipment of impellers was for. When Bablik made it disappear, he didn't just ground a few hundred fighters. He stopped four days of bombing."

Out on the station platform, commuters are gathering their briefcases and stamping out their cigarettes. We can see the train lights approaching. Charlie still hasn't looked at me or turned his gaze from straight ahead.

"One of those missions was bombing the rail line that ran to Auschwitz-Birkenau."

Charlie stops. For the first time he turns toward me.

"If those tracks had been hit, it could've saved thousands, maybe tens of thousands of Jewish lives. Because of Bablik's stunt with the impellers, the bombing mission was scrapped. Orders came and went. The mission was never reinstated."

Charlie says he's never heard the Turk speak of this. But he knows from other sources that the story is true.

"Since he got back from the war," Charlie says, "Bablik has been obsessive about getting aid to Israel in every way and by every means. He has donated tens of thousands of his own money over the years, and he's raised millions from all over the country—Blue Boxes, JNF, Plant a Tree, you name it."

The train pulls in. I have to go.

"I'm not making excuses for Bablik," my uncle says. "Ninety-nine percent he's a crook and he always has been."

I'm out the door, thanking Charlie and shaking his hand through the driver's window. He doesn't say it and I don't either but both of us, I suspect, can't help thinking about that one percent.

40.
Down in Flames

Marty meets me at the Oyster Bar in Grand Central Terminal. We didn't get the manuscript in on time, he says. Christopher Brand has gone with another young writer.

My book is dead.

"I'm sorry, my boy. We were so close."

Marty tells me that of course he'll keep submitting the manuscript. But I can see in his eyes that the moment has passed. The publishing biz is notoriously incestuous. Every editor knows which books every other editor has passed on or elected not to acquire. No one dares take the career risk of bidding on material that others have already rejected.

Marty tells me he took the train to Boston himself, hand-delivered the manuscript to Chris Brand's office at Houghton Mifflin. Chris was heartbroken as well. He even took Marty out to dinner (sole meuniere with haricots verts, I had to ask). But it was too late. Chris had signed the contract with the other writer.

"I feel so inadequate," Marty says in his Old World cadence. "I have let you down. You placed your faith in me and I have proved unworthy."

I feel ten times worse than Marty. Not for myself but for him.

"It's my fault, Marty. I'm the one who let you down by getting the book to you so late. I can't believe you took the train to Boston. No agent in the world would do that. Only you. I apologize to you, Marty. I failed you."

I order a Martini for Marty and a double Scotch for myself.

"What will you do now, son?"

"Kill myself."

Marty spends the next hour bucking me up.

"Zero for three is not the end of the world. Many writers have persevered through worse. Keep going, my boy. Promise me you will."

I give Marty my word. He doesn't believe me. He tells me he has a friend in Hollywood, a movie agent. "I sent her your second book, the one about England. She likes it very much. She'll represent you as a screenwriter if you move to L.A."

I walk Marty home. In my imagination I have anticipated a thousand ways that this book could go down in flames. But none that reflected more ignominiously on my character and lack of professionalism.

What is wrong with me?

Why do I keep fucking up like this?

Nicolette is right. I *am* an amateur. I'm possessed by demons of self-sabotage.

I have to change. I can't go on like this. I'm hurting other people, people who care about me and believe in me.

At Marty's door I ask again if he's okay. Would he like me to stay over? "I'll sleep on the couch. We'll go for lox and eggs in the morning at the Carnegie Deli."

"No," he says. "I'll be awake all night. But thank you, my boy. I maintain unflagging faith in you."

I use Marty's phone to check my answering service.

"Three messages," says the operator. "All in the last hour, all from the same person, all with the same message."

I should hang up right now, I know.

"Go ahead, tell me."

FROM:	ABBY
TIME:	9:47 PM, 9:59 PM, 10:13 PM
CALLING FROM:	505 LaGuardia Place
MESSAGE:	MARVIN OUTSIDE, LURKING IN SHADOWS. HE MAY HAVE A GUN. PLEASE COME ASAP.

41.

505 Laguardia Place

The Turk doesn't have a gun. He has a crutch. Two actually, to go with the bowling ball-sized plaster cast on his left foot, the one Yehuda stomped on after it had been nicked by a bullet in the taxi chase two nights ago.

None of these impediments stops Bablik from fleeing from me, or me from chasing him.

It's fifteen minutes to midnight. I've approached Bablik in the shadows. Is he okay? He tells me to keep outa this. Then he bolts.

I chase him across Bleecker. The sonofabitch is sixty years old, on crutches, and he's scooting away from me faster than a cockroach. I overhaul him fifty feet up the long block to West Third Street but he wheels unexpectedly and raises one crutch, whose butt-end I run into head on, full speed, spearing myself in the solar plexus. I drop like a bag of dirt.

"Help!" shouts the Turk and takes off gimping. I chase him to the corner and up the short block to West Fourth and Washington Square Park. I'm doubled-over, stumbling, on all fours. The Turk keeps bawling for help. It's nearly midnight and below freezing but the park is packed. Nobody moves. Half the people don't even look up to watch a senior citizen on crutches with a cast on one foot fleeing from a twenty-eight-year-old with the wind knocked out of him, scrambling on his knuckles like an ape.

I tackle Bablik beside the chess benches a hundred feet south of the Arch.

Snot is running out of the Turk's nose. His eyes are the color of tomato sauce. I have half a second to be reassured by this (at least I know the guy is suffering as much as I am) and then I see him ratcheting himself up onto one knee above me; his right fist descends sharply toward my left eye. He misses. His balled knuckles crunch into the concrete base of one of the chess benches. "Auuggh, fuck!"

The Turk contorts sideways clutching his busted fist.

I roll him over like a wrestler. He may be nimble and he may be scrappy but he's five foot five and I'm six foot one. "For Christ's sake, Bablik, stop fighting!"

He won't.

The Turk squirts free and takes a second swing at me, this time from on his back like a cat.

I'm no fighter. I've never punched anyone in my life. But this has gone too far. I cock my right fist six inches above Bablik's forehead and pop him crisply between the eyes. I feel the cartilage in his nose separate. Blood oozes from both nostrils.

"Godammit!" The Turk coughs and spits, clutching his schnozz. "You didn't have to do that!"

But he stops fighting.

Twenty minutes later we're back at Abby's and she's swabbing his wounds.

"Hold still, Marvin."

"Why should I?"

"Because this cut is not gonna stop bleeding until you stop squirming."

Bablik obeys reluctantly. He seems to have accepted the fact that Abby is trying to help him. Plainly he hates this. She's telling him that she won't let him go to the awards presentation the day after tomorrow. She won't permit it because he will be murdered there.

Clearly this is of minimal concern to Bablik. It's folly, he believes, to care about what happens to him, or to anybody. When Abby turns away toward the sink to rinse the blood from the towel she's using to wipe her husband's nose and lip, Bablik cranes around to me. Can it be, he's thinking, that this young man is trying to help too?

"Why did you chase me, kid?"

"Because I'm stupid."

During the first few minutes back at Abby's, everything has come out about the superchargers and the bombing mission and the dumping of toxic sludge and the bodies in the river ("Hey, I don't kill 'em," says Bablik. "I just get rid of 'em!") and that Bablik has sworn to Yehuda that he'll give him 100 percent of the expansion business and that Bablik has acknowledged, to me and Mrs. B., that he has no intention of keeping his word.

"Why," I ask, "is this award so important to you? Guilt? Atoning for some imagined crime from thirty years ago?"

The Turk opens his briefcase. Inside sits the nickel-plated .45. He takes it out and slides it across the table to me. "Take it," he says.

I push it away.

"What will the award prove? That the Jewish people forgive you? You didn't do anything wrong!"

Bablik shoves the gun back toward me.

"You're not to blame for what happened! How could you know about the bombing mission? Nobody knew. The decision was made at the level of the freakin' President! There was no way you could've known anything."

"It's not what you know," Bablik says. "It's not even what you do. It's who you are."

He draws up and turns toward Abby. A look passes between them. Abby's eyes swing toward mine. Her expression says, "This is my husband's belief. You can't change it and neither can I."

Bablik puts the gun in my hand. "Take it. I'm not letting you say no this time."

He stands with great effort and pulls a bottle from the liquor cabinet.

"You wanna be a writer?" he says. "You wanna depict life? Then stop looking for 'reasons.' There ain't no reasons. Nothing changes nobody. My crime is that I am the man I am. Do I condemn myself? Yes. But not for what I did in '44 or '57 or what I'm gonna do next year if nobody takes me out, which they probably will. I condemn myself for being the kind of man I am."

I don't believe him.

"The kind of man I am," Bablik says. "Whether you believe me or not."

The Turk pours two fingers of J&B and takes it down over his bloody lip. The whisky makes him grimace as he swallows.

He turns to Abby and me.

"I'm going to collect that award two nights from now," he says. "And you're both going with me."

Book Eight

Jew
of the
Year

42.

A Death on
Madison and 40th

First thing in the morning I phone Marty to see how he's doing. A fireman answers.

"You kin?"

"What?"

"Are you related to the old man?"

Marty has had a heart attack. He's dead.

I get up to 40th Street ten minutes after hanging up from the paramedic. Cops fill Marty's front room, along with Oscar the doorman, the super, and a couple of neighbors.

Marty's body lies on its side on the carpet. He's in pajamas. How small he looks! His slippers. His tiny hands.

"The city's gonna take him away," says Oscar.

"What?"

"He got no family. The fire department's sending the wagon to haul him to the morgue."

I tug the medic and one of the cops aside. "I'm his grandson. I'll assume responsibility for the remains."

I sign some papers. The firemen cancel the morgue wagon.

Then I phone Bablik.

"I'll take care of it," says the Turk at once. "Leave it to Uncle Marvin."

"And don't dump him in the fucking river!"

43.

Abingdon Square

I spend all morning at Marty's, arranging to have his stuff held in storage till I can go through it. I'm hoping to find a letter or document among Marty's papers that will lead me to his family, if he has any, in the Netherlands or here in the States. If not, I don't know what I'll do.

I make plans to meet Nicolette for dinner, then phone Tracy at the Burgundy and ask if I can come over.

Bablik's Jew of the Year ceremony is twenty-four hours away.

Yes, I have promised to go.

I find Tracy exiting a production meeting. She apologizes for kicking me out of the hotel the other night. I ask her to be my date for Bablik's event. If she'll bring the divorce papers, I'll sign them there.

"Why are you inviting me?" Tracy asks.

"Because I'm expecting trouble."

This is true. Tracy sees it in my eyes. Her response is an involuntary flush of gratification. She wants to go to Bablik's event now. Already she's hoping there *will* be trouble.

As I'm leaving, Tracy catches my arm. "I had a call from the band, from Death Warmed Over, their new manager." Tracy says she's meeting with him tomorrow. "Maybe we'll use one or two of the band's songs in the movie. I just wanted to make sure it was okay with you."

I'm touched. I thank Tracy for asking. "Actually it's a great idea. I should've thought of it myself."

She walks me a couple of steps down the hall. "I'm sorry about the other night ..."

"I shouldn't have been here anyway."

"No, I mean about Jake."

I pull up. "Hey, it's me who should be apologizing to you. I can never make up to you for ..."

Tracy stops me with a hand on my arm. "Don't be so hard on yourself," she says. "That's my job."

There's mail for me in the production office. A bill from my landlord for damages to my apartment and repair of its broken door, plus two phone messages from Jackie Q, the lawyer who owns Buster Weems' Club Inferno. The second informs me that he's now managing Death Warmed Over.

CALL ME. URGENT.

I get to Nicolette's around 3:30. She's on the phone to the owner of the gallery where she shows her work. She mimes to me that the call could go on for some time. I tug a pack of smokes from my jacket and sign to her that I'm going out to the park.

Abingdon Square Park is a triangle-shaped pocket of ice-crusted concrete and winter-dead grass. I find a bench, sweep off a dry spot, and sit.

Death, I'm thinking.

Tito.

Marty.

I can't make myself think about Teaspoon and what, God forbid, may have happened to him.

Not to mention Bablik, who can't be stopped from dancing right up to the precipice, and me myself with my own demons of self-destruction.

As I'm thinking this, I become aware of a shadowy form hovering thirty feet to my right, just outside my peripheral vision.

Ponytail.

I glance left. There's Ivanov, the same distance on the opposite flank.

Neither makes a move or faces obviously in my direction.

I hear snow crunching behind me.

Onto the bench, to my right, descends Yehuda.

He's wearing his same gray topcoat, with gloves and a scarf, and a fedora snugged down tight against the cold.

He doesn't look at me and I don't look at him.

"Here's how it'll go down," he says.

He asks if I can hear him okay.

I tell him I can.

"When this is over, you leave the city. You never come back. Answer me that you hear and understand."

I tell him I do.

"A Broadway show, okay. Twenty years from now your daughter graduates from Columbia?" His shrug indicates that a quick in-and-out would qualify as an exception. "Other than that, you never cross a bridge or pass through a tunnel."

"I thought," I say, "that you and your brother had come to an agreement."

"My brother, as always, is full of shit. He's been making deals behind my back non-stop since that night."

A frigid gust whips down Hudson Street. Yehuda tugs his collar up.

"We have an understanding, you and me. Say it out loud."

"We have an understanding."

Yehuda nods to Ponytail, who turns toward something or someone a few parking spaces south along the square. I hear a car start and shift into gear. Yehuda stands.

"When we were turning over your apartment," he says, "I read a couple of pages of that book you're writing."

I look up at him.

"Not bad," he says. "Not my cup of tea. But not bad."

I ask him if I can ask a question.

"Has it occurred to you," I say, "that your brother *wants* you to kill him?"

The car comes forward and pulls up to the curb behind Yehuda. It's the Ford Fairlane. Ponytail and Ivanov have already crossed to it. I can hear them opening the passenger door for their boss.

"Of course he wants me to kill him. He's wanted it for thirty years."

44.

Jackie Q

I'm waiting on the subway platform below Grand Central when Jackie Q descends the stairway from the level above. I have returned his call, from a pay phone outside Nicolette's, as soon as Yehuda and his men have driven from sight.

I raise my hand in greeting as Jackie steps off the stairs. He nixes this with a sharp glance and stops forty feet away from me, facing in the opposite direction. When the train comes two minutes later, Jackie steps aboard. I follow. I'm in one car, he's in the next.

Finally on the moving shuttle Jackie approaches. He works his way from his car into mine and grabs a strap behind me. We're standing back-to-back as the train rocks down the track.

"The band told me about the shoot-out in Ocean City—and that crazy motherfucker you sent to hide out with them. The award he's up for, the event's tomorrow night at the Waldorf, right?"

"Uh-huh."

Jackie backs closer. Our shoulder blades are touching. He tells me that he hears a lot of shit, running a club on 128th and Amsterdam. "This may be nothing," he says. "But there's word of a crew, three men, up from Haiti for one night to pop a cap into a guy in a Cadillac."

I wait.

"The night is tomorrow," says Jackie. "And the place is the Waldorf."

He gets off at Times Square. I follow. Jackie crosses to an Orange Julius and orders a hot dog, just to look like he's doing something. I wait across the platform beside a Chiclet vending machine mounted on a column that says TIMES SQ.

After a minute Jackie glides over. I thank him for delivering this intelligence. He's a good guy, even if he has stolen my gig as manager of Death Warmed Over.

"Your buddy Bablik," Jackie says, still facing away from me. "I assume he'll take a limo to the event, or the event planners will send one for him. That could be the Cadillac. I'm just saying."

Jackie says he knows nothing more. No idea who hired the Haitians. No idea who they are. No description.

I ask him how sure he is about this information.

"How sure is anybody about anything? But I'll tell you one thing. If I'm at the Waldorf tomorrow night and someone asks me to go for a ride in a Caddy, I'm gonna take a pass."

45.
Warrior Irish

From Times Square I take the shuttle back to Grand Central and catch the 6 train down to Bleecker. There I surface to street level, hike the two blocks to Broadway-Lafayette Street, where I drop back underground, grab the B train and ride it all the way to Kings Highway in Brooklyn, where I trek the final mile on foot to Joey's in Gerritsen Beach. A note says she's on duty; she's already left for the precinct. I sit upstairs with Frank and watch the Knicks fall eighteen points behind Detroit midway through the second quarter.

I know enough about Warrior Irish protocol not to ask for help directly. I wait till halftime, then do no more than explain the situation.

Frank makes no overt response. We watch the third quarter. Frank describes for me the alternative methods of winterizing a boat. You can leave the vessel in the water or you can haul it out. If you park it under covers in a storage yard, it's fifty a month and the damn thing can be vandalized and probably will be. A suspension rig for your own dock is a grand-and-a-half and two or three hundred to fix it when it breaks, which it always does. "My way," says Frank, "is fuck it. I use the boat all winter. You freeze your ass but the action keeps the hull clean."

The Knicks pull it out when Clyde Frazier hits a jumper from the top of the key with 3.4 on the clock.

At the door Frank lays a meaty hand on the back of his neck.

"That situation you were talking about. Lemme think about it."

I know enough not to thank him. I shake his hand and take the staircase down to Joey's.

We may just have saved Bablik's life.

46.
Moses

I spend the entire final day chasing Robert Moses.

Tonight is Bablik's ceremony. I have phoned Charlie late last night from Joey's. But his service says he's in Lebanon, Pennsylvania, at his main Christmas ornament plant. He's unreachable. It's too late to call Peggy so I wait for the morning.

I get her at 7:30 as she's toasting English muffins. Can she reach Robert Moses? Can she get me in to see him?

My aunt phones back in twenty minutes. She has connected with the Big Guy. He couldn't have been nicer, Peggy says. She has set up an appointment for me at Moses' office at the Port Authority, Park Avenue and 22nd, at nine. I take the B Express from Kings Highway but the power fails in mid-river; by the time I've hiked the eight blocks south from Herald Square and the three long blocks across from Sixth, I'm five minutes late. From the sidewalk I can see Moses' helicopter taking off from the roof.

I chase him to Queens to the dedication of a new elementary school on 99th Street in Corona. The chopper is gone. Moses has decamped ten minutes earlier via sedan to review progress on a wetlands reclamation project near Fort Totten on Little Neck Bay. I miss him again.

I catch the Port Authority chief finally at 3:30 at the skeleton of a forty-story tower going up on Maiden Lane and South Street in Lower Manhattan. I'm expecting bodyguards and gun-toting security but Moses is accompanied only by a driver and two aides.

I walk right up to him on the ice-encrusted construction site.

"You're Ellie's boy, Charlie's nephew," he says before I can even open my mouth. "Peggy's been phoning all day. Come on, let's take a ride."

I am handed a plastic hard hat. Robert Moses, wearing one as well, steps into a pipe-cage gondola, an external elevator that runs up the side of the under-construction tower.

Holy fuck.

Up we go in this swaying open car with our feet on loose boards and the wind howling off the river straight through the nonexistent walls. The cable supporting this bucket looks about an eighth of an inch thick and rattles ominously through the block-and-tackle rig that rides with us directly above the gondola.

"How can I help you?" says Robert Moses.

I'm shouting into the wind and hanging with bloodless knuckles onto the bars of the cage. I give Moses the short version of Bablik's story, complete with toxic dumping and illegal disposal of dead bodies. "You can't give him that award tonight."

"Why not?"

"Because he's a crook."

"And what alternative do you propose?"

"Arrest him. Throw him in jail."

I stress again the Turk's despoliation of tri-state area harbors, the human remains that his operation has fed into industrial solvent, his plan to franchise the business nationwide. "And besides, men are going to kill him."

"Really?"

The view from the gondola is, I must say, spectacular. Looking north, the Brooklyn Bridge seems close enough to touch. South and west shimmer Wall Street, New York harbor, and the Battery with the Statue of Liberty and the Verrazano Narrows Bridge in the distance. Robert Moses marvels at it and so do I.

"Are you familiar," he asks, "with Pericles' Funeral Oration from

Thucydides' *History of the Peloponnesian War*? 'You must fall in love with Athens.' That out there," Robert Moses says, indicating the harbor and the skyline, "is the American Athens, the greatest city in the world. Marvin Bablik has earned a place in it."

"Sir, he's dumping human bodies in the river and he's been doing it for thirty years. Cancel this award. You can't give it to him. It'd be a travesty."

Robert Moses is not an imposing physical specimen. But when he speaks, every syllable resonates, even in the shrieking, skull-shearing gale forty stories above the river.

"Marvin Bablik is being recognized tonight for his contributions to the state of Israel, and those contributions are apparently both substantial and significant. I'm not a party to the honoring entity. I have no power to rescind the award. I'm merely the dignitary making the presentation."

"But, sir ..."

"Please, you don't have to call me sir. I'm family."

Whatever else Marvin Bablik may or may not have done, Robert Moses says, has no bearing on tonight's ceremony. "In this city, there are criminal accusations against everybody. I can't count the number against me—and for far worse than what you're alleging about Bablik."

We reach the top floor. The gondola stops. The rig is swaying and buffeting at the precipice of this girders-only office tower.

Robert Moses asks if I intend to file charges against Mr. Bablik. Charges?

"When you do," he says, "and Bablik is indicted by a grand jury and subsequently tried and convicted in a court of law, then the state may take away his freedom. But until then, Marvin Bablik remains an innocent man whose actions over the course of a long career have done honor to the city and to his family and his people."

My kinsman takes hold of my elbow with a warm left hand and shakes my hand with his right.

"Say hi to Charlie for me. My condolences on the passing of your mother."

And he steps off the gondola to be swallowed by a crush of men wearing hard hats, some in business suits, others in construction garb. Two teamsters ride with me back down to earth.

47.

Heat

I've brought my personal stuff, which is now down to one small suitcase and a few clothes on hangers, back to the Burgundy. I get dressed there, in my old room. It's six on the dot when Tracy appears in the doorway.

My friend Peter in England once told me a story. There was a girl he fell in love with very young. They were together (married, divorced, then married and divorced again) for more than ten years. So that, Peter said, he would experience, at intervals, moments of "seeing her afresh." Maybe, he said, he'd be waiting to meet her and she would pull up in a car and step out. Or she'd come walking down a flight of stairs. "Each time when I'd see her like that I'd wonder, before the moment, if I'd still be in love with her. She had broken my heart so many times that toward the end I was actually praying, 'Please let me see her and not be in love with her.'

"Finally," Peter said, "I was meeting her for a curry at a Pakistani restaurant in the East End. Hadn't seen her for half a year. I got there early and was having a smoke on a bench outside when she came round the corner, about a hundred feet up the pavement. She hadn't spotted me yet, so I could watch her walking toward me as if she were a stranger. It hit me then. The spell had been broken. I wanted to drop to my knees in gratitude even though my times with her were the best I'd had or ever hoped to have. But the pain of it all was too much. Too fucking much. I was so relieved it was over."

That was Peter. It isn't me.

Seeing Tracy in the doorway, I feel something go funny in my stomach. I have to grab the jamb to steady myself.

"How do I look?" she says.

"You're a swell-looking dame."

Tracy adjusts my jacket, straightens my tie. She's wearing a gray, film noir-style suit: a pencil skirt and a jacket with oversize shoulders. Her hair is up. Her eyes are done in '30s fashion as well, with inky shadow and huge dark lashes.

She's telling me she's arranged for a car and driver from the production so we won't have to worry about hailing a taxi, when she glances to the nightstand and spots Bablik's nickel-plated .45.

"Are we packing tonight?"

I've been going back and forth on this all day. My final decision: No. I'm neither trained nor competent. I could hurt somebody.

"Gimme that thing," says Tracy without hesitation. She reaches past me and snatches the weapon, checks the magazine and the safeties, makes sure there's no round in the chamber, then slips the piece into her purse. "At least I know how to use it."

48.

The Green Room

The first person I see when we pull up to the Waldorf is Joey's dad, Frank. At the 49th Street corner. In uniform.

"Is this legal?" I ask as Tracy and I come up, Frank's been retired for six years.

"Fuck, no," he says. I shake his hand, introduce Tracy, and mutter something that Frank will understand as thanks without embarrassing him by actually saying the words. He acknowledges with a nod and a touch of my elbow. Frank says Joey is here too, along with her cousin Eamon, both in uniform as well.

"Who was that?" Tracy asks as we move toward the hotel entrance. I have given her the full update on Bablik, Yehuda, the Haitian hitmen and the Cadillac.

"A little extra protection," I say.

A stream of taxis and limos is pulling up on Park Avenue, disgorging dignitaries in tuxes and evening gowns. The Waldorf Astoria is one of the great hotels of the world. It's been hosting balls and galas, even peace conferences, since the early '30s.

Among the high-glam features of the Waldorf is you get to make an entrance. Just stepping out at the curb is fun. The Art Deco portal frames each entering couple dramatically. You climb the stairs with the Vanderbilt Room on one side at the top and the Empire Room on the other. Ahead you can see the famous clock centered amid the various cafes and lounges and, down the block-length hall and lobby, Peacock Alley.

My backup brainstorm for protecting Bablik has been to phone the band. Schwantz is still irate at me for the Ocean City fiasco but I manage, by citing the boys' unceremonious dumping of me as their manager, to guilt-trip him into promising to be here tonight with the van. A motor court pass-through runs beneath the hotel at mid-block between 49th and 50th. "Don't go near there," I tell Schwantz. For sure, no VIPs will depart via that route; it's a traffic nightmare. I instruct him to look for me out front on Park Avenue; I'll direct him from there to the rear canopy on Lexington. That's the sneak-out route.

My plan is at evening's end to somehow steer Bablik and Abby away from any Cadillacs and into the band's van. It's a dicey scheme, I admit. Mr. and Mrs. B. know nothing about it yet. Plus Schwantz is the least reliable operative I can think of. I make the odds at three-to-one against him even finding the hotel, let alone figuring out how to get into position at the backdoor exit.

From there, what? I have no idea.

An orchestra is playing the theme from *Exodus* as Tracy and I enter. "Wow," says my wife. "It's Jew heaven."

The scene is like opening night at the opera, or what I imagine opening night at the opera is like, since I've never actually been. A great hall, vaulted ceilings, men and women in hundred-dollar haircuts and five-hundred-dollar shoes.

We reach the top of the stairs leading up from the hotel entry. Guests are being routed past tables manned by private security officers. Men's jackets are being wanded, ladies' bags opened and searched. What the fuck? I have not anticipated this at all.

Tracy's glance is scanning the checkpoint. I feel her hand squeeze mine. "Up there. Is that Bess Myerson?"

It is.

Without hesitation Tracy makes a beeline for the former Miss America and unofficial queen of what Herman Melville once called "the insular city of the old Manhattoes."

For a moment I think, "Could Tracy somehow *know* Bess Myerson?" Not necessary, I realize. Tracy looks so glamorous and carries herself with such self-assurance that she effortlessly flags the lady down (Bess is on the far side of the security tables), stretches to take her hand, exchanges a long-distance air kiss, meanwhile passing her own handbag to Bess out of the officers' sight, while proffering some plausible explanation that I can't hear, then slipping, herself, unencumbered, through the screening portal.

By the time I catch up, the two women are gabbing like lifelong pals. Tracy introduces me as her husband and Robert Moses' nephew. "We'll be at the Babliks' table," she tells Bess, indicating the prime real estate inside the Empire Room. "Let's catch up later." In parting, Tracy hands Ms. Myerson her business card and invites her to be part of a new film and theater complex to be built next year in Tribeca.

The Empire Room is at the top of the stairs. That's where the banquet will take place. I note crystal chandeliers, floor-to-ceiling curtains, a dais at the rear. It's a dinner situation. Guests are filing in. I spot Senator Javits. There's former mayor Lindsay and his wife Mary Anne.

"What," I ask Tracy, "was that business with Bess Myerson about?" She tips her purse. "We got the gat through, didn't we?"

Where is Bablik? I spot him, with Abby, up front in the Empire Room at the center of a clutch of luminaries, but by the time I can wrangle Tracy through the crush at the entry, Mr. and Mrs. B. have vanished. Someone says they've gone to the Green Room.

I'm staring at the banner above the dais:

FRIENDS OF THE ISRAEL DEFENSE FORCES
MAN OF THE YEAR
MARVIN BABLIK

The Green Room? What the hell is that?
"This way," says Tracy.
I ask her what was that stuff about Tribeca.

"Nothing. I'll tell you later."

Apparently the Green Room is a private antechamber where the honorees, presenters, officers and board members of the FIDF and invited guests can relax before the actual event kicks off. A two-man security team guards the door. Tracy makes short work of them.

We're in.

The Green Room is enormous. As big as the Empire Room. It's packed. Atop linen tablecloths sprawls spread after spread of canapes, appetizers, hors-d'oeuvres, exotic breads, veggie dips, coffee and tea in silver samovars. Wine and imported waters are being served by handsome young men and women, actors from Joseph Papp's Public Theater, it turns out, in white jackets and ties.

"There's your girlfriend," says Tracy.

I spot Abby, turning from the bar with a martini in each hand and a metallic silver handbag draped over one forearm. She crosses to Bablik. He's in animated conversation with Robert Moses and two women I don't recognize. I come up with Tracy.

"There he is!" says Robert Moses. Clearly he has forgotten my name. I remind him and introduce Tracy. Amid the small talk, Bablik clasps my elbow. "You came," he says.

The emotion in his eyes is so intense I feel myself flushing.

"Are you okay?" I indicate his plaster-swathed foot. He's on a cane. The bridge of his nose is thick with makeup.

"Never better."

"Do you know, Marvin," says Robert Moses, "that this young man tried earlier today to get me to arrest you?"

The women laugh. They don't get the joke but they know it's a cue for appreciative amusement.

Robert Moses begins flirting with Tracy. Somehow I get the Turk aside and impart to him Jackie Q's warning about the Haitians. Has he heard this himself? He says no.

"If it's true, it's gotta be your brother. That's how he's coming after you."

Abby listens, glued to Bablik's side. She asks me, "Who do you have this information from?"

"From a source who's in a position to know and who has no reason to lie about it."

I ask Bablik what kind of limo he has rented for tonight. When he says he didn't pay attention coming here and Abby volunteers the same, I tell them whatever happens when you're leaving don't get into a Cadillac.

"I've got my guys from the band coming with their van, the red '71 Dodge. I know you remember it from Ocean City. The boys'll be out back when you exit onto Lexington. Get in that van, nothing else. I've got cops here too, friends of mine."

I tell Bablik and Abby to stay with me after the ceremony; I'll get them out of here safely.

Again, emotion wells in the Turk's eyes.

"What's your first name?" he says. "I'm sorry, I never asked."

"Steve."

"Steve." He holds out his hand. "I'm Mordechai."

We shake hands.

A gentleman in a tux appears at Robert Moses' shoulder. "Showtime!" he says. He motions Bablik and the Port Authority chief to follow him.

Bablik turns toward Tracy. "It was a pleasure to have met you," he says and shakes her hand too.

The Tux Man leads Bablik and Robert Moses away.

I call after him. "Be careful."

49.

The Empire Room

I'm out on Park Avenue, scoping the traffic, searching for Schwantz. Inside the Waldorf, the awards ceremony has started. Where is that freakin' Dodge van?

The VIPs' limos are lined up now against the curb in the security zone along 49th Street. But I know from picking up fares here in my cab that they'll maneuver via Park and 50th to their getaway stations in the rear of the hotel when the time comes. There's a Chrysler and three stretches—a Mercedes and two Lincolns—but no Cadillacs, even in the mid-block pass-through. The driver of the Chrysler tells me he belongs to Robert Moses. The others are off getting coffee. I'm on foot on Park, shuttling the length of the block between 49th and 50th, scanning the river of headlights for the two dim bulbs on the band's B-Series Ram.

How long will Bablik's ceremony take? I should've found out. I have no idea what time he and the other dignitaries will exit. Will there be presenters besides Robert Moses? How many other honorees will be receiving awards? Will each make a speech? How long will dinner take? Will there be a reception after? Will Bablik stay through dessert and coffee? How long will that take?

Twenty minutes pass. No Schwantz. I swim back inside. The passage consumes another ten minutes as I have to talk my way past the first two echelons of security, both of which refuse at first to let me by. I find Frank and Joey. Eamon is already out back.

In the banquet hall the salad course is being cleared. I spot Tracy up front at a table for eight, with Abby and the two women who were with Robert Moses and two gentlemen who must be their husbands. I work my way forward among the waiters and busboys. A preliminary award is being given. From the curtain above the dais hang two gigantic flags, one American, one Israeli. Between them, a six-foot-high photo of Bablik. I can see Frank and Joey maneuvering forward along the wall to take positions beside a brace of American flags at the right-hand wing of the stage.

Suddenly among the security staff I spot a ponytail.

I cross straight to him. "What the fuck are you doing here?"

"I'm working," says Ponytail. He indicates an official-looking ID hanging around his neck.

"That's bullshit," I say.

I tell him there're real cops everywhere. Out back too.

He tells me to fuck off and pushes past.

I bolt straight to Abby's table.

"They're here."

Abby clutches my arm. Tracy has moved tight to her shoulder. I tell Abby not to even try to exit after the award. "Stay inside. Keep with people. Don't go out back at all. Don't leave except in a group—and don't leave without me directing you."

I'm peering around looking for Ponytail. He has vanished.

Bablik is up front at the dais with the other honorees. He sees me. I flash him a look that tries to communicate everything that's going on. His eyes track me crossing to Frank and Joey. I tell them everything I know.

Back outside, there's the Dodge van. I dash to its driver's window.

"What took you so long?"

"You're welcome," says Roach. Jackie Q rides shotgun.

"What happened to Schwantz?"

"He's a pussy."

The Dodge is stopped at the curb on Park Avenue with cabs and buses stacking up behind, blasting their horns.

"Jackie, why did you come?"

He grins. "For fun."

50.

Jew of the Year

I hear applause. I hear whistles and cheers.

Again, I'm being halted by security.

I'm in the forecourt outside the Empire Room. Inside, Bablik is being introduced by Robert Moses. Through the half-closed doors I can see the Turk moving to the podium, shaking Moses' hand and thanking him, then stepping to the mike, unfolding his notes (a single sheet of paper) and beginning to speak. I can't hear him. I recognize Bablik's voice and the rhythm of his speech, but with the distance, the nearly-closed entry, and the distortion of the amplification I can't make out what he's saying. Whatever it is, the audience is responding. I can see people at the rear tables ceasing their conversations and turning, with attention, toward the dais.

"Lemme in," I tell the security guys. "That's my uncle speaking!"

"Yeah and I'm his brother."

I'm straining to hear. Bablik is saying something about himself not being the type of man this institution normally honors. He is aware, he says (I'm catching this only in snatches), that several committee members have lobbied vigorously against his receiving this award at all. He says he can understand this. In their place, he might have felt the same.

> In truth I am two men. I am the man I wish I were and the man I actually am.

Ah! Finally I find a spot, at the extreme right of the security station, where I can see and hear.

> I have two countries. One is this country, the United States, in which I dwell and where I have made my life. The other is—and I employ this term in full consciousness of its manifold meanings—the Promised Land.
>
> I do not live in the Promised Land. I live here, on these streets, in this city. I have made my way in this place. I do not apologize for it.

I can see Bablik clearly from my new vantage—and most of the rear tables in the Empire Room as well. All conversation has stopped. Every eye has turned toward the speaker's podium.

> Better men and women than I have chosen the higher way, the harder path, the nobler calling. I wish I had joined them. I would respect myself far more, had I bled and died as they did for that newer land, that loftier ideal.
>
> Tonight you honor the outer man, the one whose deeds can be counted, whose contributions can be measured. You cannot know the inner man, however. Perhaps he is not all you might wish him to be, or that he himself might aspire to. But you have saved his life this night. You have made his life. I thank you from my heart, for myself and for him.

Bablik folds the single sheet that contains his notes. He steps back from the lectern. For several seconds, the room holds silent. Then at once a wave of emotion rolls forward and up. Applause erupts. People at the rear tables (the only ones I have an unrestricted view of) are rising to their feet.

The security men are closing both doors of the entry. I can see I'll never get in this way. The kitchen apparently is upstairs, above the banquet hall. Waiters and busboys have been coming and going from a stairway at the end of the speakers' platform. I execute a 180, hang a right at the bottom of the stairs, and bolt down a hallway, seeking a staircase that leads up. If I can get to the kitchen, I can take the service staff's stairs down to the banquet hall. A concierge directs me. "Take that door."

I'm pounding up the steps now. I can hear the final swell of acclamation from the Empire Room below. I enter the kitchen. It's enormous. A full city block. Waiters and waitresses are streaming up from the banquet hall staircase, carrying trays with coffee cups and empty dessert plates. I start forward, aiming to take the down-steps that they have been coming up.

Suddenly I spot a commotion at the far end of the kitchen. Men in suits are entering from a staircase that apparently ascends from the Empire Room below. They're herding a clutch of guests. The group is so far away from me and moving so aggressively that I can't make out individual faces. I glimpse only security jackets, tuxes, evening gowns.

"What's going on?"

The party hustles swiftly across the kitchen, heading toward a service elevator at the far side of huge food-prep station. I'm pushing forward, shoving past busboys and rolling trays and dishwashing sinks.

"What's up there?"

"The exit to Lexington," says a guy cleaning a deep fryer.

I glimpse Bablik among the departing troupe. There's Abby. Fuck! I'm on a dead run now.

I chase the party to the elevator. Too late. The doors have closed. I find stairs. I come out, one floor above, into a vast carpeted hall with coat-check girls, at least a dozen, standing behind counters readying hats and overcoats for the coming rush.

Robert Moses, with Bablik and others, is just vanishing around a corner, a hundred feet ahead of me, starting down a flight of stairs. The scene looks like the Secret Service whisking the President away after the State of the Union address.

I race to the staircase and plunge down.

Ahead, the group pours through the brass doors and out onto Lexington.

I'm churning after them.

Outside. The sidewalk is wall to wall with tourists and passersby and those hip members of the press who have had this sneak-out route dialed in. A line of limos—the same ones I saw earlier on 49th—waits at the curb, doors open, drivers standing at the ready.

I see Frank and Joey. God bless 'em, they're ten feet from Bablik, covering his ass like a blanket.

Robert Moses' Chrysler is first in line. Flashbulbs are popping. I see Moses, with his two ladies and gentlemen, expertly dodging the photographers, ducking away into the limo.

Here comes the first Lincoln.

Bablik steers Abby toward it.

I'm scouring the crowd for signs of Ponytail. The movie in my head is him blasting the Turk like Jack Ruby drilling Lee Harvey Oswald.

"Get in! Get in!" I'm shouting. Bablik is fifty feet away amid the crush; he can't hear me.

Where's Roach? What happened to the band's van?

The Turk hands Abby into the back seat of the Lincoln. I feel oxygen flowing into my lungs for the first time all night.

But then he steps back.

"Get in!" I'm shouting, from thirty feet now. "What are you waiting for?"

Headlights appear on the far side of the Lincoln. I glimpse enough of the grille to recognize a Cadillac.

"Frank!" I'm shouting and plunging forward. "Joey!"

I'm twenty feet away. Big as life I see Bablik step apart from Abby and the Lincoln. He turns back toward me and meets my eye. Then he steps swiftly between the Lincoln and the limo and ducks into the rear seat of the Caddy.

The door closes. Smoked windows block all view of the interior.

The Cadillac, a Fleetwood Brougham, accelerates away into traffic.

51.

Under the Steel

I'm hauling Roach out of the Dodge's driver's door. "Getout, getout, getout!"

The van has finally appeared. We're on 49ᵗʰ pointing west. The Cadillac is all the way up the block, turning right onto Park. Frank and Joey race up on the sidewalk. Eamon hurries in their wake. I have plunged behind the wheel. "Follow us if you can!" I'm hoping Roach will bolt but he piles in back.

Somehow Tracy has caught up. She's heaving Jackie Q's door open. My wife is not the kind of damsel who consigns herself to the cheap seats. I've got the van in gear now; I'm checking traffic in the rear-view. Tracy is forcibly ejecting Jackie from the passenger seat. He springs in back. Tracy piles in up front.

"Go!" she cries.

The Brougham is ninety seconds gone. An eternity in city traffic.

"He turned uptown," Jackie shouts. I'm out on Park now, heading north. Jackie points past my ear, a block and a half, to the corner of Park and 51ˢᵗ. I can see the Caddy's taillights (or what I'm praying will turn out to be the Caddy's taillights) with its left turn signal blinking. The driver must be going all the way across town. He has picked 51ˢᵗ over 49ᵗʰ to avoid the traffic at Rockefeller Center. I've done the same in my cab.

The lights turn green. I zig into the left lane and floor it. The van crawls like it's mired in molasses.

"Roach, what the fuck did you do to this clutch?"

"What am I, a mechanic?"

The Cadillac turns west.

West?

The van slo-mos to 51st and barely squeaks through the light before it turns red. Gridlocked traffic freezes us in mid-intersection for an endless half a minute. The Caddy is five blocks gone.

I haven't had two seconds even to speculate about who's inside. Yehuda? Ponytail? The Haitians?

And Bablik crossed straight to it.

West.

Where could the Caddy be going?

Tracy: "The river."

She's right. You shoot people by the river. You dump their bodies into the current.

My mind is racing. West to the river, yes. But 51st Street is too far north to accommodate a murder or a body drop. The docks on the Hudson there are where the big cruise ships berth. Too many lights, too many people. The Brougham will be heading thirty, forty blocks south. To the no-man's-land under the abandoned West Side Highway—the meat packing district and the Chelsea piers.

Tracy: "Where are you going?"

"Trust me."

I know the piers. They're a five-minute walk from my apartment. I go there all the time at the end of the day, to be alone or have a smoke and watch the sunset.

What used to be a thriving commercial district, home to dozens of beef- and pork-packing operations, has devolved since the collapse of the West Side Highway into a scurvy demi-monde of neglected and disused industrial structures whose lofts and basements have found a second life as gay and S&M bars and sex clubs. The triangle of streets between West 14th and Gansevoort, bordered by Hudson Street on the east and the river on the west, has become a meat rack for prostitutes (straight, gay, and transvestite), heroin "shooting galleries," and squatters' nests for rough trade of all kinds. The abandoned roadway of the West Side Highway forms a ceiling of girders and crumbling concrete overhead. Beneath this, the netherworld of unpaved lots, dumping grounds, and homeless encampments is called "under the steel." God only knows what goes on inside the rusted-out sedans and derelict panel vans in this hellhole on the Hudson.

"Everybody, watch for that Cadillac!"

I take 51st across to Hell's Kitchen, then Eleventh Avenue straight downtown, past Mika's place above the Goodwill Store between 37th and 38th, blowing through red lights after a quick glance right or left, much to Jackie Q's squealing consternation. He is apparently a lawbreaker only in his nightclub. I slow for one light, at 25th, only to see Tracy's hand grab the wheel while her left shoulder bangs powerfully into my right—"Run it! Don't stop!"—and the toe of her slingback pump tromps my foot atop the gas.

Are Frank and Joey following? I shout to Jackie in back that I'm hoping some cops will spot us and chase us.

"What's that?" cries Tracy at the corner of West 22nd. She points a block ahead to two pairs of taillights—a small car following a bigger one that could be the Caddy—turning sharp and fast under the steel toward the river.

The little car is a Renault Dauphine.

Me: "What language do they speak in Haiti?"

Roach: "What are you talking about?"

"Do they speak French?"

"Who the fuck knows?"

We're under the abandoned West Side Highway now. I can see the Chelsea piers on the right.

"That's it!" Tracy points ahead. "The Cadillac!"

For .001 second her eyes meet mine with unfeigned respect.

Jackie: "What do we do?"

Tracy: "Hit 'em with the high-beams!"

I flatten the button on the floorboard. We're still a block away. The Dodge's headlamps put out the candlepower of a Boy Scout flashlight.

The Caddy and the Renault have stopped. Dark forms dismount. A group of three plunges into the darkness toward the river. The Brougham accelerates away.

"Go faster!" cries Tracy.

Now the Renault takes off. It hangs a screeching U and bolts north, right past us, into the squalid realm beneath the steel.

Tracy: "Forget that piece of shit! Keep going!"

We reach the base of the first pier. Roach is shouting, "Which one did they go out on?" There are three or four piers in a row.

"This one, this one!" says Tracy.

I snowplow to a stop. I'm out and so is Tracy. Roach and Jackie seem to be having second thoughts.

The piers jut straight out into the broad, powerful Hudson. They're abandoned, flat, nothing to obstruct a view.

"There!" says Tracy. "See 'em?"

We're on the pier now. The expanse ahead looks like the deck of an aircraft carrier, 150 yards long and forty wide. Warehouses used to stand here. Ships would tie up and be loaded or unloaded. But the pier is totally flat and open now. The deck under our feet is made up of hundreds of timbers, big and heavy, like railroad ties.

We can see the end of the pier plainly, illuminated from behind by the reflection off the river and the lights of Hoboken on the Jersey side.

At the brink: a tight group of three silhouettes.

One is on his knees. Two stand over and behind him.

A gunshot.

The muzzle-flash lights up the end of the pier, vivid and unmistakable.

The man on his knees blows forward and down, hard.

Two more shots in quick succession.

The standing men turn and start running back toward us.

I turn to Tracy. "Stay here. Keep low and don't move."

I'm advancing out farther onto the pier. Why? I have no idea. To save Bablik? Am I insane?

I hear Tracy behind me.

"Get back! Tracy, get outa here!"

She stops but doesn't withdraw. I keep going. I can see the men clearly now. They're young and fit and moving very fast. They see me and veer away. Maybe they think I'm a cop. I'm angling away from them too.

The gap between me and the gunmen is the full width of the pier—forty yards. We're each giving the other the widest berth possible.

Suddenly I hear a car engine. Headlights blaze onto the pier.

The Renault.

It's bucking out onto the timbers, heading this way.

Tracy is caught in its high beams.

It occurs to me that I have done something really stupid going out onto this pier.

Tracy runs toward me. I hurry toward her.

The two killers have lost all fear of us. They cross swiftly toward Tracy and me. I can see the guns in their hands.

We're spotlighted big as life in the Renault's headlamps.

I grab Tracy and push her behind me.

The gunmen come up, ten feet in front of us. They're young—barely twenty—and both remarkably good-looking.

I'm reading their eyes. They're thinking, Should we blast these two? In favor of this: Tracy and I are witnesses; our presence puts the killers in peril. Opposed: it ain't worth it, this wasn't part of the job, nobody's paying us to do this.

Suddenly from Tenth Avenue: sirens.

Two pairs of police headlights turn out of Twelfth Street and accelerate up Tenth Avenue, against traffic, heading this way.

Gunman #1 glances to Gunman #2. He says something to his comrade in French.

The Renault's horn blares. The driver shouts something in the same tongue.

Both gunmen turn and bolt to the car. One dives into the passenger seat, the other plunges in back. The Renault squeals into a U and tries to accelerate away, but the pier's wooden timbers are slick with lingering snow and ice; the Renault's rear drive wheels spin, seeking purchase. For a moment the vehicle hangs up, going nowhere.

I'm still shielding Tracy behind me, pinning her with both arms.

I feel her lips come up close behind my right ear. "Stand still," she says. "Don't move."

Her hand rustles inside her purse.

The Renault's tires find traction. The car squeals away.

Tracy steps around my right shoulder into the clear.

She's got Bablik's nickel-plated .45 extended in front of her in a two-hand shooting stance. It's like the final scene in *Missizombie*. The Renault is maybe thirty feet away, accelerating.

Tracy puts three rounds into its ass-end. The Renault's rear window explodes. I'm shouting stop, stop. Those heavy slugs are booming straight toward the populated buildings on Tenth Avenue.

Tracy pays no attention. She's standing tall and in balance in a two-handed pro pose that you know was taught to her by the stunt coordinator on the zombie flick. I can see the heavy recoil kick the weapon upward each time Tracy pulls the trigger. She's in control. She's not letting the kick unsettle her. Tracy blows through the whole magazine. I hear the last shot and then the metallic ping of the .45's slide locking open as the final round is ejected.

Roach and Jackie emerge from the shadows under the abandoned highway. They're peering wide-eyed from behind girders as the Renault slews past them and speeds toward Tenth Avenue.

Tracy keeps pulling the trigger. A stream of profanity pours from her. "Ah, fuck!" She realizes the weapon is empty. I'm staring at her. She turns back to me with a look that I can only describe as one of pure animal joy.

"I think I got one! Do you think I got one?"

The Renault screams away off the pier, half-rolling hard right under the steel and careening south onto Tenth Avenue. The two cop cars pass it going the opposite direction. They howl into 180s with both sirens screaming. The police vehicles give chase down Tenth Avenue.

I turn back toward Tracy. She's standing there with her eyes the size of pie plates, her hair wild and spiky, and blue-gray gunsmoke pouring from the muzzle and ejection port of the .45.

"What a rush!" she says. "I know I got 'em. I know I got one of 'em."

52.
What is Love?

Tracy's ankles are up around my ears. We're on our third time and I'm so spent, when I breathe my lungs wheeze like a vacuum pump. We've come straight from the pier to my place on Fifteenth Street, where we have killed a fifth of Remy in twenty minutes, trading pulls straight from the bottle, trying to come down from adrenaline overload. Now here we are, tangled in each other's underwear, enacting some long-overdue rite of expiation and expurgation.

This is the first time Tracy has let me touch her romantically in five years. As we're jamming our tongues down each other's throats, I'm remembering what lovemaking had been like between us when we were first married and before. The act was slow and intimate, with both of us trying to extend each heartbeat, seeking to make the moment last as long as possible, with the awareness through every instant of how precious this communion was and how incredibly lucky we were to have found it and each other. She was the one. This was forever. And Tracy felt the same about me. We talked. Not dirty talk or stupid fuck-me talk but real talk from the center of our innocent hearts. Every touch, every kiss was sent like a letter from one soul to the other, meant to fuse us, bind us together forever.

Now it's just fucking. Not a hate fuck or a pity fuck. This is a goodbye fuck. The quality of intimacy that was so present and pervasive before I ruined everything is now utterly absent. Those elements of the act that are superficially the same, our fingers clawing each other, our chests squishing together slick with sweat, that's a movie I've played in my head a thousand times and hoped for as a consummation of I don't even know what.

Now that it's here, though, I can feel that each stroke, each thrust is just bearing us closer to the end, the real end, the final end. The rite we're enacting is in fact the statement of the end. The weird part for me, and I suspect for Tracy too, though I won't say it aloud and she won't either, is that this awareness is accompanied neither by grief or regret but only by a sense of relief. We both know that something that was once extraordinary is gone and will never come back.

This woman is the love of my life. I will never find another who will make me feel like she does. But the pain of being bound to her is too much. I can't stand it any longer and neither can she. We both just want it to end. That emotion will have to suffice in place of intimacy, in the stead of love, and, in some crazy way, it does.

"Help! Stop!" I'm begging for mercy.

"Lemme finish. Hang on till I finish."

What makes you love somebody? Huh? Why this one and not that? And why do they love you? The best woman I know is Nicolette. She's the only really good one. But when I was with her I couldn't stop chasing everything in stiletto heels or blue jeans and engineer boots. What's the answer? Pick the Best Case Scenario and it still won't work. If Tracy rolled off me now and said let's give our marriage another try, I'd be the one to blow it up again, if not immediately then soon enough.

She finishes with a scream like a cheetah. Her face is scarlet. Her eyes are embers.

Me: "I can't go another time."

Tracy tucks a shoulder and crashes beside me onto her back.

"It's okay. Me neither."

I sign our divorce papers in a cab forty minutes later on the way over to Max's Kansas City for a tenderloin with sautéed onions and an avocado salad that we order and split between us.

Can it really be only a hundred and thirty minutes since Tracy and I stood with Roach and Jackie Q at the terminus of Pier Sixty in Chelsea, squinting into the black icy current of the Hudson, seeking sign of the submerged corpse of my friend Marvin Bablik?

53.
Joey, Part Two

I call Joey from a pay phone out of the neighborhood. It's six in the morning, seven hours after what I'm already thinking of as "the events of January Twelfth." I meet her at the Parthenon Coffee Shop in Sheepshead Bay ten minutes after the place opens.

I've phoned Nicolette in the interim, waking her out of a dead sleep. She's been worried sick on my behalf for weeks now, ever since I took the gumshoe job from Bablik. I tell her now (though I'm not sure she's grasping all of it through the predawn cobwebs) what happened last night at the Waldorf and at the Chelsea piers.

"Are you okay?"

"Yes."

"Are those crazy people still after you?"

"Not at the moment."

Nicolette asks where I am. I tell her.

"Come to my place," she says, "as soon as you get back."

In the coffee shop, Joey and I take the second booth in from the door, the one that's out of the draft, like we used to when we were together. Her dad is fine, Joey says. So is cousin Eamon. Neither of them were part of the pursuit last night on Tenth Avenue. They've both seen the news however and both gotten the word from their respective precincts; they know about the shooting on the pier and they know that no official entity, so far at least, has connected me to it or it to me. They're both home in bed now sawing logs, Joey's certain. When I ask her what I should do about Bablik she says, "Who?"

"The guy's in the Hudson, Joey. I gotta do something."

Nikki the waitress passes, dispensing refills. Joey waits till she's out of earshot.

Joey tells me to stop thinking like a middle-class schmuck. The Haitians have hightailed it and they ain't coming back. But Yehuda and his guys are still very much present and very much capable of wreaking havoc. "As in," says Joey, "on you, if you do something stupid like open your big mouth."

I tell her about Tracy getting off a fusillade at the fleeing gunmen. I'm terrified that my door's gonna burst open and a squad of detectives will pile in.

"What is your problem, man? Right and wrong? If you want justice, call Perry Mason."

She asks what happened to the gun.

"Tracy chucked it in the river."

"See? Follow her. She's got good instincts."

Joey and I finish our bialys. I thank her and ask what I can do to repay her and her dad and Eamon.

"I could use some smokes."

I buy her a carton of Marlboros at the Quik-Pik on the corner. A couple of quarts of Cuervo Gold, she assures me, will go a long way with her father and cousin.

By the time she drops me at the subway, I'm starting to feel better.

Joey: "Get any sleep last night?"

Me: "Not much."

54.

An Outdoor Cat

I walk into Nicolette's and there's Teaspoon. She's holding him in both hands on her shoulder.

"Oh my God." I can't believe it. "Where did you find him? Where did you find him?"

I cross the space in one stride. My first thought is, Is this really Teaspoon? Cats can look alike. I'm afraid that Nicolette has found a doppelganger on the street and mistook it for mine.

But it's Teaspoon all right. I'm certain because he's snubbing me.

"I had him all along," says Nicolette. "From the first day. Can you forgive me?"

What do I mean by snubbing? My cat refuses to look at me. When I take him from Nicolette, he turns his head away. He squirms in my grip. He can't wait for me to put him down so he can bolt from my grasp.

Nicolette snatches Teaspoon back and reads him the Riot Act. "What's the matter with you, you ungrateful little shit! Don't you know how much this man loves you? He's been out of his mind with worry about you! He's turned this city upside-down looking for you!"

My cat remains unmoved.

"Put him down," I tell Nicolette. "It's okay."

Nicolette and I cross to her tiny, galley-type kitchen. She makes tea.

"The night that your place got broken into," Nicolette says, "Teaspoon showed up at my window. I took him in. I was furious at you, as always, for letting him roam outside on these dangerous streets. I left him here when I went over to your place the next morning. I was going to give you hell for letting Teaspoon out and refuse to give him back until you promised to keep him indoors. But when I got to your apartment, the place had been ransacked, you had been beaten up, and you were freaking out because Teaspoon was missing.

"I decided on the spur of the moment that I wouldn't tell you I had him. I had to find some way to get you to break off your involvement with those gangsters. I could see how frantic you were to find Teaspoon. I thought, 'Now he'll drop everything else and look for his cat.' And that's just what you did. I was happy because now, for the moment anyway, you had stopped putting yourself in danger."

I'm listening to Nicolette thinking, This is the girl I should be with. She cares about me. She loves me ...

"But my plan backfired. You decided it was the gangsters who had kidnapped your cat. So instead of dropping out of that madness, you become even more involved in it. I was frantic. I didn't know what to do. Should I tell you I had Teaspoon? Twice you showed up at my door and I had to dash upstairs and hide Teaspoon with my neighbor. I was terrified you'd find out and hate me forever. Finally I called my sister in New Jersey and hid Teaspoon out there with her."

My cat has taken up a position beneath Nicolette's bed, just at the edge of my field of vision. I can tell he's listening to the conversation, but each time I glance in his direction, he turns quickly away, pretending to be remote and aloof.

"Bad cat!" says Nicolette. "You're a cruel, ungrateful animal!"

I tell her not to worry. "Teaspoon blames me for not rescuing him from you. He thinks I knew he was here in your apartment all along, imprisoned by you—the Mean Girl Who Won't Let Him Go Outside. That's why he's snubbing me now. To punish me for abandoning him. But I know him like a book. Give him a day or two, till he thinks I've suffered enough. When he's good and ready, he'll let me know he forgives me."

"Finally," says Nicolette, "I decided to come clean and tell you I had Teaspoon. I could see you couldn't write without him, and you were so worried and miserable. Except now my sister wouldn't give him back to me. She asked, 'Will your friend continue to let this cat go outside?' I said yes. 'Then you can't have him back.'

"It took two weeks for my mother and me to convince her. But by then things had gotten so insane with you and the gangsters that I didn't dare intervene. Can you forgive me?"

55.
Eight Million Stories

Three nights after Marvin Bablik's body vanished beneath the surface of the Hudson River, Kingie the taxi mechanic was murdered on Portsmouth Avenue just beneath the Jersey Palisades. A man walked up to his driver's window at a stoplight and shot him right through the glass. The gunman then opened the driver's door and put two more slugs into Kingie's forehead. More than a dozen people witnessed the killing. The victim's wallet with $67 in cash was still in his pocket when the police arrived.

I catch this on the WPIX Morning News in my super's office as I'm returning the keys to my apartment and trying to get a hundred bucks back from my security deposit. I'm leaving town, I explain. I'm paid up through the end of the month and I'd appreciate it if he'd prorate my deposit and give me a few dollars back for gas.

"I'll let you off," says the super. "The building won't charge you for the busted door."

I have brought Teaspoon back from Nicolette's. My original notion was to let him roam outside again, back in the courtyard, if only for the few more days we'll still be in town. You would think an outdoor cat would be excited about such a prospect after being deprived of his freedom for almost three weeks. But Teaspoon's perspective on life in the Big City has altered dramatically. He used to head out at nightfall and not pad back in till sunup or later. Now he stays glued to my side all night and only ventures onto the fire escape to use his litter box.

As I predicted, my cat has forgiven me. It took three days. I was sitting at the typewriter, blocked as usual, when he suddenly leapt up into my lap, purring.

He took his place beneath my Smith-Corona's shuttling carriage. Like magic, I could work again. In twenty-four hours I rewrote the end and the middle of the manuscript I had turned in to Marty. *Now* it was cooking.

I'm packing up. Maybe that's what making Teaspoon anxious. Our next-door neighbors Adriana the Scary Girl and her gorgeous blonde roommate are bad-vibing me 24/7. One of Adriana's other boyfriends has agreed to marry her. For about ten seconds I think, Should I insist on a paternity test? If the child is mine, shouldn't I be the one to step forward? This may be my last chance, ever, to be a husband or a father.

The newspapers and TV were wall to wall with Bablik's murder for a day and a half after the shooting. Then a senior diplomat in the office of the Saudi ambassador was gunned down in broad daylight in the Pan Am terminal at JFK. This event was followed, only hours later, by a triple homicide on 149th Street with rough-sex overtones. Finally, a Buddhist monk lit himself on fire during lunch hour outside the U.N.

As quickly as the Turk's tragedy had flared into must-see melodrama, so swiftly did it devolve into yesterday's news. The story receded in the public mind, first to a disappearance, then a mystery, at last to one of the eight million stories in the Naked City.

No one has come forward with evidence pointing to the murderers. The police have no witnesses beyond those who spotted the Killer Cadillac whisking the Turk from the Waldorf. Abby has vacated the city for her condo in Naples. When the cops interview Yehuda, it's only as the Turk's brother and business partner. I catch him on Eyewitness News, distraught with grief.

Two detectives come by and take a statement from me, but only because they're interviewing everyone on the payroll at Gotham Cab and the other taxi companies that Bablik owns. The officers are bored stiff. They can't wait to get the chore over with.

The last thing Tracy tells me the night we say goodbye at Max's Kansas City is that she has had an offer to stay on in the city. A friend has acquired a twenty-year lease on a pair of loft buildings in Tribeca, on Chambers Street south of Canal. The buildings are empty; the friend has leased them both for the first year for $28,000. His plan is to consolidate the properties and configure them into a state-of-the-art complex with film and theater production facilities, rehearsal spaces, editing suites, even a bakery and a Richard Melman restaurant. This is for real, Tracy says. Martin Scorsese is one of the investors; there's talk that Robert De Niro and Harvey Keitel may come in as well.

"I'll be Chief Operating Officer," Tracy says. She'll run the day-to-day operation, with equity in the theatrical enterprise and, in the future, the real estate as well. "It's an opportunity to get in on the ground floor of something that could be huge. I'm going to take it."

I congratulate her. The investors, I say, are getting a helluva deal themselves. "Who could do this better than you? And it gets you out of the zombie business."

We embrace in the crowd on the sidewalk outside Max's.

"So," I say. "You're with Jake now."

"He's possible."

A week ago this prospect would have put me in the physical restraint ward at Bellevue. "Hey," I hear myself saying now. "Go with God."

Me, I'm on my way out of Dodge with no forecast of return.

56.
Marty's Stuff

Four days after Bablik's murder, I take the New Haven line up to Stamford, to my uncle Charlie's Connecticut factory. He's been letting me park my Chevy van in the company garage since I came back to New York two and a half years ago.

I pick up the vehicle. Charlie and I share a brown-bag lunch in his office. I thank him for everything, including Peggy's call to Robert Moses and Charlie setting me up with a criminal lawyer. Thank goodness, it looks like I won't need him.

I tell my uncle about Yehuda's warning to me, delivered on the park bench in Abingdon Square. "How far away do you think I should go?"

Charlie peers west out his fifth-story window. "Don't stop till you hit the Pacific."

My final obligation is to dispose of Marty's belongings. Oscar the doorman has had them shipped to Manhattan Storage, which turns out to be in Brooklyn, on Kessler Street off Flatbush Avenue. I spend two days on the 19th floor of the warehouse, one of the most beautiful buildings I've ever been in—a prewar architectural masterwork with faux-Assyrian columns and facades, fourteen-foot ceilings and massive windows, all in impeccable repair. Items of value from Marty's apartment I donate to the Jewish Relief Agency, books to the public library, everything else to Goodwill.

Searching for family, I pore over three decades of Marty's correspondence, dating from his repatriation to Holland after being liberated from Bergen-Belsen on April 15, 1945 by the British 11th Armoured Division, through his arrival in the States in May of 1947, and finally to his career as a literary agent, editor, and publisher. I am spellbound.

My mail catches up to me at Fifteenth Street on that Friday, the eighteenth. On top is the bill for transfer and storage of Marty's property—five hundred and seventy-five dollars. Beneath this, my bank statement: $242.50.

The third item is a note from Marty in his elegant, Old World longhand, dated the morning of the day he died.

My dear Steven,

Below please find the address and phone # of my dear friend Marilyn Kahn in Beverly Hills. She is the Hollywood literary agent of whom I spoke. I have sent her your newest. She is crazy about it. Call her.

Martin Fabrikant

Finally, opening a stylish linen envelope, I discover a four-color brochure and a hand-written note from the Beecher Funeral Home in New Rochelle. The message is addressed to me and signed by Edwin Beecher III, Funeral Director, of whom I have no acquaintance, nor is his firm known to me.

The text advises me that the earthly remains of Mr. Martin Fabrikant have been cremated and reposed in a bronze urn, the highest-quality receptacle offered by the Beecher establishment. At the request of Mr. Marvin A. Bablik, Mr. Fabrikant's ashes have been scattered, on January 12, 1974, upon the site of a beautiful winter pasture on Mr. Bablik's horse property at Sycamore Farm on Guard Hill Road in Bedford, New York.

The fees, both for the cremation and the casting service, have been requited in full by Mr. Bablik.

57.
The End He Wanted

Nicolette helps me load my van. It's 10:20 on the morning of January 21st, the last day I will spend in New York City.

Packing a van is a science.

First I lock Teaspoon in the apartment bathroom. This is to keep him from bolting as Nicolette and I pass in and out, schlepping stuff down to the street.

Next I take my bed apart. I break the frame down to its angle-iron rails and wrap these in my one threadbare carpet. This bundle goes on the truckbed, tucked against one wall. The bookshelf in my apartment is made of four big square plastic milk cartons with plywood shelves in between. The shelves go, now, onto the deck of the van; the milk boxes I set down, stuffed with my books and junk, one in each of the four corners of the truckbed. On top of these I balance the box springs, then the mattress.

I make up the bed, neat and tight, with sheets, my old Boy Scout sleeping bag unzipped and folded out like a comforter, the Navy blanket that used to be my dad's, and finally a hand-sewn quilt that was a gift from Nicolette when we first started going to the Alliance Francaise together a couple of years ago. She helps me carry down my clothes, what few there are, folded and stuffed into cardboard boxes. These slide easily into the crawl space under the box springs, where I also stow cans of motor oil, spare tire and tools, my typewriter and writing table (disassembled) and my much-battered metal Dos Equis cooler, in which are several sandwiches that Nicolette has made for me "for the road," along with coleslaw and potato salad, an apple, and a Glad bag of oatmeal raisin cookies.

I have asked Nicolette to come with me to L.A. But even as the words are issuing from my mouth, I know it's a chickenshit play. Nicolette does too.

"My life is here," she says. "My art. Besides, what you've got to do, you've got to do alone."

Two other valedictory events have taken place over the final forty-eight hours.

First, Roach has come by to say so long. He and I go for a burger at the Broome Street Bar, sitting at the same table by the front window that Nicolette and I usually roost in when we go there. My animus toward Roach has dispelled completely. He's a good guy and a serious talent, and he stuck with me that final night on the pier.

Roach tells me that Jackie Q, in his role as my replacement, has gotten the band a record deal. I congratulate him. In three years I had never come close to such a coup. Two of the songs that the band wants to record are co-written by Roach and me. Roach buys me out with a check for $575—the exact amount I need to settle my bill with Manhattan Storage, as well as the precise tally I paid to Her Majesty's government sixty-four months ago to secure Teaspoon's release from quarantine so he could come home to the United States with me.

"One thing has been driving me crazy," says Roach, lowering his voice and leaning forward in the booth. "That night on the pier. We all saw the gunshots. You saw it better than I did, Stretch. We saw Bablik go down."

"Yeah?"

"He dropped face-first onto the timbers. Shot in the head, then shot again, twice more. We saw where he was. At least ten feet from the end of the pier ..."

"Yeah?"

"But when we got out there, after the Renault drove away ... when the four of us ran to the end of the pier … Bablik was in the river. We saw his body roll over in the current. We saw it go under and be swept away."

"I know," I say. "I've been thinking the same thing."

"Bablik dragged himself. What else could have happened? Shot to shit as he was, he somehow managed to haul his ass to the end of the pier and roll himself into the river." Roach stares at me. "But why? Why would Bablik do that? If he was alive, why didn't he try to save himself?"

The second event is with Abby. The night before she flies to Naples, to the condo she and Bablik own on the beach, she leaves a message on my service. I meet her at One Fifth Avenue, at the mahogany bar beneath the spectacular, salvaged oil painting of the *S.S. Normandie*. Makeup conceals the dark circles under Abby's eyes. When I ask her what she's feeling in the wake of her husband's death, she says, "Relief."

She orders Scotch and milk like Adam Clayton Powell.

"Don't disapprove of me for speaking the truth," Abby says. "Marvin got the end he wanted. He settled his debt in the only way that could satisfy him, given the terms by which he defined it. He's quits now." She lifts her glass. "Like I told you, he was the most moral man I've ever known."

I walk over to the pier myself the last morning. The place is completely different in daylight. Gay guys are sunbathing, shirtless, holding up reflectors in the forty-degree cold. There's no sense of menace whatsoever.

I think, Mrs. B. is right. The Turk had been setting up his own exit since the first night he called me into his office, and probably long before that, whether he understood it himself or not.

By ten forty-five Nicolette and I finish loading the van. A warm front has come in overnight. Temperature is already in the fifties. The sky looks bright to the west.

Nicolette's parting gift to me is a full tank of gas. This is no small thing, as the price of fuel has gone through the roof since the Arab oil embargo. A gallon used to be thirty cents max and as low as 24.9 in the South and Midwest. Now I'm seeing 51.9 and even 54.9. To fill my sixteen-gallon tank will cost almost nine bucks. If it takes me ten fill-ups to get to the coast, that's ninety dollars, when I used to make the trip for under forty. I break out in a sweat just thinking about it.

I have brought Teaspoon down from the apartment now. He's in the traveling case I keep for the times when I need to take him to the vet. Nicolette has his litter box, which I slide into the crawl space underneath the box springs.

As I'm taking Teaspoon out of the traveling case, something makes me glance up the block and across the street. A Chrysler Imperial sits double-parked in front of the bodega. I see a ponytailed silhouette behind the wheel.

Yehuda in a gray topcoat with gloves and a fedora is dismounting, absent urgency, from the passenger door.

I hand Teaspoon to Nicolette to say goodbye. She has an appointment and has to get going. Nicolette and I give each other a hug with Teaspoon between us. We kiss quickly and she scurries off, turning back to wave. In moments she's around the corner and gone.

The side doors of my van are both open. I set Teaspoon inside, on top of the bed, then close the doors tightly. I can see him through the two side windows. He isn't freaked or spooked. He knows where he is. He knows we're getting back on the road. He's happy. He trots straight to his favorite spot by the rear windows and settles down at once.

Yehuda has crossed the street now. He comes up to me beside the van. Ponytail remains behind the wheel of the parked Imperial.

Yehuda jerks a thumb in the direction Nicolette took when she scurried off. "Girlfriend?"

"Sort of."

He nods. "Where ya off to?"

"L.A."

"Movies?"

"Why not?"

Through the van's side windows Teaspoon has caught sight of Yehuda. He's assessing him. For whatever reason, my cat registers no alarm. He seems to accept the gangster, or at least to feel no fear of him.

"Long way to the Coast," says Yehuda, indicating my van. "This piece of shit gonna make it?"

"Hundred percent."

From inside one glove, Yehuda produces a folded bill. He extends it toward me. I take it.

"For gas," he says.

I glance down.

Benjamin Franklin.

A hundred bucks.

When I look up, Yehuda is already halfway across the street. Ponytail stretches across the front seat of the Imperial and pushes the passenger door open. Yehuda slips in, pulling the door shut behind him. Ponytail puts the car in gear. The Imperial pulls out ahead of a couple of taxis turning onto Fifteenth from Seventh Avenue. The car drives past me and accelerates away up the street.

I turn back toward Teaspoon. He has settled into his traveling spot, on one of the pillows atop the bed at the back of the van.

He's ready.

He's getting impatient.

His eyes meet mine with an expression that says, "Let's blow this pop stand."

STEVEN PRESSFIELD is a bestselling author of fiction (*The Legend of Bagger Vance, Gates of Fire, Tides of War, The Last of the Amazons, The Virtues of War, The Afghan Campaign, Killing Rommel,* and *The Profession*) and nonfiction (*The War of Art, The Warrior Ethos, Turning Pro, Do the Work, The Authentic Swing, The Lion's Gate, An American Jew,* and *Nobody Wants to Read Your Sh*t*). His weekly dispatch *Writing Wednesdays* on www.stevenpressfield.com is one of the most popular craft blogs on the worldwide web.

And yes, that's a photograph of the 1970s-era version of Steve on the back cover, courtesy of Christy Henspetter.

Special Thanks

As always to Shawn and Kate, without whom etc.; to John Milnes of the BBC for the true gen on Brit Triumph Bonnies circa 1970; to Nashville cat Brian Siewert for all things musical (and a very helpful early read); to Tor Hermansen in L.A. and London for the same, and to John Fay for assorted guitar licks; to concierge Stanley Wong, archivist Deidre Dinnigan, and tour guide Barbara Vandervloed for proffering a "look behind the veil" at the Waldorf Astoria; to Sharona Justman for the Russian proverb; to Derick Tsai for the cover design and much more; and to the Soho Grand Hotel, my home away from home.